CHRIS CURRAN

Her Turn to Cry

KILLER
READS

an imprint of HarperCollins*Publishers*
www.harpercollins.co.uk

Killer Reads
An imprint of HarperCollins*Publishers*
1 London Bridge Street
London SE1 9GF

www.harpercollins.co.uk

This paperback edition 2016
1

First published in Great Britain by
HarperCollins*Publishers* 2016

A catalogue record for this book is
available from the British Library

ISBN: 978-0-00-819606-6

Set in Minion by Palimpsest Book Production Ltd, Falkirk, Stirlingshire

Printed and bound in Great Britain

MIX
Paper from
responsible sources
FSC˙ C007454

In memory of Jim and Bedelia Curran. Dad, who passed on his love of books, and Mum, who took me to the library every week to borrow them.

Chapter One

The Pier Theatre, Hastings, Sussex – August 1953

Joycie usually loves it when Dad takes her to work with him. But not today. She wants to stay at their lodgings in case Mum comes back. She keeps telling Dad she's eleven now and old enough to be left on her own, but he won't listen.

Sid Sergeant is already in the dressing room, a fag in the corner of his mouth, squinting at himself in the mirror through the swirls of smoke. Old Harry, a conjuror they call The Great Zarbo, stands facing the sink in the corner. Joycie can hear a splashing sound and, along with the usual smells of tobacco, make-up, and beer, there's a pong of wee that makes her nose twitch.

Sid twists to look at them. 'Cover up, Harry, will you,' he says.

Harry turns on the tap and fiddles with his trousers, talking to Dad over his shoulder. 'Sorry, Charlie. Didn't know you were bringing the nipper. Someone's been in the lav for ages.' He waddles to the dressing table. 'You gonna sit with me while your dad's onstage, eh darling?'

Her dad raises his dark brows at Sid. 'That's OK, Harry; I'm going to ask Irene to mind her.'

As the star of the show, Irene Slade has her own tiny room.

She's doing her hair at the cluttered dressing table. 'Hello sweetie pie.' Irene pats the chair next to her and, looking at Charlie in the mirror, she points at a packet of chocolate cakes sitting on top of the mess of jewellery and sticks of make-up. 'I must have known you'd bring her in tonight. Got her favourites.'

When Dad has gone Joycie eats her cake and watches as Irene gets dressed, trying not to think about Mum. Irene is lumpy and middle-aged in her street clothes, but crammed into shining satin and sparkling with sequins and fake diamonds she looks as glamorous as Rita Hayworth. People say that, once upon a time, Irene performed in front of the old king, George VI.

She catches Joycie looking, fluffs out her hair and kisses the air with glossy lips. 'Not bad for an old girl, eh, lovey? Now be a darling and go ask your dad to get Sid off that stage on time tonight. I don't want to be hanging about in the wings for half an hour again.'

Joycie stops between the two dressing rooms when she hears Sid's voice: 'So what's wrong with Mary this time? You had another row?'

'No.' Her dad's voice is so low she has to strain to hear him. 'She saw Joycie off to bed, but she wasn't there when I got back after the show last night. I looked in the wardrobe and all her best clothes are gone.'

But that's not right because Joycie checked when Dad went out and Mum's favourite blouse was still there and her new black shoes in their box under the bed. She would never have left without them.

And now Joycie's thinking about what else she saw under the bed, but she doesn't want to. *Don't think about that, don't think.*

Harry the conjuror is too far away for her to hear more than a mumble. Sid is loud enough, though: 'You're better off without her, Charlie. You know what she's like. Found herself another fancy man I shouldn't wonder.'

A rustle and a waft of scent as Irene touches Joycie's shoulder. 'Never mind them, darling. They're talking rubbish. You come back in with me.'

There's a funny lump in Joycie's throat, but she bites her lip and sits at the dressing table again. Dad has come into the corridor and she can see him in the mirror, tall and handsome in his dinner jacket and bow tie. He peers in at her as he and Sid head for the stage, but she looks down and picks at the cake crumbs that have fallen into a little tray full of jewellery.

Irene sits beside her. 'Don't you worry, darling. I know Mary and she'll be back soon. Couldn't manage without you, could she?'

She pulls Joycie into her arms. Her bosom is soft and scented with powder that gets up Joycie's nose, and her hard corset digs in lower down. Joycie wishes she could cry, but there's just that awful, hurting lump she can't swallow away.

Irene is top of the bill and on straight after Dad and Sid. When she heads for the wings Joycie creeps out to watch from the other side. It's a full house with lots of laughter, but a few heckles too. Sid loves hecklers. Dressed in his trademark tweed suit and yellow tie he's fat and red-faced, his shiny bald head fringed by greasy strands of bottle-brown hair.

Sid is the star, the comic, and her dad is just the stooge, but it's her dad the girls crowd round for at the stage door. Everyone says he looks like Cary Grant. His real name is Charlie Todd, but he's called Lord Toddy in the act.

'I'm sorry, Lord Toddy, I didn't catch that,' Sid says as her dad mutters some nonsense no one can understand. At home he's cockney, but onstage Sid tells stories about Lord Toddy's family, who, he says, are filthy rich but brainless. When Sid asks a question Charlie's answer comes out as a splutter of posh noises, which Sid pretends to understand and pass on to the audience.

As they come off stage and Irene's music strikes up, Joycie steps further back into the whispering darkness.

'Shouldn't worry, Charlie boy,' Sid is saying. 'She'll be back with her tail between her legs before long. And while she's gone you might as well enjoy yourself. So what about getting Irene to take the kid tonight?'

Dad rubs his face and pulls off his bow tie. 'I don't know, Sid.'

'Go on.' He pats her dad's shoulder. 'A few drinks to cheer you up and you can come back to ours afterwards. I got a nice bottle of Scotch needs opening.'

Joycie waits until they're gone. She hopes Dad does let her stay with Irene tonight. Irene will tell her stories and make her laugh. So she won't have to think.

And she doesn't want to think. About the noises she heard in the night. Or the box with Mum's best shoes still there under the bed. Or what she found rolled up next to the box: the mat from the living room blotched all over with dark red stains that look like blood.

Chelsea, London – March 1965

Joycie kept telling herself it was all in the past, but the memories wouldn't stop flooding in. Things she thought she had forgotten; things she had tried to blank out. It was Irene Slade's death that had brought it all back, of course. Well the funeral was today so that would put an end to it.

Her face in the mirror was grey as the morning outside and the black dress didn't help. She rubbed a touch of rouge onto her cheekbones.

As she ran downstairs she could hear the wireless burbling away in the kitchen. Marcus had switched to the Home Service and on the Today programme, Jack de Manio's posh growl was saying something about snow showers forecast this morning. There was a smell of boiling milk and she stood in the kitchen doorway as Marcus made coffee. It was a squeeze to get in, even though they were both skinny, and dangerous to try when he was pouring scalding liquid.

He turned, holding the cups. 'All right? You look a bit pale.'

She sat on one of the spindly metal chairs that had to go sideways so you didn't bang your legs on the drop-down leaves of the Formica table. The latest *Vogue* was in front of her and the face that was and wasn't hers smiled from the cover through a cloud of black hair. She tapped the magazine. 'I'm not, *top model Orchid* today, just common old Joycie Todd. Don't need the false eyelashes or lipstick.'

He kissed the top of her head. 'You're still beautiful.'

For some reason that made her want to cry, but she forced a laugh. 'Shut up, you. It's your camera that makes me look good, we both know that. Anyway I need to be ordinary at the funeral. Don't want anyone to notice me.'

Marcus held out a plate of toast, but she shook her head. For once she wasn't hungry. 'Let's get going,' she said.

His old Morgan was parked outside, but a bitter wind whipped past them as they went down the stone steps of the house and, even with her coat clutched tight, Joycie was cold. Marcus drove along by the river, one hand on the wheel the other over her shoulder, rubbing her arm. She leaned into him, gritting her teeth, clamping her mind shut. *Don't think about it. It's all in the past.*

It had started to snow and she stared out of the misted window, watching a small boat chug through the filmy veil. *Don't think.* On the towpath a herring gull dragged at a slice of bread that jerked about as if it was alive. *That's it, concentrate on something else.*

But it was no good, her stomach churned and she realized it was a mistake to think she could cope with the funeral. Much better to visit the grave another day. She gripped Marcus's arm. 'I can't do this. Will you take me back?'

He stopped the car and turned to look at her. 'Come on, I'll

5

be there and you'll never forgive yourself if you chicken out now.'

She climbed out and walked over to look into the river. The water was grey, rippling with glints of steel and chrome as it slid by on its way to the sea.

When she heard the familiar clicking of his camera she turned to face Marcus. 'For God's sake, not now.'

He came close, kissing her cheek, his lips very warm. 'Sorry, couldn't stop myself. You look so wonderful all in black with the snow falling round you. Like Anna Karenina.' His head was to one side, a lock of blond hair falling across his eye, and he was wearing the naughty little boy expression that always made her laugh. She blew him a raspberry and climbed back in the car.

'OK let's get it over with.'

The stop had made them late to the church. Joycie had forgotten that Irene was Catholic and she hoped the service wouldn't be too long because her legs felt weak and her stomach was still churning. By now the snow flurries had died away, and the sun was trying to come out, but a stiff breeze bothered the daffodils growing in a couple of stone pots beside the gate.

As the heavy door closed behind them Marcus took her arm and they stood for a moment, eyes adjusting to the dim glitter inside. Joycie could feel rather than see that the church was crowded, but one short pew, tucked in beside a pillar, was empty and they slid in to sit there.

Candles flickered everywhere. Tall white ones near the altar and dozens of tiny flames on black metal stands to each side. There were plaster statues of saints beside some of the columns, their red lips smirking, painted eyes cast heavenward. As Joycie's eyes adjusted, she saw the priest in purple at the altar and a little boy in a white robe swinging an incense burner on a long chain. It sent a trail of blue vapour into the air. The sickly scent of it caught in her throat and as she watched the chain swinging to and fro, to and fro, she found herself swaying with it, until Marcus put his warm hand over hers and whispered, 'OK?'

The flower-covered coffin looked too small to carry buxom Irene, but maybe she'd lost weight before she died; the short obituary in *The Times* had mentioned something about a long illness. Joycie hadn't seen her for more than a year. A pang of guilt turned the queasy feeling into something sharper.

Latin chanting – *Pater noster, qui es in caeilis* – and tiny bells ringing. Joycie pulled her silk scarf tighter round her head, the collar of her coat close to her face, hoping no one would recognize her; wishing she'd stayed away. *Libera nos a malo.*

It seemed to go on forever with kneelings, standings, and sittings. The wafting incense made the air shimmer, the candle-light waver. Joycie gripped the pew, breathing hard.

More tinkling bells and two lines of people moving up the aisle to kneel at the altar rails. Maybe they could get out now without being noticed. She could come back to visit the grave later on – Irene would have understood. She whispered, 'Let's go.'

But it was too late. Deirdre, Irene's dresser and companion, was scuttling down the aisle towards them. She shuffled in to sit next to Joycie, her perfume clashing with the incense.

'Oh, darling, I'm so glad you came. I wasn't sure if you got my letter. Found your address in Irene's handbag. I wish she'd told me she had it and I could have asked you to visit before she went. She'd have loved to see you.'

'I'm sorry.'

'Don't you worry. She knew it was difficult for you. You will come back to the flat afterwards though, won't you?'

'Sorry, Deirdre, I can't.' She should have thought of an excuse.

But Deirdre gave her hand a clammy squeeze. 'That's all right, lovey, I understand.' She rummaged in her bag. 'I thought you might say that, so I brought this for you.' She handed Joycie a padded envelope. 'Just some things she wanted you to have.' She kissed Joycie's cheek.

The last people were walking back from the altar, hands clasped, eyes lowered.

Joycie stood. She had to get out. 'I'm sorry, Deirdre, I promise I'll be in touch, but I need some air now.'

Deirdre was such a sparrow of a woman it was easy to get past her and, thank God, the doors were already open. Outside Joycie took in a cool breath. Marcus was beside her and she leaned into him. He pulled down her scarf to kiss her ear, then patted the scarf into place again.

As they walked through the church gate a black Bentley was parking in front of the Morgan. Joycie stepped back, feeling the sharp ends of the freshly cut privet hedge pressing against her. Marcus was already unlocking the Morgan. So close it should have been easy to get in and speed away.

But she couldn't move. Had to stand there as Sid Sergeant, bigger and redder-faced than ever, jumped out and crushed her to him. Irene's envelope crackled between them. She smelled wool, tobacco, and booze and seemed to hear her dad's voice singing that old song, 'You been smokin' and drinkin' with mad, bad women', the way he used to when Sid rolled in late and hung-over before a show.

She stayed still, not breathing, her face pressed into his tweedy bulk, until Sid pulled away, holding her at arm's length.

'Oh, Joycie, I was hoping you'd be here. How are you, my lovely?'

She wanted to look at Marcus, to make him rescue her, but she couldn't. 'All right, thanks.' Her voice was a little girl's again.

A movement, not Marcus but Cora, Sid's manager and wife – in that order as she always said – getting out of the Bentley. 'Hello, Joyce, or should we call you Orchid now?' She looked older too, but good. Hair, still almost passing for platinum, black stilettos, black gloves, charm bracelet jangling at her wrist. There was a smudge of red lipstick on her teeth.

Marcus's arm came round Joycie's waist and made it possible

to move back and talk like a grown-up. 'Call me Joyce, Cora. Orchid's just my modelling name.'

Sid grabbed her hand in both of his before she could think to put it in her pocket, moving it up and down in time with his words. 'You're a very naughty girl to lose touch like that. I know you've been busy, but old friends do matter, you know.'

She stepped back so he had to let go and he turned to Marcus. 'And new friends too, of course. How do, Marcus. Don't mind if I call you that, do you? We feel like we know you already. Been following our kid's career. You've done well by her.'

Marcus squeezed her waist. 'Good to meet you, sir.'

Cora gave a nicotine-coated chuckle. 'Ooer, Joyce, he *is* posh, isn't he? And handsome with it.' She flapped the back of her hand against Marcus's chest. 'Don't mind me, dear, I'm common as muck, but harmless.'

Marcus took the hand and brought it to his lips – 'Charmed I'm sure' – as Cora gave a scream of laughter.

'Ooh, I say. You should hold on to this one, Joyce.'

Sid handed Marcus a card. 'I'll give this to you, son, because she'll only throw it away. Try to persuade her to keep in touch. We miss her, don't we, Cora?'

'You can say that again. Like our own daughter she was for a while.' Cora hadn't looked at Joycie since Marcus had spoken.

Joycie made herself move. 'We'd better be off.'

'Not going to the grave? I don't blame you.' Sid gestured towards the church. 'Can't stand all that mumbo jumbo either, but I thought we should see old Irene into the ground, at least.'

As Joycie climbed into the Morgan Sid stepped in front of her door, keeping it open.

'Don't be a stranger, eh, darling.' His hand was on her shoulder, squeezing hard, leaning close, smoky tweed filling her nostrils. 'Your dad would have been so proud of you,' he said, his voice a husky whisper. 'What happened to him, what they did to him, was terrible, but that's all in the past.'

She closed the door, and Marcus waved through the open window as he pulled the Morgan away. Cora returned the wave while Sid, hands in pockets, his paunch sticking out in front, watched them go.

Chapter Two

The envelope sat heavy on Joycie's lap. The sun made the car too warm, and she untied her scarf and slipped off her coat, letting the envelope slide down beside the door. Marcus glanced over.

'Not going to open that then?'

'It won't be anything much.' It felt like jewellery, nothing to worry about, but she wished Deirdre had forgotten it. Wished she hadn't gone to the funeral at all.

'So that was Sid Sergeant, eh? He's looking a lot older than his pictures. And the wife, Cora, you never mentioned her,' Marcus said.

They stopped at traffic lights near a park, and she watched some ducks flapping about on a big pond. Three green drakes chasing a brown female. The female was trying to fly away, feet kicking the top of the water, but the males were all around her and she couldn't get into the air. She skimmed to an island in the middle and scrambled up the bank.

Marcus touched her shoulder. 'You all right?'

'I should never have gone. Irene wouldn't have minded.'

'You didn't look too pleased to see Sid.'

It's all in the past. It's all in the past. She pulled the envelope onto her lap and tore it open. A jet bracelet and two necklaces, one a double string of pearls and the other glittering with red stones. They were things Irene wore all the time. Joycie held them to her cheek, hearing Irene's fruity chuckle so clearly she had to swallow down a sob. Marcus took his hand from the wheel and rubbed her knee.

'Ah, that's nice. Let's take some pictures of you wearing them. You can send them to Deirdre.'

But Joycie was looking at the smaller envelope that had fallen out last of all, her breath catching in her throat. In place of an address was a line of writing: *Dear Joycie, Irene asked me to get this to you. All my love Deirdre.*

Marcus glanced over. 'What's that?'

'A note from Irene, I suppose.'

'Aren't you going to read it?'

She pushed it back with the jewellery into the large envelope. 'When we get home.'

Back at the house she ran up to her room. 'I'm going to get changed.' Closed the door and emptied the big envelope onto her dressing table. Then she took the smaller envelope over to the window and ripped it open. But instead of reading it she stood with the note pressed against her chest.

She loved this house. It was tall and thin with three floors. Her bedroom overlooked a long green garden, a bit unkempt but that was the way she and Marcus loved it. Today it was full of daffodils, clumps of late snowdrops lighting up the darker corners. The trees were covered with a haze of palest green buds.

A deep breath as she unfolded the note.

My darling Joycie,
We haven't seen much of each other lately and I don't blame you for wanting to put the past and everyone connected with it behind you. Of course I have been following your progress in the papers and your photographer friend seems to be a nice

young man. So I really hope you have found happiness with him.

In that case you might decide to ignore this letter. However I can't go to my grave without saying this. The last time we met I told you someone had dropped off an address at the theatre for me with a note asking me to get it to Mary Todd's daughter. It was obviously someone who knew Mary and could maybe help you find out what really happened to your mum. You said you weren't interested because she deserted you, but you know how fond I was of Mary and I never believed she meant to leave you forever. I feel so bad that I didn't try to find her myself or make more effort to persuade you to look for her.

Anyway here's the name and address. Susan Lomax, 44 Trenton St. Manchester. It's up to you, but I really hope you decide to look into it.

I'm sorry I can't leave you anything more than a few old paste jewels, but I remember how you liked dressing up in them when you were little. So I thought you might be glad to have them.

With fondest love,
Irene

The writing was wobbly, clearly written when Irene was ill, and her signature tailed off as if she was unable to keep hold of the pen. Joycie held the scrap of paper to her lips as hot tears welled from deep inside.

I never believed she meant to leave you forever. That was what Irene had always said and for the first few years Joycie had believed it too. But her mother didn't come back, didn't try to get in contact, and Joycie told herself she'd stopped wanting her to. Irene hadn't seen the person who left the address so it could have been anyone and even if it was her mum or someone close to her, Joycie had decided it was too late. She didn't want to listen to a load of excuses. But Irene had been so good to her and this was the only thing she'd ever asked from Joycie.

Your photographer-friend seems to be a nice young man. I really hope you have found happiness with him. Irene was right about Marcus. He was more than nice and life without him was unthinkable. But as for finding happiness, well that was something else.

Marcus had declared his love for her not long after they met, but she said it was too soon. Still he asked her to move in. Said he couldn't bear rattling around here on his own. It made sense too with them working together all the time and she needn't worry, she could have her own room.

The house belonged to his parents, but they'd decamped to the country when his dad retired from the civil service. It always amazed her that people could own two houses. Her early life had been lived in theatrical lodgings in the towns and seaside resorts where Sid and her dad performed. A bedroom for her mum and dad, one for her, and another room for sitting and eating, with a tiny kitchenette if they were lucky. The bathroom was usually down the hall, shared with the rest of the tenants, and sometimes the toilet was outside. It was wonderful to have a whole house just for her and Marcus.

She knew he hoped for more, but decided not to think about that. Finally she told him she had a problem with closeness and it wasn't fair to ask him to wait for her. What she didn't say was how much she dreaded him finding another girl he felt serious about and who could love him properly. 'I do love you, Marcus, but not in that way,' she had told him. He must have guessed by then that the idea of loving anyone *in that way* made her skin crawl.

She had never admitted, because it wasn't fair to lead him on, that sometimes when he touched her the shivers that went through her felt wonderful.

***

Marcus wanted to come to Manchester with her, but she wouldn't let him. This way she could still change her mind. It was cold on the train and she felt very alone. At the station she went into the buffet to get warm, and to try and steady her nerves. She pulled up the collar of her black coat, although the woman behind the counter didn't give her a second glance. People hardly ever recognized her. Without the make-up and glamorous clothes she was just a skinny pale-faced girl.

'So you knew Irene had the address all along,' Marcus had said.

'Yeah, that was why she contacted me the last time I saw her. Must have been two or three years ago. Said someone left a note at the stage door asking if she was still in touch with Mary Todd's daughter and could she give me that name and address.'

'But you never went?'

'Irene begged me to. Even offered to go with me, but I wouldn't even take the details. Didn't want to see or hear about my mum. She dumped us, Marcus. Me and Dad. Went off with one of her fancy men, so everyone said. I reckon she heard about me getting known as a model and thought I must have money.'

That had been when the nightmares started up again. They stopped after a few months, but with Irene's death they'd come back and with them flashes of memory. Joycie knew she had to do more than pretend there was nothing wrong.

When her dad died she didn't let herself cry. It was nearly three years after her mum went and they were fine, just the two of them. But he killed himself, leaving her all alone and without a word from him. So she told herself she didn't care. There was no way to make that better, but perhaps Irene was right. If she could see her mum, or find out for sure what had happened to her, maybe she could get a bit of peace.

She asked the taxi driver to drop her at the end of Trenton

Road and come back in an hour. It seemed like an area where a taxi might cause a stir and anyway she could take a look at the place before deciding what to do.

The street lights were already on in a damp dusk and the pavement gleamed under her feet. Terraced houses, front steps shining with red polish, a couple of clean milk bottles on the pavement beside each one.

She stopped opposite number 44. There was a glow from somewhere at the back, but the front room was dim and the net curtains meant she couldn't see in.

A deep breath, collar pulled tighter at her throat, asking herself what was the point of this, what was she hoping to find? But she was outside the door now and tapping on it.

A child crying, the door opening, the woman looking back into the hallway saying, 'Watch him, Carol. Don't let him climb on the table.'

It was her mum, unchanged in all these years, just like her memories and the dog-eared photo in her bag. Joycie's breath stopped. But when the woman turned, brushing reddish hair away from her face, she was different. Not Mum then, but definitely related.

She breathed again, trying to remember the words she'd planned. 'I'm Joyce Todd, Mary Todd's daughter. Someone left this address with Irene Slade wanting me to get in contact.'

Somehow she was inside the house, the narrow hall smelling of cabbage and bacon, and then in the front room sitting on a hard sofa. The room was cold and clean; probably kept for best. A tiny boy watched her from the hall doorway, thumb stuck in his mouth, until a little girl in a dress with a torn sleeve pulled at his arm.

'Come on, Mikey, leave the lady alone.'

The woman's voice: 'That's it, Carol. Put him in the high chair and feed him his tea while I'm talking.'

Then she was back, without her apron, touching her hair. 'I'm

16

Mary's sister, your auntie Susan. Mary will have told you about me.'

Joycie tried to speak, but no words came. She bought time by undoing her coat and slipping it off. She was freezing, but it seemed rude to sit there all trussed up. Then she pushed back her own hair and met the woman's eyes. Her aunt (how strange that sounded) smoothed her skirt and gave a little cough.

'It's ages since I left that note. Never expected anyone to turn up.' Her voice was like Mum's, the northern accent just a little stronger.

'Irene has just died and your address was with the things she left me.' She didn't say she'd refused to take it in the first place.

Susan was looking hard at her, a little smile quirking the corners of her mouth. 'You know you look a lot like that model, Orchid. Did anyone ever tell you?'

Joycie could feel her face flushing. 'I am her. Orchid's the name I use professionally.'

'Well blow me down. I mean, you do look like her, like her photos, your photos, but ... ' Her face was pink now too.

For some reason this made Joycie feel better and she was able to laugh. 'It's all right. Most people are surprised at how ordinary I am. It's really all about the make-up and the way they dress me.'

'No, you're a lovely looking girl. Not much like your mam, if you don't mind me saying, but you take after your dad. He's a handsome fella.'

'Yes, he was.' A movement from Susan. 'He died a long while ago.'

'Oh, I am sorry about that. I knew he wasn't with Sid Sergeant any more. 'Cos Sid was on the bill that time I sent the note to Irene Slade. That's why I went. Hoped to see Charlie. But Sid didn't have a stooge. And I thought that was odd because Charlie told Mam he owed everything to Sid and would never leave him. You know your dad was an orphan?' Joycie nodded. 'Apparently Sid took him on when he'd just come out of the Dr Barnardo's home he grew up in. Charlie said Sid was the only family he'd ever known.'

'So it wasn't my mum who left the address?'

'No, it was me. I was hoping Irene might put me in touch with both of you.'

Joycie's breath stalled for a moment before she could get the words out. 'How long is it since you've seen my mum?'

Susan's eyes were cloudy. 'A long time. Not since before you were born.'

Something heavy seemed to drop from her throat to her stomach and Joycie knew if she tried to speak, or even to breathe, she might cry. *Stupid, stupid idiot.* She'd actually convinced herself she had no hopes or expectations. How wrong she had been.

'So why didn't you ask Irene to give your address to Mum?'

'I did. I asked her to get it to Mary Todd or her daughter.'

That wasn't what Irene had told Joycie. Was that because she had misread the note or because she thought Joycie was more likely to go searching if she thought it might have come from Mary herself or from someone who knew her whereabouts? If so then it had worked.

Susan was talking on and she forced herself to listen.

'I didn't like to send the note to Sid in case he and your dad had fallen out and that's why they weren't together, but I remembered Mary mentioning in her letters that she was friendly with Irene Slade.'

It was anger Joycie heard in her own voice when she was able to speak. 'My mother left us when I was eleven years old and I haven't seen or heard from her since.'

Susan was suddenly on her feet, one hand at her mouth, muttering something about tea. Joycie heard her talking to the children in the kitchen, her voice too low to make out the words. Then clinking crockery and a wail from the little boy. Joycie rubbed her arms. There was just one thin rug covering the brown and blue patterned lino on the floor. The fireplace was swept clean and she wondered if they ever lit it. There were no pictures on the wall and, apart from the sofa and the two armchairs, the only furniture was a spindly legged coffee table and a glass-fronted cabinet with a few china ornaments. If they had a TV it must be in another room.

Her aunt came back carrying a tray with a teapot, cups and saucers, and milk jug. She put the tray on the coffee table and looked at Joycie. 'Milk and sugar?'

'Just milk, please.'

'I expect you've got to watch your figure?'

It wasn't true, she could eat anything, but she just smiled. When Susan handed her the cup it rattled in its saucer and, looking at her, Joycie wondered if she'd been crying. She sipped the tea, strong and hot just the way she liked it, and cradled it in both hands, grateful for the warmth on her fingers.

Susan pulled a hankie from her sleeve and rubbed her nose. 'So, your mam, you've never had no word?'

'Nothing at all. When was the last time you heard from her?'

'Must have been summer '53 because it was just before I got married and I was excited to think she'd be here for that. And she was gonna bring you with her. Mam and me couldn't wait to meet you for the first time.'

'I didn't even know she had a family.'

Susan put two spoonfuls of sugar in her tea and stirred. 'When we found out she was expecting our Dad went mad. I was only a kid, but I can remember him screaming at her and her crying. He said she was no better than a common slut. And carrying on with someone like that made it even worse. He wouldn't have no more to do with her. Said none of us would.'

'Someone like what?'

'You know, on the stage. He was religious, Dad, didn't hold with that kind of thing.' She was still stirring and stirring, the spoon clinking against her cup. 'Mary left with your dad, but she used to write to Mam regular like. Dad was very strict and Mary knew he would destroy any letters so she sent them to our neighbour, who used to bring them round when Dad was at work.'

'Did your mother write back?'

'Now and then. When she could do it without Dad finding out, but it was difficult. Mary let us know when you were born and I begged Mam to take me to see you, but it was impossible.'

When Joycie shook her head, Susan did the same.

'That's how it was in those days. Dad made the rules.' She smiled. 'I can just imagine my hubby trying to lay down the law like that. I'd soon tell him where to get off. But Mam had to do as she was told. We all did. And to be fair to Dad there was no money for gallivanting around the country, especially as you kept moving.'

That probably explained why her mum never mentioned her family. If Joycie was unlikely ever to see them it would have been pointless.

The little girl had come to stand by the open door, staring in again, but the toddler staggered from behind her and crawled onto his mum's lap. She spat on her hankie and rubbed it over his face, while he squirmed and whimpered. Then he took one look at Joycie and buried his head in Susan's chest.

Joycie drained her cup. She couldn't be too long, didn't want to miss the last train and get marooned here. 'But you didn't see her in '53?'

Susan was rocking the little boy back and forth, his eyes closed, thumb in his mouth. The girl made a sudden run to her side and leaned against her, huge brown eyes fixed on Joycie. 'No, she just wrote and said she was fed up. Said things were happening that weren't right. Hoped our dad would let her stay here till she got on her feet. But if not she'd get a place nearby. She never came though and we never saw her again.'

'What about her bloke, the man she left us for. Did she say who he was?'

'She didn't mention anyone else. Just said she had to get away. And, like I said, she was going to bring you.'

'Well she obviously changed her mind. Decided to go some-where else and leave me with my dad.'

'See, I can't believe that. Like I said, our dad was a difficult man so we always thought she changed her mind about coming here. Scared he would still be angry with her. But she loved you so much, said so all the time in her letters. I just can't see her leaving you.'

'Did you try to locate her when she didn't turn up?'

'Mam wrote to the last address we had for her, but it was Charlie who wrote back.'

Joycie leaned forward. He hadn't told her about this. 'What did he say?'

'Just that he was sorry, but Mary had left him and he had no idea where she was. He didn't mention you so we thought she'd taken you with her. And soon after that Mam got ill and died. Then Dad's mind began to go so ...' She sniffed and rubbed her nose. 'I had to look after him for the next few years and by the time he died I was too busy with the kids to worry about anything else for a while. But my husband's got a big family and I started to miss Mary again because she's all I've got. And I wanted my kids to meet their auntie and their cousin.'

She put down her cup. 'I've just thought, there's a photo.' When she stood and headed for the door the little boy still clung to her and a forgotten memory came to Joycie. Her mum, lifting her and spinning her round, then clutching her close and dancing to the gramophone playing some old dance tune. Joycie's feet dangling in the air as she pressed her cheek to Mum's soft face, the powdery scent of her, an earring tickling.

While Susan and her son were out of the room the little girl stayed, staring at Joycie with those big brown eyes: so still it was unnerving.

'Hello,' Joycie said. 'Your name's Carol, is it?' A nod, the child's eyes still fixed on her. 'Mine's Joycie.'

When her mother came back Carol clutched her skirt, but

21

Susan pulled her hand away as she sat down and laughed. 'Don't pretend you're shy now.' She looked at Joycie. 'Can't shut her up normally.' She handed a silver photo frame to the little girl. 'Go on, give that to Joyce.' Carol ran at her, thrust the frame into her hand and rushed back to her mum. 'That's me and Mary, only picture I've got.'

Two girls, one a slender teenager the other much younger, still a little girl, but the likeness was obvious.

'That was taken the summer your mam met Charlie, just before the war. 1939 it was. Last holiday we had together,' Susan said. 'Mary would have been sixteen and I was eight.'

The photo was a holiday snap taken on the prom at Blackpool. Mary and Susan smiling in the sunshine, but holding onto their hats as their skirts swirled in the sea breeze. Joycie touched the glass that covered her mother's face. She looked so young and pretty.

Susan was still talking. 'Sid and Charlie were in a show there. We wanted to go, but our dad wouldn't hear of it. Then we were on the pier, just me and Mary, and Charlie was there too. He started chatting to us and bought me a candyfloss.' She smiled at Joycie. 'I expect that was to keep me quiet so he could talk to Mary. We were only there for a week, but they saw each other every day. Dad would probably have taken her straight home if he'd known.'

'But they didn't get together properly till '41 when Dad was in the army, did they?'

'They'd been writing to each other all that time. I remember thinking it were so romantic. She had a picture of Charlie in his uniform. He looked like a film star to me, although he would only have been nineteen or so. He came to see her when he was on leave and Mam took a real shine to him. But they kept it quiet from Dad.'

'And then I happened.'

'Yeah, and, of course, she had to tell Dad she was having a

baby. But Charlie wanted to marry her and was getting compassionate leave so they could do it right away. She was still only eighteen, though, and Dad refused his consent. That was when she ran away. And we never saw her again.'

They were both silent. Joycie praying that Susan might say something that would explain it all. Instead she shook her head. 'I just can't understand her leaving you as well as Charlie. Or why she's never been in touch.'

All Joycie could say was, 'Nor me, but I'm going to try to find out what I can, and if there's anything you think of that might help ...' She looked at her watch and pulled on her coat. 'I'm sorry, I need to go or I'll miss my train. Can I leave you my address and phone number?'

Her aunt followed her into the hallway and scrabbled in the drawer of a little table, handing Joycie a notepad and biro. 'There are letters from Mary to Mam in the attic. I'll send them to you.'

Joycie scribbled her details. 'Thank you. It's been good to meet you.'

In the doorway Susan moved towards her then back with a tiny cough. She was smiling, a smile that was so like Joycie's memory of her mum's it sent a charge through her. As another memory tugged, Joycie's eyes filled and she had to rub her hand over her face.

Susan touched her elbow. 'Look, Joyce, whatever happened with Mary she loved you, really loved you, and I know she would never have left you unless she had no choice.'

After they said goodbye Susan stayed in her open doorway with the little boy, Joycie's cousin, clinging to her leg and Joycie could feel their eyes on her as she walked away down the silent street.

Chapter Three

Checking her watch for the umpteenth time Joycie paced up and down by the bus stop. This was definitely where she'd asked the taxi to pick her up and she'd given him a big enough tip that he surely wouldn't let her down. But if he didn't get here soon she'd miss her train.

She moved closer to the kerb as she heard an engine approaching, but it was only a kid on a moped. He stopped right next to her and she stepped back to lean on the wall of the terraced house, looking at her watch again and then into the distance, pretending she hadn't noticed him.

He climbed off the bike. 'Hello, darlin' you're outta luck you know.' His accent was so strong it was difficult to make out the words. She didn't look at him. 'No bus due for ages,' he said.

'I know.' She brushed at her coat, still avoiding his eye.

'I can give you a lift if you like. Plenty of room for a skinny bird like you on the back.' He let out a wobbly laugh, as if his voice had not long broken.

'No thank you, I'm waiting for someone.' But now with a rush of air she seemed to be surrounded by boys on pushbikes.

'Eh, Sammy, got a new girlfriend, have ya?' A heavyset lad

bumped his bike onto the pavement, coming so close she could feel the heat steaming from him.

'Yeah, and she's dead posh.' Moped boy leaned over and pushed Joycie's arm. 'Go on, doll, say something for him.'

Joycie felt rather than saw a net curtain twitch in the house behind her. This was ridiculous, they were just kids. 'Look, go away and leave me alone, will you? I'm waiting for someone.'

A shriek from moped boy. 'Ooer, hark at it. Told you she were posh.'

The others joined in with honks of laughter and the nearest boy came even closer, looking round at his mates then back at her. 'How's about a kiss then, darling. Bet you're not too la de da for that.' She shoved him away and his face changed. 'Don't you push me, you tart.'

Loud clicking footsteps and the boys turned as a man of about forty, tall and thin in a camel coat and black trousers, rounded the corner. He stopped and looked at her. 'These lads bothering you, miss?' His accent was London, not Manchester.

The boy nearest Joycie said, 'Nah, mister, just having a chat, weren't we?' He looked at his friends, but they were getting ready to ride away. He moved his bike back onto the road. The man stared at him, arms folded over his chest, his hard gaze shifting from him to moped boy, who started his engine and rode off. The other lad followed fast, shouting, 'Bye, darling, see ya,' as he went.

Joycie looked at the man. 'Thank you.'

'Waiting for a taxi are you?' he said, his voice low and polite.

'Yes, it should be here by now.' Silly to feel scared, he was trying to help her.

A piercing whistle and there was her taxi. Almost as if it had been waiting for his signal. She reached for the door but he was there first, holding it open and giving a tiny bow as she climbed in. His hair was short and greased down, his face shiny and newly shaved. He had very pale grey eyes.

'Thank you, you're very kind.' She tried to close the door, but he held onto it.

'Station is it?'

'Yes.'

He leaned towards the driver and she caught a whiff of after-shave. 'Better hurry if she wants the London train.' She reached for the door again, but he held on. 'You shouldn't be hanging around street corners in a place like this, you know. And it's just as well those lads didn't recognize you.'

As the taxi pulled away he gave her a small wave and a little nod and turned away, shiny black shoes gleaming under the street lights.

Hastings – September 1953

Joycie and her dad have got into the habit of having their tea at the Italian café on the front before walking to the theatre. He always lets her have ice cream for afters and today it's her favourite: banana split. He smokes and sips his coffee while she eats; the ice cream cold on her lips.

When he screws up his eyes and hands her a paper napkin she scrubs at her face and he gives a little laugh. 'Your mum would have my guts for garters if she could see you.'

It's almost the first time he's mentioned Mum since she went and Joycie swallows hard and puts down her spoon, biting her lip to stop from crying.

Dad rubs her shoulder. 'Sorry, darlin', didn't mean to upset you.'

His voice sounds thick and Joycie feels bad because it's her fault. She starts to eat again even though her throat feels all clogged up.

'You mustn't blame your mum for going, Joycie. She's a great girl and I didn't deserve her. Never was much of a husband. But she loves you to bits and I bet she'll be in touch one day soon.'

When Joycie looks up he's smiling at her, but his blue eyes are bright with tears. So she gives him a wobbly grin and he sniffs, rubs his eyes and says, 'And we're all right for now aren't we?'

She finishes her banana split and holds his hand as they walk along by the sea in the late sunshine. People look at her dad as they pass, probably recognizing him from the show, but she can see that some of the women look because he's so handsome. She's proud to be holding his hand and to know he's her dad. And she's not going to think about that stained mat any more.

And anyway she looked for it when she got back from Irene's the day after Mum left and, although the black shoes were still in their box under the bed, she couldn't find the mat.

Chelsea – April 1965

Joycie woke to Radio Caroline playing The Moody Blues' 'Go Now' in the kitchen. Marcus was back then. He hadn't come home last night, no doubt staying with some girl he'd met. She was grateful that he never brought anyone back here when she was at home. She had no right to expect even that of him, but it always upset her to think of him with someone else.

A tap on the bedroom door, and he was there, holding a cup of coffee and a bacon sandwich. He sat on the bed, handing her the cup. 'All right? How did it go?'

She took a big gulp. 'It was my aunt. I never even knew she existed, can you believe that? She seems really nice, but she hasn't seen Mum since she left us and doesn't know anything about this bloke she's supposed to have run off with.'

'So what does she think happened?'

'She has no idea, although they did contact my dad just after Mum left.'

'And what did he say?'

Joycie took a huge bite of her sandwich to give herself time to think, waving her hand so he knew he'd have to wait. He smiled and folded his arms as if prepared to sit in silence for as long as it took.

When she could stand it no longer, she spoke through the food still in her mouth, and Marcus handed her a tissue from the bedside cabinet, his eyes never leaving her face. 'The same thing he told me: that she left him, and he didn't know where she was.'

'So what do *you* think now?' When Joycie shrugged and carried on chewing he said, 'I mean, if she left him for another man, who was the guy?'

'I've no idea. Over the years I realized she had other men, but it didn't affect me and never seemed to bother Dad either. I don't remember anyone being around at that time, but he must have been special if she left us for him.'

Marcus went over to the window and pulled the curtain so that the sun streamed in, making a bright halo of his hair. 'You think it was something else, though, don't you?' She didn't answer, her heart beating hard, as if by telling him it could make what she dreaded true. He faced her, half sitting on the dressing table. 'Come on, Joycie, whatever you say I can tell you don't really believe she deserted you.'

She put the plate down and began pleating the crumpled sheet between her fingers. 'I couldn't, not for a long time, even though everyone said so. Eventually I just learned to accept it because there seemed to be no other explanation. But my aunt, she's called Susan, says Mum really loved me. She doesn't think she would have left without me for any reason. But who knows, perhaps this bloke wouldn't let her bring me, and she had to make a choice.'

'What did your dad tell you?'

'That he was a rubbish husband, and he didn't blame her for going. He always said Mum left me with him because she couldn't provide for me, and because she knew it would have broken his heart to lose me too.' She rubbed her nose with the tissue Marcus had given her, but it was greasy and smelled of bacon, and she scrabbled in the box for another.

Marcus came back to sit on the bed and pulled her into his arms. They sat for a while, her head against his chest as she breathed in his lovely, familiar smell and listened to the steady beat of his heart. He smoothed her hair until she moved her head so that it rested in the curve of his warm palm, and he kissed her forehead.

'I'm scared, Marcus,' she said. 'But I can't leave it alone now.'

'I know,' he whispered.

Then they kissed properly; a long soft kiss. His heart began to thump faster against her thin nightdress. Her own heart was speeding too, and when his lips pressed harder and his fingers twined into her hair she felt a throb of longing for him.

'Little cock-teaser, that's what you are, just like your mum.'

The words echoed in her head along with the memory of cloying Brylcreem and smoke-clogged tweed, and Joycie flinched back. 'Sorry, sorry,' she managed to gasp, turning away to hide her face in the wall, gulping down the bile, afraid he would guess how she felt. For a few moments she had wanted him so much. But that voice was in her head again, and she knew she could never let go with any man, even with Marcus.

He hadn't moved, and after what seemed an age she felt his hand touch her shoulder. It stayed there for a moment before sliding down her arm. When he reached her hand he gripped her fingers. 'It's fine, come on, sit up and look at me, Joycie. It's only me.'

She grabbed more tissues and scrubbed at her face saying sorry over and over. When she was finally able to look at him, he smiled, and she longed to hold him again and tell him she loved him and one day it might work between them. But that was impossible.

'This', he made a gesture that seemed to take in her tear-stained face, the crumple of tissues on the bed, and even himself, 'is all because of what happened to your mum, isn't it?'

She met his eyes. 'I used to think someone, or something, might have forced her to go away.'

'This guy she was having it off with, you mean?'

A flicker of memory. 'Or someone else. I just don't know.' He squeezed her forearm and for a moment she longed to lean into him again. Instead she climbed out of bed.

'You're not going to leave it at that, though, are you?' he said. 'You'll see this aunt again?'

'She's sending me some letters they got from Mum.'

'Good, and in the meantime why don't we try to find out if there *was* another guy and have a go at tracking him down? I've got Sid Sergeant's phone number, so we could get in touch with him. He and your parents were close so I bet he'll have some idea.'

Her dressing gown was on the end of the bed, and she pulled it round her, swallowing to get rid of the sick feeling in her throat. 'No, I don't want anything to do with him, with either of them.'

Her voice came out louder than she meant, and Marcus raised his palms in front of him. 'Fine, fine, no need to scream at me.' She fastened the dressing gown, her fingers fumbling on the buttons, as he went on, 'I wish you'd tell me everything, Joycie, it might even help you. It's not just your mum, is it? Something happened to you as well.'

She went to sit at the dressing table, wincing at her reflection. *God, she looked awful.*

'Sid is obviously a lecherous old bastard, and it doesn't take a Sigmund Freud to see you can't stand to be near him,' Marcus said.

With her hands in her hair she stared at herself in the mirror, trying to see the whole truth in her own face. *Brylcreem, stale beer, and rough tweed smelling of sweat and wee.* 'There's things from when I was a kid I just can't remember and other things that …'

'You don't want to remember or even think about?'

A deep breath, pushing her hair back and meeting his eyes in the mirror. 'Please, Marcus, let it be for now. I think if I can find what really happened to my mum the rest might sort itself out.'

He picked up the empty cup and plate. 'OK.' At the door he turned. 'What about talking to Deirdre then? She and Irene were your mum's friends.'

Joycie had lived with Irene and Deirdre after her dad died: shell-shocked by what had happened to him. And although Irene was full of stories about her life in the theatre, they rarely mentioned either of her parents.

'We could take those photos of you wearing the jewellery Irene left you. I'm sure Deirdre would love that.'

'Yes, let's. I should go and see her anyway. I ought to have visited her and Irene more often. They were so good to me. But, Marcus, please throw away the card Sid gave you. I want to forget all about him.'

Marcus handed Deirdre the brown envelope with the photos of Joycie wearing Irene's necklaces. As she looked at them Deirdre's tiny hands shook and her eyes, when she raised them, were full of tears. 'Oh, Joycie, you look lovely. Irene would have been so pleased to see them on you. She always loved them, and she loved you too, sweetheart.' She reached over and gripped Joycie's hands. Her own were cool, the skin stretched paper-thin over the bones.

Joycie looked around at the room. It hadn't changed at all, still too warm and too crowded. Little tables covered with knick-knacks, empty candlesticks, and photo frames. More pictures on the upright piano, which was still open with some sheet music propped on it. Deirdre couldn't play, but Joycie could see she'd kept everything as it was when Irene was alive.

The time when Joycie lived here after her dad died was mostly a blur of misery, but Irene with her stories and songs, and Deirdre with her fry-ups and stodgy puddings had made it a bit more bearable. Irene had paid for Joycie to go to secretarial college in Chelsea. When she was spotted by Marcus and started earning as a model she repaid the tuition money, but she visited Irene and Deirdre less and less, telling herself she was too busy, but knowing it was because they were part of a past she wanted to forget.

She sipped her sweet Cinzano. In Irene's day it would have had a big slug of gin added. She hoped Deirdre was all right for money.

Deirdre was holding out one of the photos and a pen. 'You will both sign them, won't you, to join the collection?' She waved her hand at the pictures all around. Joycie recognized the old ones like Charlie Chester and Dame Myra Hess, but there were some more recent photos too: Helen Shapiro, all bouffant hair and big smile, and Marty Wilde in a leather jacket attempting an Elvis lip curl.

She put her name on the photos opposite Marcus's adding: *with all my love to dearest Deirdre XXX*. The signatures would make the photos worth some money, but Deirdre wouldn't want to part with them so Joycie decided she'd send her another batch telling her to do what she wanted with them. If Deirdre sold them no one need know, and it would be a way of helping out without hurting her pride.

Leaning back in her chair she was aware that Marcus was watching her, waiting for her to say what they'd come for. Deirdre refilled her own glass and waved the bottle first at Marcus and then at Joycie, who shook her head. 'Deirdre?' she paused feeling a tremor deep inside, but forcing herself on. 'I was wondering if you knew anything about that bloke my mum ran away with. I've met her sister, you see, and she said Mum never mentioned anyone.'

Deirdre put down her glass. 'So she's seen Mary, has she, the sister?'

'No, but she seems to doubt there was a man in '53.'

'Well, I'm only going by what everyone said. They all seemed sure there was someone. Your mum was a lovely girl, of course, but we all knew things weren't quite right between her and your dad even though you could tell they really loved each other.'

Marcus leaned forward. 'So Irene never said anything to you about a man when Mary disappeared?'

'No, and she just couldn't understand it.' She turned towards Joycie. 'You should ask Sid's wife, Cora. I'm sure she mentioned a fancy man, but I don't think we ever heard his name.'

Deirdre insisted they stay for sandwiches and cake, and they promised not to be strangers, but when they were outside in the Morgan again Joycie said, 'Well that's it: another dead end.'

Marcus put the keys in the ignition. 'Look, I know you don't want to see Sid, but why not try to speak to Cora? I could see her if you like. I think she took a shine to me.'

Joycie managed a small laugh. 'You noticed that, did you? OK, but make sure she doesn't get the idea we want to be friends.'

A rap on the driver's window, and when Marcus rolled it down a male voice said: 'It's Marcus and Orchid isn't it? Wonder if I could beg an autograph. Name's Bill, if you wouldn't mind putting that too.' There was something familiar about the voice, but it wasn't until Marcus had signed and passed the brand new autograph book over to her that she saw the man's face as he bent his tall frame down by the window and smiled in at her.

She scribbled her signature, aware that he was moving round the front of the car to get to her side. Then she had no option but to roll down her own window and pass the book to him, trying to avoid his eyes.

He pressed her fingers for a moment as he took the book, his own hand very cold as if he'd been standing outside for some time. She felt his breath against her cheek. 'Keep bumping into each other, don't we, Orchid?' he said. 'Glad you got home safe the other day. Take care of yourself, won't you.'

He released her hand and stood back, his trousers as sharply creased, shoes as well polished as they'd been when she'd seen him in Manchester.

Chapter Four

On the way home Marcus kept asking her what was wrong, but she couldn't tell him until they were safe inside. He made some tea, and when he was sitting opposite her at the tiny kitchen table he lit a cigarette and blew three smoke rings, which usually got her smiling. But not today.

'That man, the one with the autograph book, he was in Manchester at the corner of my aunt's street. He spoke to me, obviously knew who I was.'

'Well that's peculiar. Any idea who he might be?'

'I've never set eyes on him before.'

Marcus leaned back, staring up at the smoke rising to the ceiling. 'Most likely a journalist. Unless it's one of your fans. He looked a bit old for that, but you never can tell.'

That was as likely an explanation as any. It was disturbing to think of people becoming obsessed with her, but it had happened before. As for journalists, her fear was always that they'd get wind of her father's suicide and, of course, what led to it – his arrest and imprisonment.

When she first started modelling that was one reason she'd changed her name. They'd given out the story that she was an orphan, which had been good enough so far. And the journalists were more interested in the *romance* between her and Marcus than poking into her background. The received wisdom was that she adored him, but he wouldn't commit himself and was still playing the field. It wasn't fair on Marcus because it was she who wouldn't – couldn't – commit, but he laughed it off, saying he didn't mind people thinking he was a bit of a Casanova.

'Shall we report him to the police?' Marcus said.

'What for? He hasn't done anything, and both times he's been very nice to me. It just doesn't feel right.'

Marcus swallowed back his tea and jumped up. 'OK, go and get your glad rags on. Let's have some dinner and get drunk. Forget about all this for a while. You've got a busy day tomorrow doing that shoot for Cecil Beaton.'

'Oh God, I can't believe I've forgotten about Beaton. I've been nervous about that for weeks. Should really stay in and get a good sleep.'

Marcus came behind her chair and pulled it back. 'Oh no, you need to be distracted, and I don't want you too gorgeous for darling Cecil. He may be an old queen, but if he makes you look wonderful you might decide to dump me.' He kissed the side of her neck and as she headed for the stairs reached out to slap her bum. She managed to evade his hand, charging up two steps at a time, and thanking God yet again for letting her meet him.

Clacton-on-Sea – May 1954

It's a lovely sunny morning, but Dad was late home last night so he's still in bed. Joycie is making some tea because he likes to wake up to a cuppa and a fag. There's a knock on the door and it's Sid. He walks straight in, shouting, 'Wakey, wakey, Charlie boy,' before he slumps into a chair next to the table, pulling an ashtray towards him. 'Any tea in the pot, Joycie love?'

Sid lights up, and Joycie puts a cup in front of him as Dad comes out of the bedroom, rubbing his face. His hair has no

Brylcreem on yet and is falling over his face. 'Crikey, Sid, give a bloke a chance to come round.'

Joycie turns back to the little kitchenette, taking some bacon slices wrapped in greaseproof paper from the wooden meat safe, and trying to close it gently so the thin metal grill on the front doesn't rattle. Sid is talking about the act and she listens in. When she hears her own name she listens harder.

'We need to sharpen up a bit and I've been thinking. I know you don't like leaving Joycie at home on her own.'

'I don't, but it's not fair making her hang about at the theatre every night either. It's all right when Irene's on the bill, but now she's away I worry about Joycie when we're onstage.' Joycie can't see his expression, but she can imagine him raising his eyebrows at Sid. She knows he doesn't trust some of the men in the show.

'Well what about this then?' Sid pulls a floppy tweed cap with a big curved peak from his pocket and gestures for her to come over to him. 'Try this on, love.' When she looks at her dad, Sid laughs. 'Go on, darlin' make an old man happy, eh? It won't bite you.'

Her dad nods although his forehead is creased, and he gives Sid a sidelong glance. Joycie feels silly, but she puts on the cap and obeys the directions from Sid's waving cigarette to push her hair up into it.

Sid turns to her dad. 'She's got so tall lately and with trousers and a jacket she'd look just like a boy. A second stooge, see, that's something a bit different, which is what we need. There'd be some pocket money in it for her too, if it works out.'

He's grinning at Joycie, and her heart does a little flip at the thought of being onstage. She loves the show and hates staying at their lodgings all on her own.

'So how do you fancy it, love? Being part of the act with me and your dad? You'd like that wouldn't you?'

Her face is throbbing with heat as she pulls off the cap, and all she can do is nod.

***

Joycie arrived home exhausted. Cecil Beaton had been kindly and old-school courteous, his voice reminding her of actors in pre-war films. It had been clear however that he didn't think much of her looks, and he had spent ages rooting through boxes of scarves, fur hats, and wigs, obviously trying to find some way to disguise her flaws. Then he'd posed and reposed her until she could hardly stand.

After they finished he made her a gin and It, served without ice in a champagne bowl that made her think of the glasses Irene had let her drink Babycham from when she was sixteen.

She made herself some tea, slipped off her shoes and sat with her feet curled under her in front of the telly. There was nothing worth watching this early in the evening, just a boring programme showing bits of news too dull or silly for the main bulletin. But at least it distracted her enough to calm her thoughts.

Marcus was seeing Cora right now. He'd called Joycie at Beaton's house, much to the old gent's annoyance. 'I rang her office, and when I told the secretary it was a private matter she put me straight through. I asked Cora if we could meet and that I'd prefer if she didn't mention it to Sid.'

'I can imagine what she thought.'

'Well, let's just say she agreed pretty smartish, and we're meeting at a pub where she says Sid never goes. I'll see you about eight. If not send out the search parties.'

It was ten past eight when the Morgan pulled up outside, and she had to force herself not to rush to the door. But he wasn't alone. She heard him talking loudly as he rattled his key in the door, obviously trying to warn her. 'As I said, Cora, I'm not sure if Joycie will be in.'

She jumped up, pushing her feet back into her shoes and was in the kitchen with the door closed before they came into the hall. Feeling ridiculous to be hiding like this she listened as

Marcus got Cora settled on the sofa with a sherry: 'Make yourself at home. I'll just check if Joycie's upstairs.'

When he came into the kitchen he pulled a face and whispered, 'Sorry I had no choice. She says she'll only speak to you.'

Joycie didn't bother to pretend she'd been upstairs, just walked into the sitting room and plonked herself on the armchair opposite Cora. She was looking even more tarted up than usual: for Marcus's benefit Joycie guessed. Her legs were surprisingly slender for such a well-upholstered woman, and she stretched them in front of her, glancing down with a tiny smile at her sheer black nylons and patent stilettos.

'Hello Joyce, darling, I'm sorry to crash in on you two lovebirds like this, but Marcus tells me you have questions you want answering about your mum, and I thought it was only right to come and see you.'

'Thank you.' Joycie knew it was probably just an excuse to nose into their lives.

Cora opened her handbag and brought out a gold lighter and a pack of cigarettes. They waited as she lit up and took a long drag and a dainty sip of sherry, leaving a smear of lipstick on the rim of the glass. Joycie guessed she would have preferred a port and lemon.

When Cora spoke it was in an exaggerated whisper. 'Joyce, dear, I'm wondering if you wouldn't rather we talked on our own.' She turned to Marcus with a brilliant smile and a flutter of lashes. 'No offence, sweetheart.'

Before he could speak, Joycie said, 'It's fine, Cora, Marcus and I don't have secrets.' *If only that were true. She kept secrets even from herself.* Marcus moved back to the window seat, making it clear he was giving them space.

'You were wondering about the chap your mum ran off with, were you?'

'If there was one. I've spoken to my aunt.' Cora raised her eyebrows at that, but said nothing. 'She's sure Mum was coming to them on her own and bringing me with her. My aunt is convinced there was no other man. But Deirdre says you seemed sure about it and that you knew the bloke.'

Cora picked a tiny fleck of something from her tight black skirt, inspecting it as she spoke. 'You have been busy, haven't you?'

Joycie leaned forward. 'I need to know.'

'Well I'm sure it's no news to you that your mum usually had a boyfriend somewhere on the scene, so when Charlie said she'd run off with the latest we didn't question it.'

'But Deirdre said it was you who told everyone.'

A shrug. 'My darling, Sid and I just wanted to make things as easy as possible for you and your dad so we were happy to spread the word.'

Her heart was drumming so hard she could barely speak. 'So who was he?'

Cora leaned back on the sofa with a shrug. 'Search me.'

A fierce spurt of rage. 'If you don't know anything, why the hell did you insist on seeing me?'

'I must say, Joyce, I never expected gratitude from you, but there's no need to be rude. Your young man,' she gestured towards Marcus, 'said you were tearing yourself apart about it, and I thought I might be able to help.'

Marcus coughed in the background, but Joycie didn't look at him, just stood and said. 'I need help to find out what happened to my mum and if you can't do that then there's no point in us talking.'

She walked to the door, but Cora didn't move, just raised her empty glass to Marcus. 'Wouldn't mind a fill-up, darling. And then, if you don't mind, me and Joyce need a minute alone.'

He poured her another drink, squeezed Joycie's shoulder, saying, 'I'll be in the darkroom. Give me a shout when you're finished,' and went out, closing the door behind him.

Cora eased off one of her shoes and rubbed her foot, then did the same with the other and looked up at Joycie still standing by the door, her hands clenched. 'Look, darling, I can see what it must be like, not knowing, but sometimes it's best to leave things be.' She waved her hand to take in the room. 'You've got a good life now, and there's no call to go upsetting yourself by raking up the past.'

'Please, Cora, just tell me everything you know.'

Cora patted the sofa, and Joycie sat next to her, breathing in a fog of Chanel No. 5. 'All right, you win.' Cora didn't quite say the words, *you asked for it*, but her expression did. 'Don't get me wrong, no one could blame your mum for wanting some male company.' A little pat on Joycie's knee. 'Your dad obviously wasn't interested any more, if you know what I mean.'

Joycie moved away from her touch. 'Not really, Cora.' Why make it easy for her?

Cora pressed her fingers to her lips and gave a delicate cough. 'You know why they put Charlie in prison, don't you?'

'I've worked it out over the years, yes. They found love letters from another man.'

'Sid has always said it was the army that did for Charlie. You know, turned him queer, if you'll pardon my French. When he came back after the war he was different somehow, and I don't think things were ever the same with your mum. So, like I said, who could blame her?'

She took a sip of her sherry, dabbing her mouth with a hanky she pulled from her sleeve, then gestured with her head towards the hallway. 'Does Marcus know about Charlie?'

'I told you, we don't have secrets.'

'That's nice.' Cora was gazing towards the dark window, her eyes misty. 'Me and Sid now, I can't deny we've both strayed, but our marriage has always had that special something.'

Joycie waited, gritting her teeth.

'Anyway, the day your mum disappeared Sid tried to cheer Charlie up. Took him out for a drink after the show. You were staying with Irene if I remember right.'

'Yes, I expect Sid had a couple of girls lined up as usual.'

It was unkind, but if Cora was upset she didn't show it, just gave a small chuckle and another of those annoying pats on Joycie's knee. 'See, you probably know more than I do. I used to tell Sid to watch out for you: little vessels, big ears, I used to say. Sure you didn't hear anything the night your mum disappeared?'

If she wanted Cora to tell her everything she had to be as honest as she could. 'I woke up thinking something was wrong, or not normal anyway. There were voices and bumping sounds, and I was scared, but then the wireless came on again, and I fell asleep. Mum always had music playing.'

Cora took her hand, the red talons scraping lightly on her palm, and seemed to think for a moment. Then she took a deep breath. 'OK, here's what I know. Sid brought Charlie back to ours very late. Charlie was absolutely paralytic. I've never seen him like that, and he was crying and raving on about your mum.'

Joycie swallowed, feeling sick. 'Is that all?' Cora was staring into space, or maybe at the sherry bottle. 'I'm going to find out anyway,' Joycie said. 'There's plenty of other people I can ask if you won't tell me.' It wasn't true, but she had to push for everything now.

Cora seemed to shake herself then spread her hands on her knees. 'Next morning, your dad was still not fit to get out of bed, and Sid asked me to go round to your lodgings. He was worried about some of the things Charlie had said. We got his keys from his jacket and I went.'

Was it possible not to breathe for this long and still be conscious? 'And?'

'Everything seemed all right. I checked the wardrobe, and she had taken most of her clothes, like Charlie said. But Sid had told me to have a good nose.'

'And?'

'Well I looked under the bed.'

Please don't say it.

Cora took both her hands, squeezing hard, and Joycie made herself endure the touch. 'Darling, this might be nothing, but I found a mat with some stains that looked to me like blood.'

She could only whisper, but somehow she got the words out. 'What did you do?'

'It wasn't a big mat so I just rolled it up and walked out with it. Dropped it on a bit of waste ground on my way home.'

'And said nothing about it?'

'That's right. I reckoned that was best. Didn't even tell Sid.' She dropped Joycie's hands and leaned back. 'Wouldn't have told *you* except you seemed so sure you needed to know everything. And that is everything. So if I was you I'd leave it now. Your dad's dead and gone, and I wouldn't be surprised if your mum was too.'

It felt as if a chunk of rock was lodged deep inside her. She wanted to scream at Cora to tell her more, but she knew there was no point. Not yet anyway. She managed to stand and say, 'Thank you.'

This time Cora brushed ash from her skirt, put away her lighter and cigarettes, clicked her bag shut, and followed her to the front door.

Marcus bounded along the hall. 'I'll drop you, shall I?'

'Just take me to the tube station, please love.' Cora leaned forward and kissed the air beside Joycie's cheek. 'All right, darling? Hope I haven't upset you.'

'I'm OK, and you're right; I need to put it behind me.' Marcus glanced at her, but she avoided his eye.

When she closed the door she leaned against it, her jaw clenched. So that bloodstained mat was a real memory. There one day and gone the next. And Cora got rid of it. It all fitted. But she was certain of one thing. What Cora had told her wasn't the whole truth, and she couldn't rest until she found out what that was.

She had been bluffing when she said there were other people

she could ask, but, of course, there must be. People who had no reason to hide the truth. Joycie just had to do what she'd avoided all these years: to allow herself to remember.

Acton, London – January 1951

Joycie is nine and a bit too old to cry so she's trying to keep her chin from wobbling. She's in the school playground all alone, or, at least, there are kids around her, but she can't see them because the smog is so bad. They're playing what they call 'Hide and Seek in the Fog' but is more like Blind Man's Buff. Her friends are shouting her name and saying, 'Cooee, come and get me.' Now and then one of them taps her on the shoulder or screams close to her ear then disappears back into the surrounding mist.

She feels bad, her throat hurts, and she's hot in her thick coat. The smog smells awful, smothering her in a wet blanket. She doesn't want to play any more, and when the whistle goes she breathes again and heads for school. But she can't tell which way to go. She turns round and round on the spot. And big sobs are coming out, making her ashamed to be such a cowardy custard.

'Joyce Todd, what on earth are you doing out here?'

It's Miss Hendry, and she grabs Joycie's collar and pulls her along. And there are the lights and almost at once they're inside school. She must be in trouble, but she doesn't care, just wants to lie down on the cool floor of the corridor. Instead she leans against the wall and closes her eyes.

Then she feels Miss Hendry's cold hand on her forehead. 'Joyce, dear, where do you live?'

She parrots the address. At least this one in Acton is easy to remember because they stay in these digs every winter.

'Ah, just down the road, that's good. And Mummy will be home, I expect?'

She nods and Miss takes her hand again, and they are back in the playground. At the school gate Miss stops and points at the orange haloes of light gleaming through the fog.

'Just keep on the pavement and follow the lampposts. Tell Mummy to put you to bed with a warm drink. And you're to stay home tomorrow.'

Joycie's legs are moving, one foot floating after the other over the shiny pavement. She can see the lamppost in front of her, its light a wavering orange moon. When she reaches it she holds the post for a moment then pushes on towards the next one.

Mrs McDonald, the landlady, opens the door at her knock. 'You're early, ducks, what's up?'

'Sent me home.'

Mrs McDonald's hand rough on her cheek. 'No wonder. You're burning up. Well your mum's in, so up you go.' A laugh that's more like a bark. 'She'll be pleased to see you so early, my love. I think she gets lonely on her own all day.' Then she's gone, back to the kitchen, laughing at something as she goes. She must have a funny programme on the wireless.

The stairs rear in front like a mountain, but Joycie pulls herself up by the banisters. At the door to their rooms she taps and taps, then calls her mum, but quietly because they mustn't annoy Mrs McDonald or wake up Mr Grant next door, who does night work.

But her mum doesn't come, and Joycie is too hot and tired to knock again. She pulls off the thick coat and spreads it on the floor so she can lie on it and rest her head on the cool lino.

'Bloody hell, Mary, it's your nipper.'

Mr Grant's voice, but coming from their own doorway. A sickening feeling as the world lurches and she's up in the air, held over Mr Grant's shoulder. Hot skin against hers and stinky sweat.

Mum's voice: 'Bring her in. And for God's sake be quiet, will you. I bet old McDonald's down there earwigging again. Then you'd better go.'

She's in bed, and Mum's giving her warm milk, but it tastes

bad, and Mum smells funny too: a bit like Mr Grant. And it's all wrong anyway, because Mum is only wearing her slip, even though it's the middle of the day.

Chapter Five

'Concentrate now, Orchid baby.' Marcus always called her Orchid in public. He had been so pleased with the pictures he'd taken on the way to Irene's funeral that he'd decided to do their next shoot by the river too. So she was standing on Westminster Bridge in a red silk evening gown with the Houses of Parliament behind her.

It was very early on a morning that promised to be warm, but the ground was still shining with dew, and the mist on the water sent wafts of chill air around her feet. She wore strappy silver sandals and no underwear – nothing to spoil the line of the dress – and the black feather boa the magazine had sent to go with it gave no warmth. Marcus gestured for her to stretch out one leg to emphasize the fall of shining silk.

Joycie still remembered Mrs McDonald's address because her dad had rented the same digs every winter until her mum disappeared, so Marcus was going to drive them there after the shoot. The landlady had seemed like an old woman when Joycie was a little girl, but thinking about it now she was probably only in her forties. So there was a good chance she might still be living in the same house.

47

Marcus came forward and teased out locks of black hair to tumble round her face.

'Fantastic, baby.'

But she knew it wasn't much good. All she could think of was getting to Acton. It was likely Mrs McDonald could tell her something about Mr Grant. He was certainly living there the last time they stayed in the March before her mum's disappearance.

Joycie wondered for a moment when she had started to think of Mum as disappearing rather than leaving them.

Marcus must have realized he was wasting his time, and in any case the milky light he loved was more or less gone, and the bridge was getting busier with commuters, hurrying along, tut-tutting as they stepped between Joycie and Marcus. He took a few snaps as a couple of bowler-hatted gents wove past, then gave up. 'OK, let's go.'

She struggled after him in her flimsy shoes, the red silk twisting around her legs. As he drove she grabbed her big bag from the back seat, pulling a sweater on top of the dress, wriggling into jeans, and shoving the red silk down into the waistband. The magazine would complain that the dress was creased and grubby, but sod 'em.

'So you think this Mr Grant might have been your mum's boyfriend?' Marcus said.

'I know there was something between them for a while, at least, and we stayed in Mrs McDonald's every winter, so it could have gone on for years. Dad and Sid used to work the summer season at the seaside, but London was a good base the rest of the time. They did lots of pantos at the Chiswick Empire, so Acton was convenient.'

'Were you living there when they arrested your dad?'

Two men smelling of sweat fill the tiny living room. They wear heavy suits, not uniforms, although they say they're the police. One of them goes into her dad's bedroom and comes out waving a bundle of open envelopes in the air. He grins at Dad. 'Nice love letters from your nancy-boy pal. Charming turn of phrase he's got.' He chuckles, but Joycie can tell he isn't joking.

The other man pushes Dad from behind. 'Right, duckie, you're coming with us.'

Dad stares at Joycie, his eyes wide, she's never seen him scared before and she can't breathe. He sounds like he can hardly breathe either, looking from her to the men and back again. 'My daughter?'

They turn to Joycie as if they've forgotten her and one of them says, 'We'll get the landlady to look after her for now.' Then he shakes his head and mutters, 'Poor kid.'

The other man looks down at the letters he's holding, and says, 'Disgusting.' She feels her armpits prickle and smells her own sweat – does he mean she's disgusting?

'Joycie?' Marcus touched her knee. 'I said, were you in Acton when your dad was arrested?'

'Oh no, we never went back to those digs after Mum disappeared.'

'It was disgusting …' Marcus said. How strange to hear him echoing the policeman's word. '… the witch-hunt they ran against homosexuals in the '50s. No one could be more conventional than my father, but apparently when he was at the Ministry he met the journalist who was involved in the Lord Montagu case.' He lowered his voice to a posh growl. 'He said, "Seemed a decent chap. Couldn't help the way he was made." And *decent chap* was high praise from Dad. It's ridiculous that it's still illegal even now, but at least they don't persecute them the way they did then.'

'It was a while before I even realized what my dad was supposed to have done,' she said. 'Some of the guys in the shows were very camp, and one or two of them were obviously friendly with Dad, but I was so green I didn't guess. And, like I told you, Dad was really popular with the girls too.'

They were passing the iron gates of a school, the playground full of children just arriving, and Marcus slowed to a crawl as a small boy in grey shorts charged across the road in front of them. As he pulled away again he said, 'From what your aunt told you your parents were in love at the start.'

'And they seemed to love each other when I was a kid.' A lump filled her throat. 'But then I thought they loved me.'

Marcus reached out and rubbed her knee, and once again she saw her dad looking back at her as the police led him away. He did love her. She couldn't imagine what he went through in jail, but it must have been terrible to make him commit suicide, knowing it would leave her alone.

'Did you ever find out who turned your dad in?'

She twisted to look at him. 'What do you mean?'

'Well you said the only evidence they had was the letters.' He changed gear as he turned the car into a narrow street, but he must have heard her breath catch. 'What's wrong?' he said.

'The police. When they came to our lodgings they didn't really have to search. They seemed to know exactly what to look for and where to find them.'

'So whoever tipped them off was someone he knew.'

'Someone he must have known really well.'

You could have knocked Mrs McDonald down with a feather when she realized she had Marcus Blake and Orchid on her doorstep. She was even more astonished when Joycie explained she was Charlie and Mary Todd's daughter.

'Come in, come in.'

The landlady was almost quivering with excitement as she bustled ahead of them into her overheated kitchen: somewhere little Joycie had only glimpsed through a half-open door. Over tea and custard cream biscuits she told them Mr Grant – George – had been a long-term lodger until he left to get married. 'Ooh, that must have been five years ago now. She was a widow with a bit of money and they moved out to Surrey, but he still sends me a Christmas card every year.'

'So he was living here for some time after we stopped coming.'

'Yes, it would have been '59 or '60 when he left.'

'My mum and he were close for a while, weren't they?'

Mrs McDonald chuckled. 'That's one way of putting it, darling. George was a real ladies' man, and your mum wasn't the only one by a long chalk, but it was never serious with him. Not until his rich widow came along.'

'Was Mum serious about *him*?'

'I shouldn't think so. Only doing it to make your dad jealous, I thought.' She looked suddenly suspicious. 'This isn't a divorce thing, is it? I wouldn't want to get George in any trouble.'

'Oh no, my dad's dead.'

Mrs McDonald reached a hand towards Joycie, but then put it to her mouth. 'Poor Charlie, that's terrible, he was no age.'

'But Mum left us in '53, just after the last time we stayed here, and I wondered if she went off with Mr Grant.'

'No, darling, George was just a bit of comfort for her. She was a lovely girl, and what with Charlie being the way he was …' She looked at Marcus as if for help, and when he nodded she let out a heavy breath. 'He was a theatrical, wasn't he? And like a lot of them he was light on his feet, as they say. Probably should never have married, but then your mum was a slim little thing, boyish like, and they must have been very young when they got together. But they were still fond of each other, you could tell that.'

Marcus leaned forward. 'Do you think Charlie knew about the affair?'

'I shouldn't be surprised, but she would never have left him for George, and George wouldn't have asked her to.'

They managed to avoid more tea and said their goodbyes, but on the doorstep Joycie said: 'So you knew my dad was homosexual?' Mrs McDonald pursed her lips, as if the word was too rude to respond to, and crossed her arms over her acreage of bosom, but Joycie carried on. 'It's just … I wondered if you ever mentioned it to the police?'

Mrs McDonald squeezed her bosom tighter, hands high in her armpits. 'Certainly not. Apart from a couple of commercial travellers, like Mr Grant, I've always had theatricals staying here. If I reported everyone who was that way inclined the place would soon be empty. Anyway, live and let live is my motto.'

Joycie touched her beefy forearm. 'I'm sorry. I didn't mean it like that.'

They thanked her and turned to go, but she said, 'Why do you want to know all this after so long?'

'My aunt just got in touch with me hoping to trace Mum.'

'Only I was wondering. Because someone else was asking after your mum and dad a week or so ago. I thought he was a debt collector, but perhaps it was your uncle?'

A chill down her back. 'What did he look like?'

'Smart chap, fortyish, and as I say looked like a debt collector to me. Wouldn't want to get on the wrong side of him, if you know what I mean. Lovely shiny shoes, though.'

'It was the same man – the one from Manchester – the one with the autograph book,' Joycie said.

'Surely not.'

'The way she described him, I just know it's him.'

'But why would he be calling on your old landlady?'

'I don't know, but it scares me.'

'Do you want to go to the police then?'

'They'd just laugh at me, you know that,' she said.

They were both quiet for the rest of the journey, but when she got out of the car and was climbing the steps to the house Joycie found herself looking up and down the sunny street. Marcus put his arm round her as he slotted in his key. 'Relax, there's no one there.'

There was the usual pile of post on the hall floor, and Joycie put it on the little table and began to look through it, trying to calm herself.

'There you are – Fort Knox,' Marcus said, attaching the chain to the front door and slapping the heavy wooden frame. 'And we could get a dog, if you like. I wouldn't mind an Afghan or something.'

Joycie only half-heard him because she was opening a big brown envelope, her heart beating hard.

Dear Joyce,
These are the letters from Mary to our mam or all the ones Mam kept anyway. It was lovely to see you and the kids haven't stopped talking about you. It would be nice if you could come for a proper visit sometime.
Your loving aunt,
Susan

Marcus came behind her and rested his warm hand on her shoulder. She put her head against his cheek. 'You'll want to read those on your own I expect?' he said. When she nodded he rubbed her arm. 'I'll be in the darkroom. Call me if you need to talk.'

It was sunny outside now so she made a cup of Earl Grey and took the bundle of letters into the garden. Marcus had dragged a couple of old wicker chairs out from the shed the other day, and she put the brown envelope on one and sat on the other. A deep breath, a gulp of tea, then with her cup carefully placed on the grass beside her she took out the letters.

They were in no particular order. One from '43, another from '52 and one from '49, all signed: *Your loving daughter Mary*. The careful handwriting wasn't familiar, but then she'd only ever seen a shopping list or two scribbled by her mum. Odd phrases jumped out at her as she tried to organize the letters by date.

The postal order is for Susie's birthday. Please buy something nice for her.

Joycie is walking really well and is into everything.

Charlie and Sid are doing the summer season in Clacton …
… in Margate,
… in Blackpool. Perhaps you could try to get over sometime while we're there. If you drop a note at the box office I can arrange to meet you. I'd love you to see Joycie. She's so pretty and she never stops talking.

Joycie held the crinkled paper to her lips, looking down the garden. Most of the daffodil flowers had gone now, leaving just their spikes of green to catch the sun, but the tree in the middle danced with pink blossom. The date on this letter was 1947: her mum hadn't seen her family for six years.

She took a breath and carried on organizing the bundle by date. This must be one of the first: August 1941, not long before her own birth.

I don't know when Charlie will get his next leave, but I'm not on my own because I'm staying with a friend of his, Irene Slade. She's very kind, but I do miss you all.

Just before Christmas that year:

We're calling her Joyce after Grandma. Charlie hasn't seen her yet. I'm still staying with Irene and I've put her address above. I know it must be difficult, but if you could get down here it would be lovely to see you.

December '45: *Charlie's home and we're so happy, but Joycie is still not sure of him!*

She skimmed through them all, but could find no mention of Mr Grant or any other man. There were only two from that last year: 1953. The first was just chit-chat about them going to Hastings for the summer season and the new shoes she'd bought for Joycie. She remembered those: they were red patent leather, and she'd worn them till they were so tight her toes began to bleed. *You should see her in them. I think she might turn into a dancer one day.*

Then what must be the last, sent in August 1953.

I'm coming back home. Please tell Dad I only need to stay for a day or so until I find somewhere permanent. Charlie won't be with me, just Joycie (something scribbled out here that was impossible to read). *Please, Mam, something has happened and I have to get away from here and to get Joycie away too.*

Joycie pressed her hand to her throat where a lump of ice seemed to be stuck. For a moment she thought she could hear the ice cracking, but it was only the breeze catching at the tree's thin twigs and whipping a whirl of pink blossoms onto the grass.

Chapter Six

She was rocking back and forth, the letters clutched to her chest, when Marcus came into the garden. 'Come on,' he said, 'you must be starving. Let's have some lunch at Franco's.'

She was still wearing the silk evening gown under her jeans and sweater so she changed into slacks, a blouse, and flat shoes and hung the silk on the hook behind the door, hoping some of the creases might fall out. Then she shoved the brown envelope into the box on top of her wardrobe where she kept the few things she still had belonging to her mum. She wouldn't think about the letters for now.

As they walked down to the Italian restaurant at the end of the street, Marcus smiled and took her hand, but didn't speak. The restaurant was a tiny place with roughly plastered walls and checked tablecloths. It was busy at lunchtimes, but the customers were all regulars, mostly middle-aged, and if they recognized Marcus and Joycie they avoided showing it.

Their usual table was in a dim corner, where no one else wanted to sit, so it was still free. The waiter brought the Chianti right away, but Joycie's stomach felt hollow, and she made herself crunch on a breadstick before taking a deep drink. She was very aware of Marcus's blue eyes on her, but shook her head at him. 'Can we wait till the food comes?'

They were halfway through their spaghetti when he said, 'You know it just might help to talk about it.'

She sat back and put down her fork. 'Either she was lying to her mother or she really was planning to take me with her.'

'Any mention of a man?'

'No, and if there was one I really don't think he was her only reason for leaving. She said something had happened.'

'That could mean your dad had found out she was cheating on him, I suppose. But it sounds like their relationship was very open, and he would have understood that she needed someone. More likely it was the boyfriend who gave her an ultimatum.'

Joycie dipped a chunk of bread into her bolognaise sauce. It made sense, but something told her it wasn't right. Perhaps because she didn't want to believe it. She shook her head. 'But if she had a boyfriend, why would she want to stay with her family?'

'I don't know,' Marcus said.

The food was delicious, and suddenly Joycie wished she'd never started all this. What she wanted more than anything was to enjoy the food and wine, maybe even get drunk, and put the whole thing out of her mind.

Marcus was still talking. 'I wonder if we should stop looking for the boyfriend and just try to find out everything we can about your parents' lives at the time.'

She was tempted to tell him to leave it alone just for an hour or so. But instead she gazed over his shoulder at a young couple sitting by the window. They were sharing an ice cream sundae and kissing between mouthfuls. The girl was very pretty, in the way Joycie had always longed to be, small and curvy with blonde curls and a turned-up nose.

'I said, what about school friends?' Marcus's voice jolted her back.

She blinked and forced herself to look at him. 'What?'

'If we want to find out what really happened I think we need to stop focusing on the boyfriend and just talk to anyone who was around in those days. Another of the acts, or even someone you knew from school.'

She laughed and spooned more grated parmesan onto her spaghetti. 'I was only in one school long enough to make friends. The one in Acton. Even there it was difficult because I was away every summer. And we moved lodgings after Mum disappeared, so I never went there again. By the time I was thirteen I'd more or less stopped going to school altogether. Explains why I'm so ignorant, I suppose.' She emptied her glass, poured them both more wine and leaned back to drink hers.

'There must be someone we can talk to,' he said.

A wave of heat flooded through her, and she wanted to scream at him to leave her alone. She needed to think, but didn't want to think now. Certainly didn't want to talk about it. 'Look, this isn't your problem, Marcus, so please stop going on about it. Let me figure it out for myself.' It came out all wrong, as if she was angry with him.

He sat looking at her for a moment then beckoned the waiter and asked for the bill. When it arrived he said, 'Are you coming?'

'You go. I'm going to have another glass of wine.' Again it came out wrong. Too loud; too sharp. She had no reason to be angry with him. The kissing couple were staring at them, and their eyes followed Marcus as he left without looking back at her.

She ordered some more wine and forced herself to drink the whole glass although she no longer wanted it. At the door she stumbled and heard a giggle from the pretty girl. The door clanged hard behind her, and she could feel the couple's eyes still on her as she passed the window where they sat.

Marcus had left their front door ajar. *So stupid, anyone could have got in.* She locked up and went into the living room. He was sitting on the sofa with two cups of coffee in front of him. 'I made it nice and strong,' he said.

She tried a laugh. 'Not strong enough for me,' and went to the sideboard. 'I need a brandy.' Some of it spilled on the polished wood as she poured, and she wiped it away with her sleeve, slumping down in the armchair opposite him.

He leaned forward. 'Those letters must have upset you. You need time to let it all sink in. I shouldn't have pushed you.' His hands were on her knees, and when she flinched he pulled back. 'Sorry.'

That hank of blond hair was falling over his eyes again, and his face was so sad and sweet she felt a sob rise into her throat. She stood and looked down at him, trying to smile. 'I'm the one who should say sorry.' She stroked his hair, and he pressed his face into her waist.

They stayed like that for a while then she knelt to give him a gentle kiss. But when he drew back she found herself looking at his lips and kissed him again, hard and greedy this time. He returned the pressure and moved to pushed her down onto the sofa, his hand pulling at the buttons of her blouse.

'Oh, Joycie, I love you so much.'

She was aware only of him, the musky scent of him, the warmth of his hands and his lips, the length of his body against hers. She opened her mouth to him and let her knees fall apart.

Dirty little tart, I know what you want.

She was standing, heart thumping, breath catching. On the sofa Marcus stared up at her. Then he twisted to sit straight, elbows on his knees, hands covering his face. She touched his shoulder, but he pushed her hand away. 'Don't.' She had never heard him sound like that before. As if he hated her.

She left him there, went to her room and lay on the bed, her chest heaving so hard she felt as if she was having some kind of attack. She longed to cry, but her eyes were dry and all she could do was turn and press her face into the pillow.

It might have been a few minutes or an hour later when she heard the front door slam.

Clacton-on-Sea – May 1954

Joycie has been rehearsing her part as the second stooge for a few days, and she's going to be in the show tonight. They're calling her *Our Kid*, and she's practised walking heavily with her feet turned out and her hands in her pockets. The difficult bit is following her dad on to the stage and bumping into him. Dad keeps telling her she's doing fine, but Sid's face says something different.

Now she's standing in the wings, her tummy twisting so hard it hurts. At least she doesn't have to speak, doesn't think she could, because her throat is so dry she can't even swallow.

The audience is a good one and they're laughing a lot, but her ears have started buzzing so she can't hear what Dad and Sid are saying. But she does hear her cue when it comes because Sid speaks louder than usual. 'Go and get our kid, Lord Toddy.' Dad does his usual gormless stare at Sid before looking towards the wings. 'I said get the kid,' Sid repeats even louder.

Dad ambles over, and she knows Sid must be saying something else because there's more laughter, but all she can see is Dad. He steps into the wings, touches her shoulder and whispers, 'OK darlin'?'

She nods, and he turns so she can press herself against his back, and they march back to Sid, in step, just like they've practised. There's laughter and she knows it's for them. She can feel the audience out there in the dark, like some big animal watching and waiting to see what they'll do.

Dad turns fast, and her face is against his waistcoat. She knows he's looking helplessly back to the wings because the laughter gets louder. She waits for a moment, like Sid has told her to, then pulls back her foot and kicks Dad's shin. He jumps away, looking from his leg to her and back again, as if he can't understand where she came from. Then he takes off his top hat and whacks her round the head with it. She runs back a few feet and faces the audience rubbing her head, careful not to dislodge the cap. Then she stands looking down at the stage, pulling the sad face she's practised.

'Oh, poor little chap.'

A lady's voice, just like Sid hoped, and more laughter. She's done it. But Sid has warned her to be careful. *The worst moments are when it's going well. That's when you can get carried away and lose them.* She feels good, but knows she has to do it right or she won't get another chance.

'Tell our kid,' Sid is talking to Dad, 'to take this note to that lovely lady down there.' He points to a fat woman in the front row.

Dad turns and does his posh stutter at Joycie, his eyes telling her it will be OK. She knows it will, and she runs down and gives the note to the woman, who makes a big show of opening it, enjoying every moment. When she reads it she lets out a scream and flaps Joycie on the arm. Before she can say anything Joycie hurries away, running up the steps to the stage.

The woman shrieks something, but Sid talks over her. 'Hear that, Lord Toddy, you've upset the lady.'

Dad hangs his head, but when Joycie reaches them he turns on her and hits her with his hat over and over until she jumps away. She runs towards the wings, but stops just before them and sticks out her tongue at him. The audience roars with laughter, and a voice shouts, 'Cheeky young blighter,' as she steps into the darkness, feeling so happy she's sure everyone must hear her heart thumping.

The rest of the act goes fine, and when her dad comes off he pats her shoulder. 'Well done, love. That was great.' Sid says nothing, but she doesn't care; she knows she was good, and he'll want to keep her.

She has to wait in the dressing room after the show while Dad and Sid go out to do autographs. Sid says he doesn't want people to know she's a girl so it's best if she stays inside and keeps her costume on. But the cap is itchy and she takes it off to scratch her head.

When the door opens she shoves it back on, but the girl who comes in laughs. 'It's all right, only me.' It's Pauline whose mum, Mrs Shaw, runs the box office and seems to do pretty much everything else too. Pauline is about Joycie's age, but they've never spoken. Joycie has seen her sitting behind Mrs Shaw, reading a comic while her mum sells tickets, but she never even looks up. Once Joycie saw her in town with a gaggle of girls all laughing and screaming over something Pauline was saying. She was the prettiest of them all.

Now she hitches herself up to sit on the dressing table near the door, swinging her legs. She has blonde curls and a wide smile, and she reminds Joycie of a girl she saw once in a film: a bobby-soxer they called her. And Pauline is chewing gum just like the bobby-soxer did. 'Mum let me stay and watch tonight 'cos it's half-term holidays. You were funny. Don't like those clothes though,' she says.

Joycie has to cough before she can speak. 'They're horrible. All scratchy.'

Pauline jumps down and opens the door. 'See you.'

Don't go, please don't go.

She's in the corridor when she turns back. 'I'll ask Mum if you can come to tea on Sunday. OK?'

Chelsea – May 1965

It was nearly 4 a.m. before Marcus came back. Joycie was lying on her bed, fully clothed. She listened as he moved about in his bedroom on the floor above. She waited for the silence that told her he was asleep, then grabbed her weekend bag and crept downstairs. She scribbled a note and left it propped in front of the kettle.

I'll call you in a couple of days. Just need to sort a few things out by myself. Sorry. J

Then she left, closing the front door, quietly, behind her.

Chapter Seven

Joycie was glad she'd bought a first class ticket to Clacton because she had the compartment to herself, and the rest of the train was crammed with families heading for a Sunday outing. But her seat was too soft, enveloping her in its cushions so she felt suffocated. It was hot, and when she pushed down the window beside her the breeze stirred the thick air, but didn't cool it.

Why had she been like that with Marcus? Getting angry when he tried to help her and pushing him away when he said he loved her. It would be her own fault if he wanted nothing more to do with her. It hurt her so much when she thought of him with other girls, but she had no right to object.

And she couldn't bear talking about the past with him either. He thought there was more she could tell him, and that was true. Her memory of some things was acid sharp, but there was so much she seemed only to half-recall. Things she might have imagined. Until Cora mentioned that bloodstained mat she'd been almost sure it had never existed. So what else had she buried?

Marcus had guessed that the way she was with him had something to do with Sid. He was right about that too. It was Sid's voice and his ugly words that shivered through her when her feelings for Marcus took her close to the edge. But she had refused to think about what happened with him, what he did to her, for so long that the details were hazy. Her mind shrank back when she tried to bring them into focus and the idea of trying to tell someone else, even Marcus, horrified her.

Whatever the truth, she knew it was best to leave Marcus out of it, at least for now. The only way she could face up to the past was by doing it on her own.

Pauline's mum, Mrs Shaw, would surely be able to help. She had worked at the theatre in Clacton forever and must have known Joycie's dad and Sid for years, as well as lots of the other acts. Joycie wasn't sure how well Mrs Shaw might have known her mum, but Pauline had certainly heard the gossip. The only fight they had was when Pauline said, 'Everyone knows your mum ran away with her fancy man.' Joycie kicked Pauline for saying that, and Pauline pulled her hair and told her. 'I'm not your friend any more.' But she came to the dressing room before the show a few days later to ask Joycie to meet her the next morning, and they made friends again over Pepsis and sweets.

Mrs Shaw was lovely, and tea at her house was Joycie's favourite thing during those summers. She and Pauline would tuck into an enormous spread laid out on the table beside the French windows. Pauline's dad was a lot older than his wife, and Joycie always thought of him as a kindly granddad rather than a father. He sat in his rocking chair with the wireless on, laughing at comedy programmes or humming along to music while his wife waited on him.

Like Joycie, Pauline was an only child, and it was obvious both her parents adored her. The Shaws had a proper house, and Joycie was in heaven when Pauline took her up to her own bedroom. On the window ledge she had a collection of spun-glass ornaments: fairies, birds, and butterflies. Best of all was the brimming bookcase. Joycie had read *Heidi*, *What Katy Did*, *The Chalet School* and the rest, but had to get them from the library.

As the train chugged through the Essex countryside she felt

her eyelids drooping – she'd hardly slept last night. She tried to stay awake by watching the landscape, but it was just field after field stretching flat and green to the misty horizon.

The train jolted, and she dragged herself awake to find they were pulling in to Clacton station. She must have slept for half an hour or more, and her eyes were blurred and sticky.

Walking down towards the pier she still felt half-asleep. The bright sun gave the shop windows a harsh glitter, and on Marine Parade she stood by the railings, resting her eyes on the silent sea. Even under the blue sky it had a muddy green tinge.

Ahead was the theatre, but it would be closed today. Instead, she booked into the Royal Hotel. She had fantasized about staying there when she was young. Now all she could think of was lying down for a while to clear her head.

Up in her room she kicked off her shoes and pushed up the sash window, expecting to fall asleep as soon as she lay on the bed. The window let in a cool breeze, but with it the sound of traffic and the screech of seagulls, and she was soon wide awake. She swung her legs to the floor. It was Sunday so they'd almost certainly be home. Probably having one of Mrs Shaw's huge roast dinners. So there was no reason to wait.

She'd been to the house so often that her feet took her there automatically, but standing in the neat front garden she felt a tremor of anxiety. The door opened to her knock and there was Mrs Shaw; her fair hair permed in the same style as always with just a few strands of grey at the temples. She was a little rounder, but otherwise much the same. When she saw Joycie she beamed.

'Oh, Joyce love, how wonderful to see you. This is such a surprise, come in, come in.'

As she followed Mrs Shaw into the front room Joycie had the feeling of being in some kind of dream. The room was just as she remembered. Comfortable sofa at one end and French windows open to the back garden at the other. And yet it was utterly different. Mr Shaw's rocking chair was empty, the cushions neat and plump. The place smelled of furniture polish not tobacco. They both looked at the chair.

'I lost my Ned a good while ago now,' Mrs Shaw said. 'He was a lot older than me, of course. Still, you're never prepared.'

Joycie plonked onto the sofa and managed to say, 'I'm sorry.' It wasn't so surprising, but she felt a lump in her throat. *Poor Pauline; she doted on her dad.*

Mrs Shaw was already heading for the kitchen. 'Tea all right for you?'

It was so quiet, so still in here, and so clean. It had never been grubby, just felt wonderfully cosy and lived in. Of course, Pauline was probably married by now.

When Mrs Shaw came back with the tray she poured for them both and offered a plate of chocolate biscuits. 'Sorry they're shop bought. It's not worth baking just for me.' She was smiling hard and in the bright light from the window Joycie saw that her face was feathered with lines that hadn't been there before. 'Who'd have thought it?' she said. 'Little Joycie, who used to play in our garden and loved my Victoria sponges, turning into a famous model.' She pointed to the bottom of the bookshelf where a neat pile of magazines was stacked. 'I knew it was you the first time I saw your picture. And you're calling yourself Orchid. That's lovely.'

Joycie smiled. Orchid was the nickname her father had given her when Sid and some of the others kept referring to her as *Our Kid* offstage. Pauline must have heard it when she came to their lodgings for tea. 'How *is* Pauline these days?' she said.

Mrs Shaw balanced her cup and saucer very carefully on the arm of the sofa, staring out through the French windows. 'You haven't seen her then?'

'Well, no.'

Mrs Shaw was still looking away. 'I thought – I hoped – she'd looked you up and that's what you were here about.' Her voice was muffled.

'No, I haven't seen her. Is she in London then?'

Mrs Shaw stood, ignoring the wobble of her cup and saucer. She moved one of the cushions on the rocking chair and replaced it in a slightly different position, paused, and moved it back, then went over to the empty fireplace, looking towards the French windows and the garden again. 'I don't know.'

'Is she married?' *A problem with the husband maybe?*

Mrs Shaw sat in the armchair opposite the rocker, her hands tugging the hem of her cardigan. 'Truth is, I don't know. I hope she is, but ...'

Joycie waited, wanting to know more, but not sure how to ask. She was very thirsty, but it seemed wrong to drink her tea when Mrs Shaw was clearly upset. The cup rattled on the saucer as she put them on the table, and the sound seemed to bring Mrs Shaw to life again.

'How old were you the last time we saw you?' she asked.

'Nearly fourteen and Pauline was a few months older. You made a Victoria sponge because we were going back to London next day. Sid and Dad were hoping to get booked here for the next summer season so I thought I'd see you all then.'

'Oh, Joyce. I heard about Charlie. I'm so sorry.'

Joycie gave her a little smile and a nod. This wasn't the time to talk about her family. 'I still don't understand about Pauline.'

'She was so upset when you didn't turn up the next year. And, of course, Sid was on the bill so it wasn't until he got here that we realized Charlie wasn't with him. It was only then we found out what had happened. I asked Sid for your new address so Pauline could write to you, but he didn't have it.'

Oh yes he did, the bastard. 'But what happened with Pauline?'

'Don't think I'm blaming you, love, but she went right off the rails that summer. It must have been this boy she took up with.' Mrs Shaw's face was pink, and she twisted her cardigan between her fingers. 'You're a grown-up now so you know how things are. The fact is Pauline got herself in the family way. I guessed, of course, and we had a big row. The first I can ever remember. She begged me not to tell her dad. She worshipped him and, of course, he would have been upset because he was old-fashioned.'

Joycie's heart thumped hard. Poor Pauline. 'Did she run away?'

The ends of the cardigan were twisted into a knot now. 'It was my fault. I'll never forgive myself, but I was so angry. Told her to make the boy come and explain himself to her dad.'

'Who was it?' Pauline was so pretty and lively; she had lots of boys hanging around her, but she never seemed interested. A sudden vision of her eating ice cream on a bench, swinging her legs the way she always did.

'We never found out. She left and that was it.' Mrs Shaw took a hanky embroidered with blue flowers from her sleeve and dabbed her eyes. 'It killed her dad, I'm sure of it. He couldn't go on without her. And once he got over the shock he would have forgiven her, she should have known that. He would have loved being a granddad.'

After that Joycie couldn't ask any of the questions she'd prepared. All she wanted was time alone to try and process everything she'd just heard. She told Mrs Shaw she was staying the night and would call at the theatre in the morning. Mrs Shaw seemed pleased.

'It's a good show this year. You'll probably know some of the acts on the bill.'

Joycie walked down to the theatre and checked the names outside. There was one act she had hoped to find: The Bluebirds. They were a brother and sister singing duo and had been great friends with her dad. Dennis, the young man, was often at their lodgings and once or twice Joycie had woken early in the morning to find them smoking and drinking tea together. She'd been a bit jealous of Dennis, to tell the truth, even though he was always sweet to her.

When Joycie and Marcus talked about who might have betrayed her dad to the police she had thought of Dennis. She knew they wrote to each other when they were working in different towns. She would have to try and speak to him tomorrow.

As she stood looking at the billboard she felt the back of her neck tingle and turned quickly around but, although there were lots of people about, no one seemed to be watching her. Still she decided to head back to the hotel along the quiet residential streets away from the seafront.

She could hardly believe what Mrs Shaw had told her about Pauline. It was an old story, of course, not that different from what had happened to her own mum, but Pauline loved her parents and she knew they doted on her. Even if she'd run away in panic it didn't make sense that she had stayed away all this time and never even written.

As Joycie turned the corner by the hotel she thought she heard the rapid click clack of smart shoes behind her. She whipped round fast but whoever it was didn't turn onto the seafront road. A revolving door led to the hotel foyer and she stood just inside for a couple of minutes, watching people stroll by. There was no one she recognized; no one wearing formal shoes, and as the adrenalin wore off exhaustion flooded through her so strongly it was all she could do to collect her key and get into the lift. Back in her room she lay on the bed again. Her stomach ached with hunger, but Joycie was too tired to move.

Chapter Eight

Eventually she got herself off the bed, pulled a cardigan over her thin blouse and headed down. The hotel restaurant was just off the foyer and the air was thick with chatter and perfume. Middle-aged couples were arriving for some kind of fancy dinner, the men wearing lounge suits, the women in pearls and stilettos, their dresses rustling as they moved. A heavily made-up blonde drew her skirt back from Joycie's crumpled slacks in a flounce of stiff petticoats as they passed at the revolving doors.

Outside it was still warm but all the little cafés were closed at this time on a Sunday night, so Joycie followed the smell of vinegar and found a fish and chip shop. She took the parcel of food to a bench on the seafront, pulling at the cod and grabbing handfuls of fat chips, chewing and swallowing fast until the worst hunger pangs were gone. When she was able to eat more slowly she leaned back and tried to relax, looking out to the dark horizon and listening to the gentle shush, shush of the waves.

She thought again of Pauline, in her candy-striped dress, sitting on a bench very near here all those years ago, eating an ice cream and swinging her legs as she talked. 'Do you know who all the girls at school fancy?' she said with a laugh.

'Tony Curtis?' Joycie had written off for a signed photo of him that she kept propped up in her room and she was getting ready to boast about it.

But Pauline laughed again. 'No, silly, someone in your show.'

'Not Dennis from The Bluebirds?' She knew he often had girls asking for his autograph.

'Some do, but most of them like your dad best. Can you believe it?'

'But he's too old.' For some reason Joycie felt angry.

Pauline bit the end off her cornet and sucked the ice cream through the hole. 'I know, but at least he's a real man, not a silly kid.'

Joycie turned away. *Did Pauline only want to be friends to get close to her dad?*

'What's the matter?' Pauline tugged at her shoulder. 'I was only saying some of my friends think your dad's a bit of all right. What's wrong with that? I told them he's past it. And I said he can't be much cop anyway because everyone knows your mum ran away with her fancy man.'

That was when Joycie kicked her and Pauline pulled her hair.

A few days later, friends again, they were back on the same bench sharing Pepsis and sweets. Pauline said, 'I only wanted you to know *I* don't fancy your dad. He's almost as square as mine.' She blew down her straw turning the Pepsi dregs at the bottom of the bottle into a froth of brown bubbles. 'And I don't fancy that Dennis either.'

That was the only conversation about boys or men she could recall having with Pauline. Boys would try and chat her up, but Pauline either ignored them or said something clever that sent them off even quicker. No boy ever paid attention to Joycie back then.

She scrunched her fish and chip paper into a ball and tossed it into the bin, wishing the woman at the shop hadn't been so free with the salt.

That and thinking about Pepsi had made Joycie thirsty and

she looked across the road to The Ship pub, wishing she had the nerve to go in on her own.

'Can I get you a drink?'

The voice came from nowhere and she whirled round, heart drumming as she scanned the promenade. She was completely alone, twisting back and forth, almost convinced she had imagined the words.

A tiny sound behind her. She spun back towards the dark beach and saw him climbing the steps to reach her. The man from Manchester; the man with the autograph book who called himself Bill. Another look along the promenade, but it was still empty, the little pools of light cast by the street lamps making everything outside them even gloomier. He could have been there all the time, his dark clothes hiding him from view; watching, as she sat eating, imagining herself alone.

A burst of laughter floated across from the pub and she couldn't stop herself from glancing over again, wanting to run in and shout for help. Instead she took a breath and crossed her arms, trying to stop her voice wobbling. 'Why are you following me? What do you want?'

He was as smartly dressed as always, a suit and tie, trench coat over his arm, and he was smiling at her, his cheekbones sharp and shiny in the lamplight. Eyes glinting like splinters of glass. 'Let me get you a drink and we can talk about it. You'll feel safe in the pub.'

Joycie's instinct was to tell him to get lost, but she needed to know what was going on, and he was right: she would be safer in the busy pub than alone with him. She headed across the road, determined to get there first. But as she opened the door a cloud of smoke wafted out and she caught her foot on a ledge, unable to suppress a small yelp of pain.

'Careful now.' He took her arm, pulling her close beside him. She felt his breath on her cheek. 'What can I get you?'

She freed herself as discreetly as she could. 'A Pepsi or a Coca

Cola.' Then sat at a table close to a group of old men who were playing dominoes, smoking, and drinking pints with whisky chasers. It wasn't the kind of pub that expected female customers and the old men stopped playing and looked at her. She tried to seem relaxed and smiled over at them. One old guy raised his pint to her. 'Cheers, darling,' and they went back to their game.

She was surprised to see Bill come back with Cokes for both of them; she imagined Scotch was more his style. He saw her looking at the bottles as he put them on the table, hanging his coat neatly on the back of his chair. 'I never drink when I'm working.'

A sudden thought. 'Are you a policeman?'

He smiled, but it was a smile for himself not her, and poured his Coke. 'Let's just say I'm looking out for you. Minding your back.'

'And is your name really Bill?'

He took a long swallow from his glass and flashed crooked white teeth at her. 'You remembered, that's nice.' His voice was very soft, but Joycie felt a sharp spike of fear. Couldn't breathe.

She held her glass to her lips; trying to calm herself. Then drank some warm Coke pretending she couldn't feel those pale eyes watching her. A swallow, a deep breath, and she was able to speak in a voice that hardly trembled. 'I asked you why you're following me.'

'Like I said, I've been told to keep an eye on you.'

'Who by?'

'Can't tell you that, I'm afraid, and I shouldn't be talking to you either, but I like you and I want to help you if I can.' He spoke softly. His accent was a smoothed over cockney that reminded her a bit of her dad's. But this man's voice had a note that sent a chill through her.

Somehow Joycie knew she would get nowhere with him unless she stayed strong. 'I don't need your help or anyone else's, thank you very much.'

He reached over and grabbed her wrist. 'You need to go back

to the Smoke, back to your poncey boyfriend, and get on with your life.' His grip was hard. 'Until you do that you won't get rid of me and you won't be safe. And, although you might not believe it, I really want you to be safe.'

She looked down at her wrist, making sure her face didn't show how scared she was. 'What I do is none of your business.'

He let go of her wrist, running a finger down the side of his glass. 'Ah, but it is, which is why I'm warning you. You could be in danger if you don't stop this lark.'

'There is no lark. I'm just here to see old friends.' She tried to stare him out, but couldn't prevent her eyes from dropping first. 'Who could possibly care about that?' she asked aware of how weak her voice sounded.

He leaned back and finished his drink. 'That's for me to know, Orchid love.' Another flash of teeth as he said her name. 'What you need to know is that I'll be sticking around until you see sense. Unless that takes too long, of course.'

She was shaking, although whether with fear or anger she wasn't sure. 'And what if I go to the police?'

He took his coat from the back of his chair and stood looking down at her. He was smiling a different smile now and shaking his head. 'Night, night, darling. Take my tip and have a good sleep then get the train back to London. I hear lover boy is missing you.'

She forced herself to finish her Coke, waiting for her heart to stop fluttering and her breath to calm. The barman called, 'Last orders,' and the old man who'd spoken to her tipped the last of his pint into his whisky glass, swilled it round and swallowed it. 'No more for me, lads, I'd best get back.'

She followed him when he headed for the door. As she'd hoped he set off towards the Royal. But it didn't matter because there was no sign of Bill, or whatever he was really called.

***

Next morning the sun had gone and the green sea lurched under a light drizzle. She hadn't slept much, but when she scanned the street from her window there was no sign of Bill. She intended to go back to London today anyway, but she was glad she hadn't weakened and told him that.

She had breakfast in the restaurant. The bacon was too crisp, the fried egg almost solid, and the toast barely warm, but she was hungry again and ate it all, thinking about last night. What the hell did Bill want? Who was he working for?

Outside she took an indirect route to the theatre and lingered staring at the billboards until she was sure Bill hadn't followed her. The box office was open and a small queue waited for Mrs Shaw's attention, but Bill wasn't there either. The foyer was a bit tattier than Joycie remembered and looked smaller to her adult eyes, but otherwise much the same.

When Mrs Shaw had issued the final ticket she called out. 'Come into the office, Joyce.' It was a tiny room opening off the box office and Mrs Shaw sat behind the desk where she could see into the foyer. 'I felt terrible after you went yesterday, love. I should have asked you to stay for dinner and I never gave you a chance to say why you're here. It was such a shock seeing you after all this time, but that's no excuse.'

Joycie smiled. 'Of course it is. After what you told me about Pauline I couldn't think of anything else either. But I was hoping you might know something about what happened to my mum. Why she left us like she did.'

Mrs Shaw walked to a shelf in the corner where a kettle stood. She held up a tin of Nescafé. Joycie shook her head and Mrs Shaw spoke as she made herself some coffee. 'I only know what everyone said. That she'd fallen for someone else. Have to admit I was surprised. Your mum and dad were really fond of each other, you could tell that, and they both doted on you. But Mary was still young so …' She shrugged and put her cup on the desk, looking over to the door as voices sounded from the foyer. 'Won't be a minute.'

When she came back after selling the tickets Joycie didn't speak and Mrs Shaw looked into her cup as she stirred the coffee. 'Did you notice The Bluebirds are here again this year? Dennis Bird should be in soon, so why not talk to him. You probably remember he was very friendly with your dad.'

***

Kay Bird was alone in the dressing room when Joycie opened the door. She stared for a moment, then her face creased into smiles and she jumped up to envelop Joycie in a scented hug. 'Oh my giddy aunt, what are you doing here, you little star?' She didn't wait for an answer, just pulled Joycie to the dressing table, perching on it and gesturing for Joycie to take a chair.

Joycie felt herself flushing hot under Kay's gaze. The Bluebirds were the youngest performers Sid and her dad appeared with regularly, and she had been in awe of the curvy blonde with her turned-up nose and infectious giggle. Kay had aged, must be in her thirties now, but still looked good, although her outfit – pink slacks and a mint green blouse with a huge bow at the neck – was like something Doris Day might wear. As always she was fully made-up and Joycie could see that her own appearance didn't impress. 'Who would have thought it, our little Joycie a famous model? I remember you in your scruffy trousers and boots with that awful cap they made you wear.'

Joycie laughed. 'Don't remind me.' But Kay had jumped up and was pulling a white jacket from a hook on the door.

'Come on,' she said. 'Let's get out of here, have a coffee and a sticky bun, and you can tell me all about your glam life and that dishy boyfriend of yours.'

Joycie didn't move. 'I was hoping to see Dennis too. Is he around?'

Kay's face seemed to freeze and she put her jacket on slowly, buttoning it up and then undoing it again. 'Look, Joyce, let's go out and talk. Dennis hasn't been too well and he doesn't like being reminded of the old days. Things haven't been easy for him.'

She opened the door, but when they heard footsteps in the corridor, she began to close it again. She was too late. Dennis, so changed Joycie hardly recognized him, stood staring at her. She made herself smile and say, 'Hello, Dennis,' surprised at how cheerful she managed to sound.

Dennis looked at his sister as if for help and she took his arm, talking with fake jollity as if he was very old or ill. 'Look who's come to see us, sweetie. It's Joyce.'

Dennis seemed to shake himself and gave a tiny smile that was more like a wince. 'Hello, Joyce, lovely to see you.' His voice, which had always been so sweet, girlish even, sounded hoarse and he coughed, his eyes sliding sideways at Kay. 'This calls for a drink,' he said.

He came over to the dressing table and opened a drawer, taking out a bottle of gin and two glasses. 'Kay doesn't approve of drinking on show days,' he said as he poured, 'but this is a special occasion if there ever was one.'

`Kay was still by the door. 'It's only eleven o'clock, Dennis. Let's take Joyce for a coffee instead.' She didn't look at either of them, but Joycie could hear the pleading note in her voice and moved towards the door hoping Dennis would follow.

Instead, he almost pushed her back into her seat saying, 'You go if you like, Kay. I want a nice chat with my old friend's daughter, if that's OK with you.'

Kay took off her jacket and sat next to Joycie. 'Of course it is. Just don't drink too much.' Again that *talking to an invalid* tone. And Dennis certainly didn't look well. Unlike Kay he had aged badly. He had always been small and slender, but now he was very thin. His hair, as thick and blond as ever, only emphasized the ruin of his face. There were deep grooves down his cheeks and lines across his forehead. Something had happened to his nose too, which had been as delicate as Kay's, but now was bent and flattened.

He swallowed his gin in one gulp and poured another, tapping Joycie's untouched glass with his own. 'Come on, darling, never let a man drink on his own.'

She raised the glass. 'Cheers, Dennis, but it's a bit early for me.'

'Funny you should turn up now. I was just thinking about Charlie.' He gave a little laugh that could almost have been a sob and when Kay made a sound he inclined his head towards her. 'She doesn't like me talking about him, but I bet you'd love to hear some stories of the old days, wouldn't you?'

'Only if you feel like it, Dennis.'

At that Kay pushed back her chair. 'Oh for God's sake.' She stopped when she got to the door. 'Try and stop him getting drunk, Joyce. I'm fed up of going on alone. Unbelievable though it is, he's the one they come to see.' She banged the door behind her.

Dennis took a sip of his drink and sighed. 'Poor old Kay. She used to think we could make it big. Thought we'd be the next Pearl Carr and Teddy Johnson, only we'd actually *win* the Eurovision Song Contest. But we were never that good anyway and now we're out of date and my looks are shot so ...' His lips curled in another of those wincing smiles, but his eyes were glassy as he gulped more gin.

She closed her own eyes, but a vision of the handsome boy she remembered laughing with her dad flashed behind her lids and she opened them again. 'What happened, Dennis?'

A wobbling laugh. 'Your dad happened, the police happened, jail happened.'

So he had been arrested at the same time as her father. 'I'm sorry, I didn't realize you were involved. Was it your letters they found him with?'

He nodded. 'They wanted me to say he took advantage of me

79

when I was underage, but I wouldn't do it. Couldn't let Charlie down. That's when I got this.' He gestured to his nose. 'And there was worse when they locked me up.' He gazed into space, his eyes fixed, reliving what horrors Joycie couldn't bear to imagine.

'I'm so sorry, Dennis.' She wanted so much to say more, but could think of nothing that would help. Instead she reached for his hand, and when she squeezed he looked back at her with another of those painful smiles. 'I didn't even know you were arrested.'

'Funny thing is they let me go after a week. Came and said I had no charges to answer. I couldn't understand it, but when I got out Kay told me Charlie was dead.'

'So they didn't actually prosecute you? Was that because Dad had died?'

'I suppose so, although they could still have used the letters to prove I was a raving pansy if they'd wanted to.' His face crumpled and he looked suddenly young again, like a little boy in pain. 'I loved Charlie, you know. Never believed in love at first sight, but that's how it was with him, and I felt so angry when I heard he'd killed himself.' He rubbed his hand over and over across his chest. 'But then it was probably even worse for him than it was for me.'

For a moment the world seemed to stall as a series of nightmare images flashed in front of her. Her dad beaten and bloody, his handsome face destroyed, and worse, so much worse. *Don't, don't think.*

Dennis's hand on her cheek brought her back. 'Sorry, darling, shouldn't have said that. And it's all right, they can't hurt him now. Charlie's at peace.'

She was sure he didn't believe that any more than she did. 'You were very brave,' she said. They sat for a while. Then he scrubbed his face and tried to smile at her, and she stood up. 'Come on. We've upset Kay. Why don't we find her and get that cup of coffee?'

He shook his head. 'It was probably her, you know. Charlie and me were talking about throwing in the towel, getting out of the business and setting up on our own. Going in with some pals who had opened a nice little club in Soho. Charlie wanted you to have a real home too.' A tear trickled down his lined cheek. 'We were saving up.'

'You think Kay reported you to the police?' She hadn't even thought of that.

'She was jealous and scared. I said she could come with us, but she wanted to keep the act going. She would never have told on me, of course. Didn't know about the letters. Must have expected them to follow him; to catch him doing a bit of cottaging or out trolling for rough trade.' He looked at her seeming to realize who he was talking to. 'But Charlie wasn't like that, Joyce. We loved each other.'

'Was that why my mum left him then? She found out about you?'

'Oh, my darling, no. We didn't get together until after she went and he always told me they loved each other. She had known what he was like for years and trusted him never to betray her. He couldn't understand why she'd gone.'

When he reached for the bottle again Joycie put her hand on his. 'Don't, Dennis, please.'

They stayed looking at each other for a while then he lifted her hand and pressed it to his lips. She felt his tears trickle through her fingers.

Chapter Nine

Dennis turned away and scrabbled in his pocket for a hankie as the dressing room door opened. It wasn't Kay, but a young girl Joycie didn't know. She held out a piece of paper, her face very pink, obviously star struck. 'Sorry to bother you, but Mrs Shaw has had to pop out and she asked me to give you this.'

Joycie opened the note, hearing the girl's breath loud beside her.

Dear Joyce,
Please let me make up for being so rude yesterday by giving you a proper tea. I'll expect you about 4 o'clock, but if that's not convenient of course I understand.
Yours,
April Shaw

Joycie smiled. She'd never known Mrs Shaw's first name – Mr Shaw always called her, *love* or sometimes *Mother*. The girl was still panting beside her like a little dog with pepperminty breath. When Joycie looked back at her she flushed even redder and pulled a biro from her pocket. 'Can I have your autograph? My name's Sandra.'

Joycie turned the note over and signed the back: *To Sandra with best wishes from Orchid XXX.'* She handed the paper to the girl with a smile. 'Tell Mrs Shaw I'll see her at four. And when I get back to town I'll send you a photo,' she said.

The girl almost bounced out of her shoes. 'Oh, thank you, and can you get Marcus Blake to sign the photo too, please?'

Dennis looked at her. 'All right, you've had your eyeful and your autograph, now bugger off.'

The girl twisted on her heel and flounced to the door. 'OK, Dennis, keep your hair on.'

Dennis laughed, 'See the respect I get. Come on, let's go and find that bloody sister of mine.'

Kay was in a coffee bar close by. There was no sign of Bill, but the seafront was busy despite the drizzle and he was obviously good at keeping out of sight. Joycie ordered a coffee and an iced bun, but Dennis said he had to go. 'Got to see a man about a dog.' As he walked out he gave an airy wave looking, just for a moment, like the long gone young man Joycie remembered.

Kay shook her head. 'Don't worry, he'll be all right.'

It was obvious she didn't believe this so Joycie just smiled and stirred her coffee. The iced bun was bright pink and when she took a bite it tasted bright pink too.

Kay made patterns with her spoon in the layer of froth at the bottom of her wide glass cup. 'He blames me for what happened to him and your dad. Thinks I reported Charlie.'

'And did you?'

'Of course not. Why would I?'

'Dennis thinks you were scared the act would break up.'

Kay slammed her spoon onto the chrome tabletop. 'So why doesn't he suspect Sid? He was in the same boat.'

She'd thought of that, of course, but what Dennis said seemed to make more sense.

Kay pushed a blonde curl behind her ear with a sigh. 'And it could have been someone else altogether. Someone who was jealous of your dad. I mean, the girls really went for him, but he wasn't interested so who knows.'

Joycie nodded, looking over to the door as the bell rang, but it was only a young couple with a little boy. She wished she'd been able to sit where Kay was so she could see outside.

Kay was still speaking. 'I remember the first time we worked with Sid. I saw Charlie and went all weak at the knees. That was when your mum was still around, must have been just before she left.' She smiled. 'I couldn't help thinking what a shame it was that Charlie was married. Never thought he'd prefer Dennis to me.'

'So you remember my mum? Do you have any idea what happened to her?'

Kay looked at her. 'Ah, that's what you're after.' She drank the foamy dregs from her cup. 'Well she didn't go because of Dennis, if that's what you're thinking. Like I said we had no idea Charlie fancied fellas. I just thought she went off with a boyfriend like everyone said.'

'You see, I've found out she was planning to take me with her and I want to know why she didn't.'

Kay touched her hand. 'Oh, darling, all I can say is that in my experience most men are bastards and I can't see lover boy, whoever he was, wanting a kid tagging along.'

It was the same thing she'd told herself all these years. But she no longer believed it. 'I've been wondering if it was something to do with Sid. I mean, he was very possessive of Dad.'

Kay snorted a laugh. 'Now come on, love, you can't think there was anything like that going on between them two.'

'That wasn't what I meant.'

'You must know what Sid was like. It was the birds he fancied and the more the better. He tried it on with me once, but Dennis isn't as girly as he looks and he soon saw him off.'

A real little tart aren't you? Just like your mother. Joycie pushed the iced bun away and swallowed a gulp of coffee. It was like dishwater. Surely her mum must have known what Sid was like. So how could she leave Joycie in a situation like that? What had the letter said? *I need to get away and I need to get Joyce away too.*

'Of course, Charlie was the one the girls went for. Always hanging about the stage door for him.'

'I know they sometimes used to take girls to the pub or a club after the show.'

'And your dad would slope off after a couple of drinks leaving good old Sid to take his pick.'

'Do you think Sid had a go at my mum and that's why she left?'

'Oh no, darling. He wouldn't have wanted to upset Charlie and anyway she was a bit old for him.'

'She was only in her early thirties.'

A chuckle. 'Like I said, a bit old. Sid likes them young. Told me that himself. I was, twenty, twenty-one, when we first worked with him and when he made that pass at me it was like he was doing me a favour.'

So how could Mum leave me there?

Kay was looking at the iced bun. 'Are you going to eat that?'

'No.' Joycie pushed the plate over and Kay cut a chunk from the end.

'Shouldn't really.' She patted her round tummy, but took a huge bite.

There was no point in asking any more about her parents, but maybe she could find out something useful for Mrs Shaw. 'I don't suppose you know what happened to my friend, Pauline, Mrs Shaw's daughter?'

'She got herself knocked up, didn't she? Mrs S kept it quiet, of course, but that was the rumour. And honestly, Joyce, it was so awful that year after your dad died. Dennis was in a hell of a state and I could hardly think straight. Certainly wasn't interested in other people's problems.'

'It just seems odd that the Shaws never heard a word from Pauline.'

'Yeah, that's a real shame. Mrs S is a nice woman and the girl was a good kid. You two were great pals, weren't you?' Joycie nodded and Kay asked. 'So when did *you* see her last?'

'The year before, when we were in the show here. When Dad died I lost contact with her. It was my fault, but I was so unhappy. Unhappy and ashamed too. Couldn't face telling people what had happened to him.'

Kay licked her fingers. 'Yes, I remember now. At the start of the season she asked me if I had your new address, but I didn't. I meant to ask if she'd heard from you, but she stopped coming to the theatre shortly after that. Must have been when she took up with the boyfriend.'

She arrived at Mrs Shaw's a little before 4 o'clock. The table was laid by the French windows, just the way Joycie remembered, but that only made the room seem emptier. The rocking chair, its cushions undisturbed, sat unmoving beside the silent radio and when Mrs Shaw came in with the teapot and took what had always been Pauline's seat Joycie had another of those dreamlike moments.

'It's so lovely to have you here, Joyce.' Mrs Shaw poured them both tea and held out a plate of white bread sandwiches cut in neat triangles. 'I think I've remembered the ones you liked best. There's cucumber, here, and fish paste and those are egg.'

They sat for a moment eating. The drizzle had stopped, the sun was trying to break through, and it was pleasant sitting by the open French windows. The garden was lush and very green. A little more overgrown than she remembered, but Mr Shaw's favourite pink roses were as pretty as ever and she could smell the lavender from here.

Mrs Shaw said. 'Ned used to love his garden, but I don't have time to keep it up.'

'It's still beautiful.'

'Joyce, love, do you remember Helen Crawford?'

She nodded, unable to speak for the cake in her mouth. Helen was a school friend of Pauline's.

Mrs Shaw went on, 'She's Helen Banks now. She got married and they moved to London.' She reached into the pocket of her flowery apron. 'This is her address and phone number and I just wondered, if you had time, you might speak to her and ask if she's heard anything about Pauline.'

'You haven't called her yourself?'

Mrs Shaw folded and unfolded the note. 'I did but, well, I thought she might tell you something she wouldn't say to me.'

'You think she's seen Pauline?'

'I don't know, but I got the idea she was keeping something back.' She picked up the milk jug and put it down again then stirred the sugar in the bowl. 'I just need to know she's all right; she doesn't have to come and see me unless she wants to.'

Joycie took the paper. 'Of course. I'll try.'

'You can send me a note or call the theatre if you find out anything. Ned hated telephones. Wouldn't have one in the house. I thought of getting one when he died but there wasn't much point. I've got no one to phone me.'

There was still no sign of Bill when Joycie got to the station. She found a phone box and called Marcus.

'Thank God. Where are you?' he said. She told him and he was quiet for a moment.

'Marcus?'

'I've been going mad worrying about you. Why the hell couldn't you have told me where you were? Picked up the phone just to let me know you were all right?'

'I'm sorry. I just needed time to think everything through on my own.'

'So when are you coming home?' The word *home* brought a

sharp pain to her throat and she couldn't speak. 'You are coming home aren't you?'

'If you still want me to.'

'Of course I do, you daft cow. Now get on that train and I'll meet you at Liverpool Street.'

Alone in a first class carriage again she tried to make sense of it all, but there was so much to take in she didn't know where to start. And she could hear that familiar voice in her head telling her to leave it alone; to bury it. There was Bill, too, warning her she could be in danger if she went on. But went on with what? And why was he and whoever he was working for so worried?

She looked at the paper bag on the seat beside her. Mrs Shaw had insisted she take the rest of the Victoria sponge. 'It's so nice to have someone to cook for.'

Joycie's mum had never made cakes; never had a proper oven. It must have been hard for her, moving from place to place, having nothing of her own, and Joycie had always thought that had a lot to do with her leaving. But that was just another of the stupid things she'd told herself to avoid facing the truth. The truth of that bloodstained mat.

There were only two real possibilities. Either the boyfriend had forced her to go with him, hurting her in the process or … She raked her fingers through her hair. Or someone had more than hurt her. And if it wasn't the boyfriend there was only one person it was likely to be.

Cora had described the way her dad was the night afterwards: *'I've never seen him like that and he was crying and raving on about your mum.'* And why had Sid sent Cora to check their lodgings? It must have been because of something Charlie told him.

The sky had filled with dark clouds and the light came on in the carriage, turning the window next to her into a hazy mirror. Her eyes looked enormous. It was no surprise: she had known it all along, just didn't want to know. And it could have been an accident. Her dad got home after the show and her mum told him she was leaving and taking Joycie with her. He might have been drinking and they argued: *those noises she had heard, the bumps and then the silence.* He wouldn't have meant to hurt her. Joycie was sure of that.

She sat for a long time, staring at her own dark image until they drew into a station and an elderly man got on, nodded to her and flipped open his evening paper.

Perhaps her dad killed himself because when he was in prison he had time to think and for the first time had to face up to what he'd done.

Now it was her turn to face up to things.

The Chiswick Empire, near London – February 1956

Joycie is alone in the dressing room for once. She shares it with Cathy, the magician's assistant, and three girl singers, but they've all rushed off and Sid and her dad will be ages chatting to people at the stage door. She isn't allowed to go out with them in case someone guesses she's a girl, but she doesn't care. Dad often comes back with autograph books for her to sign. The other day he gave her a note, with a name and address, saying: *Please, please, write to me,* and last week a girl left a message at the box office asking *The Kid* to meet her in the park.

It's a shame it's always girls who want her autograph and she has to keep pretending she's a boy. If these girls saw her outside the theatre they wouldn't know her and certainly wouldn't want to go anywhere with her. But she loves the fact that they like her. The older people in the audience like her too. She knows because of the way they laugh and ooh and ah when she's onstage.

She hangs the cap she has to wear as *The Kid* on a hook and unfastens the clips from her hair so it tumbles to her shoulders. Then she slips her braces down and takes off the scratchy collarless shirt. Although she still doesn't have much on top, she wears a bandage around her chest to be *The Kid* and she's just taken that off when the door opens. Even though it's probably just one of the girls come back for something they've forgotten she holds the bandage against her chest.

It's Sid and he's looking at her in that way she hates. He closes the door and leans against it. 'No need to be shy with me, darling. I remember when you used to sit on my knee with your chubby little arse all bare. Hated wearing knickers when you were a nipper, do you remember?'

She swallows and shakes her head, looking at the chair where her shirt is hanging, but she's scared to reach for it in case she drops the bandage. 'Cathy'll be back in a minute, if you're looking for her.'

He smiles. 'Cathy's gone, darling, and I sent your dad off to get some Mackeson's. Thought we could all have a drink together later on. You're old enough now and looking so grown up.' He's walking towards her very slowly, his eyes raking her up and down and smiling in that horrible way he has.

She looks at the door, praying for her dad to come, and holding the bandage tight against her chest.

'It's funny the way you're such a hit with the girls,' Sid says. 'Wouldn't they be surprised if they could see what I can?'

He's still moving closer and all Joycie can do is to press back against the dressing table.

But then Sid takes the shirt from the back of the chair and hands it to her. 'Put this on, sweetheart, you're getting cold.'

He doesn't take his eyes off her, but somehow she manages to pull on the shirt and let the bandage drop. As she buttons up, Sid sits down and gestures for her to take the chair next to him. She looks at the door again, but he isn't doing anything wrong and she feels a bit better with her shirt on, even though she has nothing underneath it.

'I just want a word about the act without Charlie around, darling. Think he's getting a bit jealous with you having more of the spotlight.' He starts talking about some other bit of business they could do, looking at himself in the mirror and fiddling with the hair clips on the dressing table. She tries to concentrate.

But all at once he's standing and moving behind her chair. He grabs her hair and lifts it up. 'See I'm wondering if we need to get this cut. I know you won't like it, but there's lots more we can do if you can take off that cap now and then. The kind of business Charlie does with his hat, you know.'

He leans down so that his cheek is close to her ear, his chin almost resting on her shoulder, and she can smell tobacco on his breath and the tweed of his jacket. There's a tang of sweat too, but when she tries to move away he keeps hold of her hair and it hurts.

'I can see why those girls go for you, darling,' he says. 'But it's the boys you like, don't you? Not so innocent as you make out are you, eh?'

His head is pressed hard against her ear and he's still holding her hair so she can't move. Her breath catches in her throat and her heart is beating so hard she can feel it thumping right through her body. He reaches down, unbuttons the top of her shirt and squeezes her bare bosom so tight it hurts and she opens her mouth to scream, but there's no sound. And now, *oh God*, his other hand is into the loose waist of her trousers, his fingers pulling aside the front of her knickers.

He mutters. 'A real little tart aren't you? Just like your mother.' *Scream, run, do something.* But she can't and he twists round so that he's standing in front of her, moving both his hands to the back of her head and pushing it, pushing it, towards the buttons on the front of his trousers. The rough cloth is painful against her face and she can't move although the stench of tweed and wee is making her gag. One of his hands pushes in front of her face groping at his buttons, the other still hard on the back of her head, pushing and pushing …

***

'All right, my dear?' The elderly man opposite was folding his newspaper and looking at her with concern as the train pulled into Liverpool Street Station.

She managed to gasp out that she was fine, but had to wait until he'd got out and walked away before she could stop shaking. She wanted to sit there and cry and cry, but the carriage door was open and there was Marcus, shaking his blond fringe out of his eyes, smiling at her and holding out his arms. When she fell into them she pressed her face into his neck, breathing in the clean cotton smell of his shirt and the fresh, warm scent of his skin.

Chapter Ten

Marcus didn't speak until they were in the car, then he looked at her and said, 'You can tell me about it when you're ready.' She wondered if she'd ever be ready to tell him everything.

When they got indoors she kissed his cheek and said, 'I'm sorry about disappearing like that.'

'I didn't behave too well myself so let's forget it shall we? Why don't you go up and have a nice bath and I'll make us some sausage and mash.'

She looked at him for a moment, but could only manage to say, 'Thank you, that would be lovely.'

In the bath she forced her mind to go back to that dreadful night. The memory she had tried so hard to suppress. The worst thing was that she still couldn't recall what had happened afterwards. It wasn't just the arrival at the station that had stopped her remembering. Every time she tried to bring back the *after* her mind flinched away. So it must have been worse.

Eventually she allowed herself to stop thinking about it and let her mind drift, lying in the warm scented water with her eyes closed. She had almost dozed off when Marcus called up that food was ready. He had put the plates on the coffee table and as she came in, wearing her old candlewick dressing gown with a towel on her head, he poured a glass of red wine for her. 'I reckon you need this.'

She took a long drink then put the plate on her lap and started eating. He'd done the sausages just the way she liked with lots of gravy and a pile of crispy onions on top of the mash. She ate quickly, aware of Marcus turning to smile at her every so often. After a while he stopped eating and sat back with his glass. 'Was it any use then?'

She told him first about Dennis and Kay and he said, 'That's interesting, so you think this Kay was the one who did the dirty on your dad, do you?'

'She swears she didn't, but Dennis knows her best and he's sure she did. As she said, though, there could be any number of people who might have had it in for him.'

Her hunger was gone now, but she carried on eating as slowly as possible. She wanted so much to tell him about Sid, but the words wouldn't come. Instead when the food was all gone and he'd refilled their glasses she said, 'I was hoping to see a girl I knew in Clacton. Her name is Pauline, but she seems to have disappeared. Her mum wants me to visit another friend who lives in London in case they've been in touch.'

Marcus gave a little laugh. 'Don't forget we've got work booked.'

'This shouldn't take long. All I can do is ask Helen if she's seen Pauline and pass the news to Mrs Shaw.' She tucked her feet under her and pulled her dressing gown collar up around her chin.

Marcus rubbed her knee. 'But none of this is what's upset you so much, is it?'

Don't think about it, don't think. Her breath caught in her throat as she looked into her glass where the wine seemed to swirl blood-red.

'You haven't seen that guy again, have you? The one you think is following you.'

Breathing easier she told him about the encounter with Bill.

'Bloody hell, that's weird. Was he threatening you or trying to help?'

She sipped her drink. 'I don't know. He seemed concerned about me, but he wouldn't tell me who he was, or if he's working for someone else. The way he talked scared me though and I still can't figure out why he's following me.'

'He didn't tell you what he wants?'

'Not really, just said I could be in danger. But it has to be something to do with my mum or dad.' She saw Marcus glance at the phone. 'And before you talk about calling the police again, I've already thought of that. In fact I threatened him with it, but he just laughed. And he's right. What can I tell them? What has he done wrong?'

'Following and threatening you, of course. That's got to be against the law.'

'If it is I don't know how I could prove it. Even if they could find him it would be my word against his. You've only seen him once and no one heard what he said to me. We don't even know if Bill's his real name.'

'Well we should get you a bodyguard then.' When she laughed he said, 'I'm serious, Joycie.'

'I know and thank you, but let's leave it for now. We'll be back to our normal routine this week so he may lose interest. And you'll be with me all the time.'

He picked up the plates and headed for the kitchen. 'OK, I prescribe a cup of coffee, some telly, then an early night.' He switched on the TV as he passed it and Joycie stretched her legs out along the sofa, leaning back into the soft, soft cushions.

She woke in bed and for a few moments couldn't think where she was. Marcus must have carried her up after she fell asleep on the sofa. The birds in the garden were in full voice with the dawn chorus and she listened for a few minutes, enjoying the tunefulness after the squawking seagulls that had woken her in Clacton.

She pulled on her dressing gown and padded down to the kitchen, made some tea and took it out into the garden. It was only 6 a.m. and her mind had that kind of early morning clarity that always made her think she could find a solution to anything. Sipping her tea she let the birdsong and the early morning quiet of the green garden soak through her as she tried to sift through all the things she had learned in Clacton. Kay had talked about Sid's interest in young girls so what he had done to her probably wasn't an isolated incident. She still couldn't remember how that had ended and … her mind flinched back again. Surely it couldn't be worse than the things she was imagining so why did it stay out of reach?

But there were other implications to what Kay had said. Her dad had helped to attract the girls, so he must have known something at least of what Sid was like. Of course, those girls they'd taken out after the show had gone willingly. Presumably they were old enough to drink and old enough to understand what they were getting into.

A shiver as she remembered Sid's words to her. *Thought we could all have a drink together later on. You're old enough now and looking so grown up.* But she wasn't old enough, only fourteen, and certainly not old enough for what he tried to do to her.

And now she was thinking about the really young girls. The ones she had attracted as *The Kid.* Was that the reason he had wanted her in the act? The reason he wanted to build up her involvement?

She jumped and almost spilled her tea when Marcus put his hand on her shoulder.

'You're up early. Are you OK?' When she nodded he sat next to her and took her hand. 'Are you ready to tell me the rest of it yet? It's obvious something else happened while you were in Clacton.'

His hand was warm on hers. Joycie took a deep breath. It was time to talk. If she was ever going to unlock all the doors in her mind, the ones that refused to be ignored since she started digging into the past, she had to share with him what she had been able to confront so far.

There in the green quiet of the garden she began to tell him. As soon as she started to speak the sense of calm lifted and it was so difficult to breathe she had to force each word out. It was disjointed and she could only give him the barest details, but he heard her out and did nothing more than squeeze her hand once or twice when she stumbled into a choked silence. At the end they sat together for a long time until she turned to him and he held her and kissed her hair while she rested her cheek on his chest.

After a while he moved away. 'Breakfast, I think, don't you?'

In the kitchen she made toast and scrambled eggs while Marcus heated some milk for coffee. When they were sitting at the little kitchen table she said, 'I don't understand why I can't remember the rest.'

Marcus slammed his toast down and his voice was hard. 'I can. That filthy bastard, I feel like going over there and beating the daylights out of him.'

She looked at him. 'In the garden earlier I was thinking about what Kay said. Sid liked them young so I probably wasn't the only one.' They sat for a moment, neither of them touching their food. 'I just hate that he must have met girls through my dad and even through me. I think that was why he wanted me in the act, Marcus, to attract the younger ones.'

He said, 'Can you remember if you told your dad what Sid did to you?' His face wavered in front of her eyes as a rush of dizziness swept over her. She gripped the edge of the table, hearing him say as if from miles away. 'What's wrong?'

His chair scraped on the floor and he was kneeling beside her, his arm around her shoulder when she was finally able to blink and look up at him. She took a breath and tried to smile. 'I'm OK, just tired. Got up too early.'

He sat opposite again. 'I know we're booked to do that shoot for Yardley, but I can cancel it if you're not up to it.'

'No, I need to get back to work.' Working would mean she didn't have to think about any of this for a while. And that was what she wanted more than anything.

The Yardley shoot took two exhausting days. It was for a new range of hair products and they didn't finish until late in the evening of the second day. By then her head and neck were aching and her hair felt as if it had been shocked by several thousand volts of electricity. She longed to go home and sleep but Lucy, the stylist, had worked hard and when she suggested they all go to the Marquee Club with her boyfriend later on she couldn't say no.

They arranged to meet for a Chinese meal in Soho before going on to the club and when they got home Joycie had a quick bath and tried to wash some of the gunk from her hair. Then she threw on a pair of black slacks and a purple silk shirt – she didn't bother much with clothes when she wasn't working.

Marcus was still in the darkroom when she came down and she decided to phone Pauline's friend, Helen, who was now apparently called Helen Banks.

The girl who answered had to shout above the music playing in the background, Tom Jones belting out 'It's Not Unusual', but Joycie managed to get through to her that she wanted to speak to Helen Banks. Thankfully someone had turned the music down by the time Helen came to the phone and Joycie explained that she was Joyce Todd, a friend of Pauline Shaw. 'I saw Pauline's mum when I was in Clacton the other day and she said you were living in town now. Suggested I look you up.'

There was a moment's silence then Helen said, 'Are you the girl who used to come with the show? Worked with that comic?' It was obvious she didn't realize Joycie was also Orchid, but she grudgingly agreed to see her next day. 'You'll have to come to the boutique where I work. Expect you've heard of it – Plumes.'

When Joycie said she didn't know it Helen made a noise that could have been a sniff and said, 'It's in Foubert's Place just off Carnaby Street. All the mods come there and the pop stars. We had Lulu in last week.'

Next day Joycie dressed as plainly as she could in a blue shift dress, gathering her famous black hair into a pony tail.

The Sandie Shaw song that was in the charts, 'Long Live Love', was blasting through the tiny shop, which certainly appeared to be popular. Racks of clothes filled the place and girls were trying on hats, wrapping feather boas around them or holding dresses and trousers to themselves in front of the mirrors that lined one wall.

The girl behind the counter must be Helen, although she had changed dramatically from the pretty redhead Joycie remembered. The ginger curls had somehow been transformed into a dark shiny bob and the freckles were hidden under pale make-up. Her eyes were made enormous with false lashes and bright blue eyeshadow.

Unfortunately the wall behind the counter was covered by an enormous poster of Orchid/Joycie herself and, sod's law, her hair in the picture was scraped back in a ponytail just like she had it now. As she approached, Helen's eyes seemed to bulge from her head and she plonked herself onto a tiny stool as if too surprised to stay standing.

Joycie spoke quietly, hoping no one else would spot her. 'Hello, Helen, it's Joyce, I phoned about Pauline.'

Helen seemed to shake herself and glanced around at the shoppers, speaking in a loud whisper. 'Good grief, are you really, you know …?' She breathed the word, '*Orchid*,' and her mouth opened in a silent scream as she pointed a finger over her shoulder at the poster behind her.

Joycie nodded. 'That's my working name, yes, but I'm just here as a friend, as Joyce, so can we keep it quiet please?'

Helen seemed unable to stop nodding, her thickly coated lashes fluttering like giant insects. She took a couple of steps to a beaded curtain and called through. 'Norma, mind the counter will you, I've got to pop out.' Without waiting for an answer she grabbed Joycie's arm and led her out of the shop. There was a café just up the road and, thank God, it was blissfully silent inside. The band they'd seen at the Marquee last night, The Yardbirds, had been good, but her ears were still buzzing.

When they were settled at a table, Helen with an ice cream soda and Joycie with a piece of chocolate cake, Helen leaned forward. 'So how did you get to be a model? You never used to be all that good-looking.'

Joycie had heard this kind of thing before and she just smiled. 'I met Marcus Blake and that was it. He's a brilliant photographer. Could make anyone look great.'

Helen smiled and relaxed, shaking her shiny bob so that her big plastic earrings, which Joycie saw were made to look like bunches of purple grapes, rattled and glinted. 'A photographer was in the other day. Said I could be a model if only I was a bit taller. You're lucky like that.'

'But your shop looks a fun place to work.'

A little shrug. 'It's OK. Better than the bank where I used to be.'

'Mrs Shaw said you got married.'

Helen stirred her thick drink with the striped straw. 'We aren't really together any more. He works in an office and we had this flat in Hounslow.' She pulled a little face. 'The only good thing about that place is it's on a tube line, but it takes ages to get into the centre. Before we moved from Clacton Dave promised we were going to see a bit of life, but he just used to come home at 6 o'clock, watch telly and go to bed before midnight with a cup of cocoa. But I'm still young. Wanted to live a bit before I fell for a baby and got really trapped. Haven't told my folks though. They'd go mad.'

Helen looked at Joycie's chocolate cake. 'You're so lucky to be able to eat stuff like that. If I so much as look at a cake or biscuit I gain half a stone.' She took a breath. 'It's so funny, you being a famous model. I never saw the show when you were in it but Pauline told me you looked just like a boy. So why did you stop coming to Clacton? Pauline said something happened to your dad.'

'Dad died and I had to go and live with friends.'

'Oh, I didn't know. That's a real shame and he wasn't that old was he? Pauline said he was a lovely man and some of the girls at school really fancied him. Not like that horrible comic. He was a right creep and I know Pauline couldn't stand him.'

'Mrs Shaw said you might have been in touch with Pauline.'

Helen sucked her straw so hard it made a gurgling sound. 'I told her when she rang me. I haven't seen Pauline since she left Clacton.'

'You've no idea where she went?'

'She was so miserable that last summer. I thought it was because you didn't come down. And then she got the boyfriend and we didn't see much of each other after that.'

'Who *was* the boyfriend?'

'Don't know, she kept him quiet, but then her parents were so fuddy-duddy I guess she had to.' She reached into her tiny black and white bag and fished out a box of Sobranie Cocktail cigarettes, flipping it open and offering them to Joycie. When Joycie shook her head Helen pursed her pale lips, her fingers hovering over the coloured cigarettes as if choosing from a box of sweets. In the end she settled for a bright pink one and lit up, breathing in deeply.

To stop herself from checking her watch, Joycie rubbed a hand over her hair, which still felt sticky from its two day torture. 'You know Pauline got pregnant?'

Helen looked down at her cigarette, flicking her nail against the gold band near the tip. 'That's what people said.'

101

'She never told you?'

'Like I said, she wasn't around much. And I was already going out with Dave.' She was still looking at her pink cigarette, still flicking at its gold tip. Mrs Shaw had been right, she was holding something back.

Joycie leaned on the table, pushing her plate out of the way. 'I won't tell Mrs Shaw if you think I shouldn't.'

Those enormous eyelashes flipped back, the blue eyes considered Joycie for a moment. Then Helen said, 'Look, I only got this from my sister, Sally. She's three years older than us and she said one of the girls she worked with lived in Pauline's street. This girl, Mandy, was a right slut and she told Sally that Pauline asked her about ...' She looked around then shifted closer, the insect lashes fluttering fast. 'Apparently Pauline was asking about getting rid of it, you know ...' she mouthed rather than said the words, '*an abortion.*'

Joycie couldn't speak, just swallowed down a rush of sharp bile as Helen sat back looking satisfied at having delivered her bombshell. 'So I reckon she came up to the Smoke to get it done. Well I've heard about them so-called doctors, the backstreet ones, and I wouldn't be surprised if it didn't go right. Could even have killed her.'

Joycie's breath had stopped and her stomach seemed to have plummeted deep down inside. It shouldn't have been surprising and it would make sense of why Pauline had never been in contact with her family, but she couldn't bear to think of it. She certainly couldn't share it with Mrs Shaw.

'That's awful,' she said, trying to push away the image of pretty, smiling Pauline in a dingy room with some horrible quack. She swallowed, looking at Helen who was stirring the ice cream in the bottom of her glass. 'But you don't know any of this for sure?'

'Oh no and I hope I'm wrong. Maybe she's emigrated to Australia or something.'

Joycie managed to get away after promising to send a big signed photo to hang in the boutique and giving Helen her telephone number when she said, 'I'll have a think in case there's anything else I remember about Pauline. And we should keep in touch anyway. Maybe go out one night soon.'

As she walked away down the sunny street the voices of The Righteous Brothers screamed at her from the open doors of the boutique: telling her she'd lost that loving feeling. She moved faster and faster until she was almost running. Trying to put Helen, the music, and the whole conversation behind her.

Poor, poor Pauline. Joycie had always imagined her still in Clacton with a lovely husband and a tribe of kids, making cakes and having Sunday dinner with her mum and dad every week. The idea that she might be dead had never entered her head.

She jumped on a bus to head home and the motion soothed away the buzz in her ears and let her think more clearly. Underneath the horrible image of Pauline, all alone as she bled to death, something else had been niggling at her brain.

Why had no one seen this mysterious boyfriend? And why was she unable to stop thinking about what Helen had said right at the start. Something about Sid. '*He was a right creep and I know Pauline couldn't stand him.*'

Chapter Eleven

'You're not thinking Sid forced himself on Pauline and got her pregnant, are you?' Marcus said. They were sitting in the garden drinking gin and tonics, the ice chinking in their glasses, and Joycie had just told him about her meeting with Helen. He had been in his darkroom as usual when she got back and she had knocked on the door, desperate to speak to him right away.

'It's so horrible I can hardly bear to think of it, but it does make sense,' she said. 'Nobody ever saw the boyfriend and she obviously couldn't turn to him for help when she needed it. So maybe he didn't exist.'

Marcus pulled at the lavender bush next to his seat, breaking off a spike of flowers and twirling it in his fingers, so that Joycie caught a hint of the sharp, clean scent. 'And she never contacted you?' he said.

'No. I blame myself for that. When I was living with Irene and Deirdre I didn't want to see or even write to anyone. Tried not to think about how things had been before Dad died. But Mrs Shaw asked Sid for my new address and he said he didn't know it, which was a downright lie.'

They were silent for a while, sipping their drinks. Joycie's was too strong, and she went into the kitchen to add more tonic. As she was pouring, and putting in another ice cube, Marcus's voice came to her through the open back door. 'Hang on a minute. You said Mrs Shaw asked Sid for the address, but he didn't tell her.' When she came out to sit beside him again he twisted in his seat to face her. 'Well what if Pauline went on to ask Sid herself?'

Acid in her mouth and goose pimples chilling her arms. She put her drink carefully on the grass beside her. 'You think he offered to tell her, but not her mum? Oh God, Marcus, he could have used that as a way to get her on her own.' A wave of dizziness that she forced herself to ignore. 'He could have lured her to his dressing room or his lodgings. And he had a car too. So he might even have offered to take her to see me.'

Marcus must have heard the wobble in her voice because he put down his own drink and took both her hands in his. 'Now stop that. I agree it's possible, but not all that likely. And even if it's true it wasn't your fault.' They sat without speaking as the sky turned paler with evening, the air cooled, and streaks of pink began to stain the clouds on the horizon.

Then Marcus said, 'I was supposed to have a drink with Tommy Green tonight. Do you want me to put him off?'

She stood, arms folded, hands rubbing at her chilly skin. Tommy was a tailor – a real East End character who had realized there was money to be made catering for the new fashions. The friendship was important to Marcus. It had helped him shed some of his public school mannerisms and fit in with the other young photographers, who all seemed to be cockney lads.

'No, you go. You won't be back late, will you?' She hadn't realized how anxious she was not to be left alone at night and had to fight to keep the pleading note from her voice.

'Just long enough for a couple of drinks. Tommy's a good bloke and I've got a favour to ask him, but I'll be home before the pubs close.'

She followed him into the kitchen, turning the key in the back door. He kissed her and said, 'Lock and bolt the front door after me.' A smile. 'Just so I won't worry.'

After he'd gone she sat on the sofa trying to read. She had a book by a new author, John le Carré, on the go but it was about spies and was so sinister it made her look behind her every time the house creaked. She knelt by the bookcase in the corner to check what Marcus's mother had left behind and pulled out a Miss Read novel – a story about life as a teacher in a country school – that might help calm her down.

She felt better when she'd read a couple of chapters and she got up to make herself some coffee, but when she sat down again she couldn't face the book. Would she ever be able to think of Pauline without the hated shadow of Sid getting in the way? The thought that he could have used her friendship with Joycie to get to her was sickening.

But what about her dad? All those years when he was Sid's stooge. Did he know what Sid was like with young girls and look the other way? Or, worse, did he help?

And all at once she felt the memories stirring. Another locked door in her head beginning to creak open. She wanted to close it tight again, didn't want to know, or to see. But she thought of the way she was with Marcus and the way she wanted to be. And most of all she thought of Pauline. If uncovering those horrible memories might shed even a little light on what happened to her friend she had to face them.

The Chiswick Empire, near London – February 1956

The rough cloth of Sid's trousers is harsh against her face and she can't move although the stench of tweed and wee is making her gag. One of his hands shoves down in front of her face, groping at his buttons, the other is still hard on the back of her head, pushing and pushing.

And just when she thinks she's going to faint – and almost hoping she will – he shoves her chair away from him.

'What the fuck is going on?' Her dad's voice.

Her heart jumps into her throat and she twists round. Dad is standing in the open doorway.

'Go on, Joycie love, hurry up and get changed.' Sid gives a hoarse laugh, as if it's all a joke.

Dad's face is so white it's almost green and there are deep creases she's never noticed before running like scars down his cheeks. He looks from Sid to her and back again.

She wants to die, wants him to say it's all right, but most of all she wants to run away. Her face, already sore from rubbing against that rough tweed, throbs with heat. She's so ashamed and longs to tell Dad she's sorry, but she's afraid to speak.

He's still looking at her with that terrible expression and his voice is cold. 'Go home, Joyce. Right now.'

Burning tears fill her eyes and she bites her lips to hold back the sobs that are trying to force their way out. Her hand is shaking so much she can hardly pick up her bra from the back of the chair and when she stumbles towards the clothes rail for her dress and shoes, Dad is there already, shoving them into her arms without looking at her. His voice is very quiet, coming from miles away, and it still isn't her dad's voice. 'Go home now, Joyce. Get changed there.'

At the door a shoe drops from the bundle of clothes and as she stoops to pick it up she can't stop a sob from bursting out. She doesn't dare look back, but when she gets to the end of the corridor she's too exhausted to keep moving. She leans on the wall and presses her face into the bundle of clothes to muffle the sound of her crying. How can she go home? How can she ever face Dad again?

The voice she hardly knows as his is still going on, low and bitter. 'You fucking bastard, I warned you.'

Another of those croaky laughs from Sid. 'Calm down, Charlie boy, it's not the way it looks. We were just talking about the show. Joycie wants a bigger part and was trying to persuade me. You know what girls are like ...' His voice cuts off and there's a rush of sound that makes Joycie jump – heavy feet moving fast. But they're not coming out here so she stays where she is, clutching the bundle of clothes to her chest.

A thump and then another. Her dad's voice: quieter but oh-so hard. 'Don't you dare, you arsehole. That's my daughter you're talking about. I'll fucking kill you.'

Sid coughs a couple of times and when he speaks it sounds like he's choking on something. 'Ok, Ok, Charlie. You got me. I'm a right bastard and I should have known better. Just couldn't help myself ...' This time it's obvious her dad has hit him and he must have collapsed into one of the chairs because she hears it creak under his weight.

'That's it, Sid, I've had it with you. I'm getting out.'

Sid sounds muffled, but angry now. Like he's given up trying to get round her dad. 'You try that, Charlie. Just try it. You're past it anyway and I'll be better off without you. The act is about me, not you, and certainly not about that little tart. If I want another stooge I'll get one a damn sight better than you ever were. So clear off and see how you manage.'

'I will.' It sounds like Dad has turned away and she opens the door to get out.

But Sid is still speaking, his voice very calm. She thinks he might even be smiling. 'Of course, if you're not working with me any more I might have an attack of conscience and need to see the cops. And not just about you and your little boyfriend.'

Joycie freezes, her hand still on the door. She wants to go, but she can't move.

'What are you talking about?'

'About getting them to look into what happened to your darling wife. Cora told me what she found when she went to your place the day Mary left you. Or did she leave you, Charlie? I've never been sure about that after what Cora said she took from under your bed.'

'What do you mean?'

'It was a mat covered in blood, so she told me.'

Say something, Dad, Joycie begs him silently.

But he doesn't speak and there's silence for what seems like hours. Then he says, 'Don't be stupid. Cora was never at my place.'

'Have you forgotten the way you were that night? Drunk as a lord and shouting about Mary. We thought it best if Cora went and had a look and she found the mat.'

'You're lying.' Dad's voice has gone all quiet.

'Am I?' This time Joycie is sure Sid is smiling. 'Well we can ask Cora, if you like, but it was all so long ago it would be a shame to let it spoil our friendship.'

Dad doesn't speak, but Joycie thinks she can hear him breathing, great loud breaths as if he's going to be sick or something. Then Sid says, 'Of course, if you were to change your mind about leaving, it wouldn't be in my interest to cause trouble for you and little Joycie, would it?'

'Fuck off, Sid, just fuck off,' is all her dad says, his voice sounding like he's being strangled. And she hears him move. He's coming her way. And she runs out of the door, out of the theatre and keeps running.

As she runs she tells herself not to think about it – any of it. Because if she doesn't think about it, it didn't really happen.

She doesn't stop running until she's back in their lodgings. She goes straight to her room, takes off the horrible boy's clothes and puts on Mum's old candlewick dressing gown. Then lies curled up in her bed staring into the dark. *Don't think, Joycie, don't think.*

She doesn't hear her dad come back.

***

It was only 9.30 when Marcus got home, but Joycie had drunk several more gins by then. She was lying on the sofa and had to wobble to the door to unbolt it for him. She knocked her shin on the coffee table as she passed, but it didn't hurt. Nothing hurt, nothing mattered. 'You're early,' she said.

He smiled. 'And you're drunk.'

'Just a bit. Haven't had anything to eat.' She collapsed back on the sofa, closing her eyes, but opening them again when the world tipped. The trouble was she hardly ever drank a lot so she couldn't take it. She didn't go in for pot or pills much either, but she would have liked something now.

Marcus must have gone to the kitchen because he came back with a big lump of cheese, a packet of cream crackers, and some coffee. 'There's not much to eat, but get this down you before you go to bed or you'll feel awful in the morning.'

After she'd eaten and had two cups of coffee she felt almost sober again. And wished she was still drunk. She looked at Marcus. It would help so much to tell him what she'd remembered about her dad and Sid. But Marcus was rubbing his hand over his face and she realized he looked very tired, almost ill.

She touched his arm. 'Are you all right?'

His smile wasn't really a smile. 'Yeah, fine.'

Those goose pimples had sprung up on her arms again even though the room was very warm. 'Marcus, what is it?'

He shook his head. 'Nothing. Really, it's nothing. We can talk about it tomorrow when you're more yourself.'

She looked at him, telling him with her crossed arms and her raised eyebrows that she could wait as long as it took, and trying to ignore the heavy thump of her heart.

Finally he said, 'You know I saw Tommy Green tonight?'

'Yes?'

'Well the reason we met was because I knew he had contacts

on the shady side so I asked him a couple of days ago if he could find a bodyguard for you.'

'And could he?' She swallowed. Her lips and throat were suddenly very dry and the food she'd just eaten felt like a pile of rocks in her stomach. Somehow she knew the answer already.

'No.' He was staring into the corner of the room and biting his lip. Joycie forced herself to stay silent.

Marcus took a noisy breath and looked back at her. 'He said no one would take the job on for any amount of money.'

It was hard to speak because her breath seemed to have stopped completely. 'Why not?' He shook his head again and closed his eyes. 'Marcus, please tell me.'

'Apparently the word has gone out that we've upset some important people.'

She pressed her fingers to her mouth. 'Who? What people?'

'All Tommy would say was that he knows the guy who's been following you, and who really is called Bill, apparently. He's a member of one of the big London gangs.'

'Oh my God.'

Marcus pulled her to him, but she could feel his own heart drumming so fast it didn't really help. She looked over to the front door. He had bolted it when he came in.

'It's all right, it's all right,' he kept saying. Then he pushed her gently away, still holding her shoulders and looking into her eyes. 'I've asked Tommy to spread the word that we've got the message and you'll be keeping your head down from now on. Told him we haven't found out anything that could bother anyone and you're going to focus on work.'

She couldn't speak, just shook her head at him.

'I had to tell him that, Joycie.'

'I know.' She leaned close again and spoke into his shoulder. 'I might have put my aunt and her family in danger. And he was in Clacton as well, so there's Mrs Shaw, Dennis and Kay too.'

'It'll be all right,' he whispered into her hair.

After a long while he pulled back, head to one side, his blue eyes crinkling at the corners as he tried to smile at her. 'And there's one bit of good news. Tommy can get us a lovely dog. She's an Afghan, called Fatima. Her father won prizes apparently.'

She tried to laugh, although it came out like a sob. 'Don't suppose it was for being a guard dog, was it?'

He did laugh. 'I doubt it. Probably for most glossy coat or something, but Tommy swears she's got a very loud bark.'

They looked at each other, and when he held out his arms she fell into them. His heartbeat was slow and steady now, and he held her without speaking.

After a long time she looked up into his blue eyes. 'Will you stay with me tonight?' she said.

Chapter Twelve

They lay on her bed fully clothed, her head on Marcus's chest. Just hearing his slow breathing helped her to relax. 'I don't think I can give up now,' she said.

He moved to look down at her. 'But you know what Tommy said. You'd be in real danger and we can't get you any protection.'

She sat up, her hands in her hair. 'So what do I do? The fact that they're so desperate to stop me means there's something serious to find out.'

'Let's go to the police then.'

'And tell them what? That my mum disappeared years ago and I've never bothered to look into it till now. Or that some man has helped me get a taxi and asked for my autograph.'

He twisted to face her. 'But we can tell them who Bill is. And they're bound to know him if he's a gang member.'

'So what can they do? If they try to warn him off that could make things worse.'

Marcus brushed back her hair, his hand lingering on her cheek. 'Can't you just let it go?'

'If I do I'm not sure I'll ever get over the things that have happened to me. I want to be happy, Marcus, and to be with you properly.'

'At least put it out of your mind for a while and see how things go.'

She shook her head. 'I can't. Now I've come this far I know I'll never get any peace if I do.'

He kissed her forehead then held her to him for a long time, while she listened to his heart and felt his warm breath stirring her hair. Finally he sighed and said, 'But you do understand that we need to be a lot more careful, don't you?'

There was an ache in her throat, but along with it a surge of happiness. 'Thank you, thank you.'

'What for?'

'For understanding why I can't stop. And for saying *we*.'

He kissed her hair. 'Silly girl. We're in this together.' He stood up then and smiled down at her. 'Do you still want me to stay?'

Joycie felt her face flush and the pain in her throat grow worse. There was nothing she wanted more, but she shook her head. 'It's not fair on you. I'll be all right.'

He grabbed her nightdress from the end of the bed and threw it at her. 'I'll take that as a yes then, but you'd better put that on or I might not be responsible for my actions.'

He'd seen her almost naked any number of times, but he made a show of turning his back. Then began to take off his own shirt and jeans. She undressed and got under the covers saying, 'OK I'm in.'

Marcus slid under the eiderdown, but on top of the blanket. 'I'll be warm enough here, just make sure you keep your hands to yourself, eh?' He lay on his side facing away from her and she listened until his even breathing told her he was asleep.

After that she was awake for what seemed like hours, feeling the heat from him, longing to touch him. If only she could wake him now and tell him how much she wanted him. But it wouldn't be fair because she knew that awful voice would spoil it again.

***

114

When she opened her eyes it was light and Marcus was gone. She lay listening to the hum of voices from the radio in the kitchen and the rattle of cups. Last night she had come so close to asking him to make love to her. How would she be feeling now if she'd done that? Horrible probably and so would he because she would have ended up rejecting him again. If only she could stop hearing that voice, stop feeling dirty.

It was all to do with her memories of what happened with Sid; she knew that. But she also remembered how terrible it had been thinking Dad might blame her too.

And it was just before his arrest, so they never had time to talk about it properly. The nightmare of the police arriving and taking him away, and everything that came after, had wiped their few last hours together from her mind. But she thought about them now.

Chiswick – February 1956

When she wakes next morning Joycie is still curled up in Mum's candlewick dressing gown with the eiderdown pulled tight around her. She's hot and shoves back the covers to sit up, taking a shaky breath when she hears Dad snoring. He must have gone to the pub after the bust up with Sid, but he didn't blunder about and wake her when he came in so he couldn't have been all that drunk.

She feels like crying again. She wants so much to hear him tell her it's all right and he knows it wasn't her fault, but his face and voice were like a stranger's yesterday. So angry and cold.

At least in these lodgings, unlike some of the others, she has a sink in her room, and when she's splashed her face and got dressed she feels a bit better. There's enough bacon and eggs in the kitchenette for Dad's favourite breakfast too. But when she starts frying the bacon she can't hold back a sob. The lovely salty smell reminds her of so many other, ordinary, days. And she wishes more than anything that this was one of them. That yesterday had never happened.

Dad's door opens and she scrubs her face with her sleeve before she dares to look round.

He's tying his dressing gown and scratching his head just like always. 'Smells good,' he says. His voice is a bit quiet, but he sounds almost like Dad again. She breaks the eggs into the pan, glad of the excuse not to look at him because if she does she'll really start to cry.

When she brings the plates to the table he rubs his hands, like he always does, and dollops on the brown sauce. Joycie turns back to the kitchenette for the bread, hardly daring to breathe, but when she sits opposite him he gives her a little smile before looking quickly away.

It's hard to eat because her throat feels swollen, but she wants him to know she's all right. That everything is just the way it was. So she forces the food down.

Dad has finished before her and wipes his plate with a slice of bread, folding it in half then mopping the last smears of sauce up with the folded edge. Still without looking at her, he says, 'We'll need to be careful with money for a bit, love. Won't be working with Sid any more.' He takes a bite of the folded bread and she breathes a bit easier. He doesn't know she overheard the argument then. She watches him wiping his plate again although it's almost clean. 'But not to worry. I've been thinking about breaking with him for a while now and I've got a few irons in the fire. We'll be all right and we won't have to travel all the time either.'

'That's good, Dad.' She wants to say more but is frightened to spoil things, so she takes the plates to the sink and starts washing up.

After a few minutes Dad comes over and rests his hand on her shoulder. His hand is warm and heavy. 'Thanks, Joycie, you're a good girl.' Then she knows it's going to be all right.

***

116

Marcus came in with some tea and Joycie rubbed her eyes before sitting up to take a mug from him. The tea was hot and strong and when she smiled at him he put his head to one side and she nodded. 'Just right.' He must have been back to his own room because he'd put on some different jeans, and a clean shirt still open at the front. He sat on the bed with a bounce that made her lift her mug to stop the tea from spilling. She wanted to push back that lock of blond hair from his forehead and to kiss him, but instead she squeezed his hand. It was important to talk now.

'I'm so sorry for the way I am, Marcus. I do love you and want to be with you. But I have no right to ask you to wait for me.'

He touched his finger to her lips for a moment, shaking his head. 'I can wait. Just you try and stop me.'

She took a deep breath. 'I've been thinking. About what happened with Dad after Sid attacked me.'

The smell of tweed and wee and rough cloth hurting her face. She put down her tea, hand to her throat where a surge of acid was burning it.

Marcus touched her knee. 'It's all right. Take your time.'

A deep breath pushing away those horrible thoughts. 'I think I've managed to remember it all. Dad came in and stopped him. But he was so cold, and sounded so angry, I thought he was blaming me.' Marcus moved towards her, but she raised her hand. She had to get through this. 'It was all right next day, though. He called me a good girl and said he was leaving Sid.' Marcus kissed her ear, and she wanted to turn to him to kiss him properly, but she had to keep going. 'I already knew they were breaking up because I overheard them arguing.'

'So it must have been Sid who reported him to the police. If your dad was going to leave him he had nothing to lose, the vindictive bastard.' He stood up, beginning to button his shirt. 'Look why don't we go out for breakfast. Down to that greasy spoon by the river? You can talk as I drive.'

She grabbed his hand and pulled him down to sit beside her again. 'I need to tell you this now.' There was a flutter of birds just outside the window. It sounded as if they were fighting.

Marcus looked hard at her. 'What is it?'

'When Sid and Dad were arguing, Sid did threaten him with the police, but not just for being homosexual.' Her heart thumped loud in her ears. She longed for Marcus to say something, to stop her telling him and making it true, but he just put his hand on her shoulder, rubbing gently.

'He was going to accuse Dad of killing my mum.'

Marcus's hand stopped moving. 'What?'

There was a roar like a stormy sea in her ears and her throat was almost closed up. 'And he might have been right. You see, I found a bloodstained mat under their bed the morning after my mum disappeared.'

Marcus twisted onto his knees to look her full in the face. 'You've never said anything about this before,' he said.

'It was gone next day and I told myself I'd imagined it, but when Cora came to see me the other day she said she found it and disposed of it. She swore she didn't tell Sid, but she must have been lying because that's what he threatened to go to the police about.'

Marcus scratched his head. 'Well why didn't he?'

'I've been thinking about that. He turned nasty because Dad was going to leave him. But without the mat there was no real evidence. And even if they'd believed him Cora could have got into trouble for throwing it away. And I know Sid wasn't keen on the police so I think he decided to report Dad for being homosexual instead. That way he could do it anonymously.'

'Let me get this straight.' Marcus pressed his fingers to the crease between his eyebrows. 'You heard Sid say this? About the mat and your mum?' She nodded, swallowing hard, but that burning sensation was still in her throat. 'So what did your dad say?'

'That was the worst thing. He said Sid was lying, but he sounded so upset I didn't know what to think. I was longing for him to give some kind of explanation. But he didn't. And I never dared to ask him about it.'

Chiswick – February 1956

Dad doesn't tell her what his ideas for making money are, but after breakfast he goes to his room. 'Need to write a few letters and sort some things out, Joycie love.' An hour or so later, while she's tidying the living room, he goes out to post the letters and make a call from the phone box on the corner.

Joycie checks the old biscuit tin where they keep the housekeeping money. Dad said they need to be careful, but she decides to make his favourite tea tonight: pork bangers with crispy onions. Walking to the shops she keeps telling herself everything will be all right now. The pavements are icy, but it's sunny and the sky is a clear pale blue.

The butcher is laughing with the woman in front of her and when the bell clangs as she comes in they carry on laughing, looking at her so she has to join in. She doesn't know what the joke was, but it's nice to laugh. When it's her turn the butcher says, 'Cold enough for you, ducks?' as he wraps up the sausages.

She answers, 'Just about,' and he laughs and puts a couple of slices of spam in a bag. 'There you are – make yourself a nice sandwich, eh.'

As she walks back she feels almost cheerful. When they have the sandwiches Dad might tell her about his plans and it will be just like always.

But when she gets to their lodgings she stops halfway up the stairs. The door to their rooms is wide open and she can hear men's voices. At first she wonders if they're something to do with the ideas Dad's got for finding work, but the way they sound scares her.

She forces herself to go up and stand in the open doorway. Two big men in heavy suits fill the tiny living room and Joycie's nose wrinkles at the musty smell coming off them. One of them turns to look at her and it's then she sees Dad.

He's sitting on the threadbare sofa, still in his shirtsleeves, and the expression on his face makes her want to cry. His eyes seem to have sunk deep into his head and all she can see are two dark holes. His mouth is all crumpled, as if he's about to cry.

The men are looking at her and one of them says, 'Who's this then?'

She's not sure if he's talking to her or her dad, but Dad answers his voice so quiet she can hardly hear it. 'That's my daughter.' He looks at Joycie and she can see he wants to say something to her, but the second man speaks before he can.

'What's he say?' he cups his hand to his ear as he turns to the other one. 'Couldn't hear that.'

The first man barks out a hard laugh that scares Joycie so much she's afraid she might wet herself. For a minute she thinks about running back out into the street, but she can't leave Dad. 'He says it's his daughter, if you can believe that, the dirty sod.' He pushes Joycie past them into the room. 'You go and sit over there, darling. We won't be long. And there's no need to be scared. We're the police, see, and we just need to have a little look around.'

Joycie can't help staring at them, wondering if they really are policemen. She's never seen one without a uniform. Her legs have gone all watery and she heads for the sofa to sit next to Dad, but the man says, 'Not there. Sit at the table.' His voice is too loud.

'Right let's get on with this.'

One of them goes into her dad's bedroom while the other walks around the living room, opening drawers and cupboards. She can hear the same kind of noises coming from the bedroom.

She wants to speak to Dad, but his back is to her, very stiff and straight, and all she can see are his hands twisting around each other. After just a few minutes the policeman comes out of the bedroom waving a bundle of open envelopes in the air. He grins at Dad. 'Nice lot of love letters from your nancy-boy, pal. Charming turn of phrase he's got.' He chuckles, but she can tell he isn't joking.

The other man flaps his hand at Dad to make him stand up, and the one with the letters pushes him from behind. 'Right, duckie, you're coming with us.'

Dad stares at Joycie, his eyes wide. She's never seen him scared before and she can't breathe. He sounds like he can hardly breathe either, looking from her to the men and back again. 'My daughter …?'

They turn to Joycie as if they've forgotten she's there and one of them says, 'We'll get the landlady to keep an eye on her for now.' Then he shakes his head and mutters, 'Poor kid.'

The other man looks down at the letters he's holding, and says, 'Disgusting,' and Joycie feels her armpits prickle with sweat. Do they think she's disgusting?

Her dad is still looking at her and she knows he wants to say something, but he doesn't speak. Her hands go to her mouth as she tries to hold back a sob. To stop them hearing, she turns to the hook in the corner for Dad's jacket. But they're already shoving him out and she has to follow them down the stairs.

When he gets to the front door her dad pulls away from the man who's holding his arm and stares back at her. She lifts up the jacket, but he shakes his head and says, 'It's all right, love, I'll be back soon.' But his eyes are like black pits and although he's trying to smile his mouth doesn't seem to work properly and his chin is wobbling up and down.

Then they push him out the door and slam it behind them, while Joycie stands on the stairs, still holding his jacket.

Marcus pulled the Morgan up beside the café and smiled at her. 'You've been miles away. Were you thinking about your dad again?'

She nodded and they headed inside. It was busy at this time in the morning, the air thick with the smell of frying and the windows misted over. 'Ferry Cross the Mersey' was playing in the background, but as they opened the door Joycie heard one of the men call out, 'Can't you shut that rubbish off, Linda?'

Behind the counter, Linda, a bouncy middle-aged redhead, just laughed and carried on pouring tea from her huge metal teapot. Marcus and Joycie came here quite often so she waved them to a table calling out, 'The usual is it?'

Joycie smiled, and Marcus said, with the hint of cockney accent he always used in here, 'That's right, Linda. Two full breakfasts and two teas, please.'

Joycie slipped off her jacket and went to the counter to collect the tea, and as Linda passed over the thick white mugs she gestured with her head towards the man who'd called out. 'Dead old-fashioned some of them are, but I love Gerry and the Pacemakers, don't you?' She didn't seem to expect an answer, just turned away to check the pan with a, 'Breakfasts won't be long, I'll bring them over.'

Joycie smiled as she took the tea back to their table. Nearly all the customers here were local workmen, and apart from the occasional, 'Hello Marcus, hello, darling,' she and Marcus were mostly ignored.

When she sat opposite him she rubbed a patch of window clear of steam. It didn't make much difference because it was grey and cloudy outside, and she could barely make out the dull metal river sliding along beside the empty towpath.

Marcus pushed his mug to one side and leaned towards her. 'Gonna tell me what you were thinking about in the car?'

She looked around, but no one could hear them because Linda

had turned up the radio and was singing along to the Beatles' 'Ticket to Ride', and the babble of talk from the other tables had become louder.

'I just wish I could stop being angry with my dad for killing himself. He promised he'd be back soon, you see. And I believed him.'

Linda was heading over with their food and they both smiled and thanked her. She looked as if she was going to linger for a chat, but a man in the other corner shouted, 'Hey, Lin, you forgot the bread.' So she pulled a face and went back to the counter.

Joycie poked at her fried egg. Linda always did a lovely breakfast, but she had no appetite. Marcus, cutting his sausage very neatly into even segments, said, 'He couldn't help it. Think about his friend and what it was like when he was arrested.'

'I know, and if it was bad for Dennis I'm sure it was even worse for Dad. He was older and he was on remand for longer.' She shook her head. 'Not that long, though. Only a few weeks. Never went to trial or anything.'

'And they told you right away?'

'That he'd died? Yes, but I didn't find out he'd killed himself until the funeral. We had the wake at Irene and Deirdre's flat and I overheard it then.'

The room is stuffy and the collar of her new black dress rubs her neck. Irene has asked her to bring the sandwiches from the kitchen and when she comes back in she stands by the door for a minute because people are moving about, holding sherry glasses or pouring beer from bottles, and she's scared she'll knock into someone.

She looks at the sandwiches – Deirdre has stuck little paper flags to show what's in them: ham and tomato, egg, sardine – her tummy rumbles, but she also feels a bit sick and the smell of booze in the air is horrible.

Then she hears a woman's voice. 'Poor old Charlie. Terrible way to go.' And she stops breathing and presses back against the door, trying to make herself invisible.

A man answers. 'Coward's way out if you ask me.'

The woman again. 'Oh, Ron, that's an awful thing to say. He must have been desperate.' She lowers her voice, but Joycie can still hear. 'Irene says he hung himself with his bed sheets, poor soul.'

'Still, it was suicide and in my day they wouldn't even bury you in the churchyard if you did that.'

Joycie forced herself to look at Marcus. 'I made Irene admit it afterwards. I was furious with her for keeping it from me, which was so unfair. But then I was pretty awful to her and Deirdre in those first weeks.'

Marcus had been working steadily through his food and he rubbed his mouth with the back of his hand and took a glug of tea, saying, 'I suppose it's possible he didn't really kill himself.'

She swallowed the sliver of sausage she seemed to have been chewing for ages. 'But he did it with a bed sheet. How could that be an accident?'

'Well we're pretty sure he was beaten by the cops, aren't we? So what if he died of that? They'd easily be able to fake a suicide I should think.' It was a terrible thought and yet, and yet … It would mean he hadn't wanted to desert her. Marcus reached for her hand. 'And prisons are violent places, so it could have been one of the inmates, or even a group of them.'

He must have seen the surge of horror she felt as the scene flashed through her mind because he brought her fingers to his lips, saying, 'Sorry, Joycie, I'm sorry.'

She glanced out of the window, which was already steaming up again. A scruffy little dog was trotting past all on its own and it stopped to chew at something on the towpath before looking up at her and scuttling away.

Chapter Thirteen

Tommy Green turned up with the dog, Fatima, next day. She was beautiful, her eyes peeping through long pale hair. Joycie took her straight into the kitchen where she'd put out a bowl of food and some water.

Tommy was talking quietly to Marcus, but she heard him say, 'So I've been spreading the news about you minding your own business in future. And be sure you do that, mate. Keep an eye on your girl too because if you let me down it won't just be the pair of you in the frame.'

As Joycie came back into the living room she said, 'So who is this Bill? And who does he work for?'

Tommy looked at Marcus. 'I told you to keep all this to yourself. No point in frightening the young lady.'

'I'm sorry, Tommy,' she said, 'but it's me Bill's been following and I want to know why.'

Marcus smiled and shook his head at Tommy. 'Better tell her, mate. She won't give up.'

With a sigh Tommy sat on the sofa, nodding as Marcus went over to the drinks cabinet and held up a bottle of Scotch. 'You'll have heard of Ernie Georgiou?' he said. When Joycie shook her head he gave an even heavier sigh and gulped at his Scotch.

125

'Gang leader, darling. His firm has rackets going all over the place. Bill was one of his faces for years.' He smiled when she shook her head again. 'One of the big names in his mob, I mean.'

'And does this Ernie Georgiou have connections with Sid Sergeant?'

'I wouldn't know.'

Joycie leaned forward. 'Please, Tommy.'

He looked pleadingly at Marcus, who was crouched down stroking the dog, but Marcus just raised his hands in a *there's nothing I can do* gesture.

Tommy took another swallow of Scotch and turned back to Joycie. 'The thing is, love, Sid and his lady wife go way back with Ernie. During the war Sid was resident comic at one of Ernie's nightclubs. And Ernie never forgets a friend. So if Sid came asking him to put the frights on someone Ernie would get one of his faces onto it – no questions asked. And if he's picked Bill then you're honoured. He's the best of the lot.'

'The kind of honour we could do without, eh Tommy?' said Marcus as Tommy drained his glass and stood to go.

'That's right. And the funny thing is, it's common knowledge Bill decided to go legit a few years ago. Settled down and opened a couple of betting shops. So it really put the wind up me when you mentioned his name. Because it looks like he's come out of retirement especially for you.'

Tommy turned back as he opened the front door. 'Listen to your fella, my lovely, and leave it alone whatever it is.'

Chelsea – June 1965

Marcus bought the dog a name tag with Fatima on one side and their address on the other, but he was soon calling her Fatty, which was ridiculous because she was so slender, but she seemed happy to answer to it.

Joycie had written to her aunt Susan shortly after the bundle of letters arrived, but now she wrote again saying she was sorry she couldn't leave London for a while so wouldn't be able to visit any time soon. They'd probably put her down as a stuck-up cow, but she didn't dare go again until she was sure it was safe.

She also wrote to Mrs Shaw saying: *I've spoken to Helen Banks and I'm afraid she really doesn't know anything. She hasn't seen Pauline since before she left Clacton.* It was true as far as it went. And it certainly wouldn't help Mrs Shaw to hear Helen's suspicions. With the letter she included a note for Mrs Shaw to pass on to Dennis telling him she hoped her visit hadn't upset him. She added: *if it helps I'm pretty sure it was Sid, not Kay, who reported Dad to the police. I'd made myself forget a lot that happened around that time, but I remember now that they had a big row and Dad said he was going to leave the act. So Sid had every reason to be angry with him.*

After that, and although she had said she couldn't stop trying to get to the truth, she found she was able to do just that for the next couple of weeks. There were more and more times when she realized she had walked for several minutes without listening for the click of footsteps or glancing behind her. And although Fatty seemed to be frightened of cars, cats, bikes, children, and pretty much everything else that moved it was still comforting to know she was there.

Joycie was booked to work with another photographer, John Burns, on a *Vanity Fair* spread and Marcus was out and about taking pictures of London for an American magazine. So they didn't see each other during the day. But they always took Fatty for a walk when they got home. She was supposed to be trained, but when they let her off the lead she would charge madly away so that they spent most of the time chasing her. When they finally caught her they were sure she was laughing at them, tongue hanging out as she looked from one to the other to make sure they were sharing the joke.

Something had changed between Joycie and Marcus since she'd been able to tell him everything about Sid and about her dad. Although she didn't dare ask him to sleep in her room again she often found herself gazing at him in a new way, and his smile when he caught her doing so told her he had noticed. He'd always been affectionate, but now when he touched her his hand would linger a little, his blue eyes on her face, making sure she was all right.

***

John Burns decided to do the *Vanity Fair* shoot in Victoria Park and around the whole Bethnal Green area. Although the weather wasn't all that good it stayed dry and Joycie loved being in the open air. John was attractive and fun to work with but as she posed for him she found herself looking at his hands and thinking of Marcus. And when John smiled she saw, not his brown eyes, but Marcus's blue ones. She was sure she was too distracted to give her best, but John seemed happy enough.

Amazingly Cecil Beaton had also asked for her again. It must mean their first session hadn't been the disaster she'd imagined. He worked her hard and at the end he brushed back his white hair with an elegant hand and said, 'I think we deserve a drink, my darling.' She perched on a delicate antique armchair while he was out of the room. There were so many lovely and expensive-looking objects on every surface she was afraid to move in case she broke something.

He came back with champagne. They clinked glasses and he lolled on the blue velvet chaise longue he had used for many of the pictures. 'You were positively sparkling today, my dear, so this seems more appropriate than gin.'

It was hardly raining, but even so Beaton insisted on paying for a taxi to take her home. Although the session had turned out well she was tired and she couldn't face the thought of going out tonight. There was nothing to eat in the house so she asked the taxi driver to stop at a delicatessen and bought some bread and gorgonzola, a melon and Parma ham. The off-licence next door didn't have much choice in wine so she settled on a bottle of Mateus Rose.

When she got in she found a note from Marcus:

Fatty was going mad for her walk so I thought I'd better take her. Back soon XXX

Maybe it was because she was so tired, but it upset her to think this was the first time they hadn't done the walk together. But she knew she was just being silly and got on with putting the food on plates. Then she made herself a cup of tea and sat in front of the telly, waiting for him to come back.

The next moment Fatty was licking her face as she struggled to wake up fully. She pushed the dog down, shaking her head to try to clear the remnants of a dream, which she knew hadn't been a good one. She must have been trying to call out in her sleep because her throat felt raw, but she forced a smile for Marcus. 'Beaton gave me champagne and it really knocked me out.'

The rain had gone so they lugged the little kitchen table into the garden, rubbed the chairs dry and laid out the food. She'd forgotten to put the wine in the fridge and it wasn't cold. Marcus said it was fine, but after the champagne and tea it tasted horrible to Joycie. The sky was a soft grey tinged with red at the horizon and it was cool after the rain. Perhaps the picnic had been a bad idea.

Marcus reached for her hand. 'You're shivering.' He pulled off his big sweater and she put it on, grabbing a handful of wool and holding it to her face so she could smell his lovely musky scent. 'You were having a bad dream when I got back, weren't you?' he said.

'I think so.' A dark haze filled her mind as she recalled some-thing of the nightmare. *Her dad being held down by huge figures, his face all bloodied as he looked at her for help and she tried to scream, but could make no noise.*

When she shivered again Marcus reached over to pull her to her feet. 'You go in and get warm. I'll clear up here.'

'No, come in with me, please. You've got an early start in the morning. I can do it then.'

Sitting on the sofa, Joycie leaned against him as he played with her hair.

'I wasn't going to tell you till tomorrow,' he said, 'but when I got in this afternoon there was a phone call for you.' A thump from her heart. 'It was your dad's friend, Dennis. He said he's onstage tonight so he'll ring same time tomorrow.'

She drained her glass. 'I know I said I couldn't let it go, but now I'm not sure I want to get back into all that.'

'You don't have to answer the phone.' He smiled and shook his head. 'But you will, won't you?'

'I think I have to. It might even help with the nightmares.'

He didn't say anything, but she could guess what he was thinking. *Or it could make them worse.*

The remnants of their picnic were still in the garden next morning, soggy from overnight rain. She dumped them in the bin, dragged in the table, then took Fatty for a walk. The streets were Friday morning quiet and that sense of being watched had come back so she kept the dog on the lead. It was probably a mistake because Fatty was so skittish, jumping at every sound or movement, that by the time they got home Joycie was doing the same. As she opened the front door the phone on the hall table began ringing. She grabbed it with a breathless, 'Hello,' as she tried to untangle herself from Fatty's lead and unclip it from her collar.

Not Dennis – a young female voice. 'Is that Orchid, I mean Joyce?'

'Yes.'

'Hi, this is Helen,' a pause, 'Helen Banks from Plumes,' a little laugh, 'and Clacton.'

Helen had been right to guess that Joycie needed a nudge to place her. She had been running through the list of models, stylists, and journalists she vaguely knew, trying to recall a Helen. 'Oh, hello.' A catch of breath: Helen must have remembered something more about Pauline. 'How are you?'

'I'm fab, thanks. Just wanted to say how lovely it was to see you again and to remind you we said we'd get together one evening this week.'

'Did we?' She couldn't recall that, but her mind had been on Pauline. She must have agreed to it to keep Helen talking.

'Yeah, and I thought tomorrow might be good, if you're free, because my sister's staying with me and I want to take her out on the town. She's got two little kids, a really boring hubby, and hardly ever gets away from Clacton. She'd love to go to one of the clubs I've told her about. So I was thinking the Ad Lib?'

Although there was nothing Joycie fancied less, she remembered the sister was the one who might know something more about Pauline. 'That'd be nice. Shall we meet you there?'

A pause and some clinking that Joycie guessed were Helen's earrings tapping on the side of the phone. 'Well, it might be better to go in together. I mean, I haven't been there for ages and ...' Sounded as if she knew she was unlikely to get in. 'Why don't we come to your place first?'

'No.' It sounded sharp, but it was possible Bill was still watching, and she couldn't get Helen and her sister involved. 'I mean, we won't be here, so we'll pick you up.'

'Fine, you know my address.'

It was clear she was put out, but Joycie couldn't worry about that. She wanted to clear the line in case Dennis rang.

She fed Fatty and let her into the garden then cleaned the kitchen. The house was always a mess because neither of them had time to do it and they hated the thought of having anyone in, but when she was free Joycie actually enjoyed cleaning. She didn't dare use the Hoover in case she missed Dennis's call, but she scrubbed the kitchen floor then had a go at the bathroom.

The phone rang about four o'clock, and she grabbed it feeling a quiver of sickness in her stomach. 'Hello?'

'Hello, Joyce darling, it's Dennis.'

Her legs were suddenly weak and she had to hold onto the banister and sit on the stairs.

'I had to ring to thank you for your little note, my sweet,' Dennis was saying. 'Can't tell you how much it meant. I really did think it was Kay who betrayed your dad and me.'

She leaned back and took a slow breath. So that was all. Fatty had come in from the garden and she trotted over, resting her warm chin on Joycie's lap and gazing up with big brown eyes. Joycie rubbed the soft hair on the top of her head until she sighed and her eyes closed.

'I'm so glad it helped, Dennis. Kay loves you to bits and I can't imagine her ever doing anything to hurt you.'

'I know and I've been an absolute bastard to her. The drinking's bad enough, but accusing her of that was the worst.'

'Don't be too hard on yourself. You didn't know Dad had told Sid he was leaving the act.'

'But Kay told me and I wouldn't believe her.'

'What do you mean?'

'Charlie rang that last day. Must have been just before the police turned up. Wanted to tell me what happened with Sid and that we needed to make our move as soon as we could. Get our stake in the club we were interested in right away. I wasn't there so he left the message with Kay.'

That phone call her dad said he was going to make just before she went out to the butcher's. It must have been to Dennis.

He was still talking. 'Like I told you Kay wasn't too pleased about the whole idea, so she didn't get round to telling me. Thought she was just delaying the inevitable, but a couple of days later the police came for me.'

'Oh, Dennis. And when she finally told you about the call you didn't believe her?'

Poor Kay and poor Dennis.

'That's right. But now you've set me straight.' His voice wobbled and she knew hers would if she tried to speak. 'But, darling,' he said, 'I've been thinking about Charlie and you know I've never been able to believe he would have killed himself however bad it got. He would never have left you and I flatter myself he wouldn't have wanted to leave me either.'

Unless he'd done something terrible and he thought we were about to find out. 'I don't want to believe it either, Dennis, but Sid said some awful things to him that last day. Did Kay say how he sounded when he called?'

'No, just that he said he knew it was a bit sooner than we'd planned, but we'd make it work.'

'He didn't seem worried about anything? Or scared?'

'If he was Kay didn't notice.'

When he rang off Joycie sat for a long while, stroking the silky hair on Fatty's head and thinking of the argument she'd overheard. When Sid threatened to tell the police about the mat she'd imagined her dad staring at him, too shocked to speak, not knowing what to say. But perhaps he knew nothing about the bloodstained mat. Perhaps he had simply turned away, wondering how desperate Sid must be to make up such a story. How Joycie longed for this to be true.

Chapter Fourteen

It was only when she reached out to rub Fatty's ears that Joycie realized the dog had moved away from her to lie on the hall carpet. She had been crouched on the stairs for so long she was cold and her legs felt stiff as she got up and headed to the kitchen. While she waited for the kettle to boil she looked out of the window. The day was so cloudy that although there should be hours to go before dark it felt like evening already.

She needed to look at her mum's letters again. She had put them in the box on top of her wardrobe where she stored a few keepsakes, but when she got upstairs the bed looked so inviting she couldn't resist lying propped up on the pillows to drink her tea.

Was it possible her dad had never seen the bloodstained mat and thought Sid was making it up to scare him? If he had nothing to do with her mum's disappearance then the answer was yes. Although Joycie had found the mat rolled up under the bed there was no reason for him to look there. She had only done it because she knew where her mum kept the new shoes. Hadn't noticed the mat was missing before that. It wasn't very big and there were several others scattered around the living room. Mum often shifted them about when she cleaned the place. When they left the lodgings in Hastings a few weeks afterwards she asked her dad if she could have the shoes and her mum's favourite blouse, and he seemed surprised when she slid the box out and showed them to him.

'Looks like they've never been worn,' she remembered him saying. 'So mind you take care of them and the blouse too. She'll …' He had stopped then and turned away, but Joycie was sure he was going to say that Mum would want them kept nice for when she came back.

The bedroom door was ajar and Fatty nosed it open and came in, lying on the sheepskin rug beside the bed and closing her eyes with a gusty sigh. Joycie closed her eyes too. She wanted to reread the letters before Marcus got home, but she was so tired she didn't know if she could make any sense of them.

She was jolted awake by a bang. A door slamming? Marcus must be back already. She swung her legs to the floor and Fatty shook herself and headed for the door. 'Marcus, is that you?' A low growl from Fatty, who stood on the landing looking down the stairs. Joycie held onto her collar. The front door was closed. Maybe he'd gone straight to the darkroom.

She walked quietly down, still holding onto Fatty. The living room was cold and for a moment she thought she smelled cigarette smoke. 'Marcus?' A cool breeze was coming from the kitchen. The back door was wide open. She'd forgotten to lock it when she let Fatty in from the garden. Hadn't even closed it properly if a gust of wind had managed to blow it open.

She locked up then realized that the frosted glass in the back door meant someone could break it then reach through and get the key. So she took it out of the lock and put it into the cutlery drawer.

The darkroom was empty. It was too early for Marcus to be back anyway. She double-checked the front door and headed back upstairs. As she did so she thought she smelled smoke again. Nothing to worry about, Joycie told herself; it must have wafted in from someone's back garden.

Fatty followed her and watched as Joycie took the keepsake box down and sat with it in front of her on the dressing table.

The black shoes and the blouse were in the box along with the letters and the few keepsakes Joycie had from the past. There was a tatty photo album and some programmes and newspaper cuttings her mum had collected about the shows her dad and Sid had been in.

The blouse was neatly folded in tissue, and Joycie pulled the paper aside and rubbed her fingers over the silky fabric. In the early days she often held it to her face breathing in the familiar scent. All too soon the smell was gone, the blouse crumpled and sad-looking. So she had washed and ironed it and packed it neatly away.

She'd read the newspaper cuttings before so she leafed quickly through them. There was one whole newspaper folded small and when she opened it she saw it was the *Hastings Observer* from a week or so before her mum disappeared. Presumably she hadn't got round to cutting out the review of the show.

The photo album tempted her. Perhaps a look through would give her some clues, but she had stared at the pictures so often over the years she knew she would just be giving in to sentimentality. The letters were the important thing.

The first time she had read them Joycie had been trying to find some hints about the boyfriend her mum might have run away with, but now she was searching for anything to do with Sid. That phrase from the final note: *something has happened,* had been playing over and over in her head and she had started to wonder if her mum had suspicions about Sid's behaviour towards young girls. Maybe she'd heard talk about it or even seen something.

It was just as likely, of course, that what had happened was closer to home. Something to do with her parents' relationship.

She took out the pack of yellowing envelopes and clicked on the lamp beside her. In the early letters from during the war, when her mum was pregnant and living with Irene, there were a couple of references to Sid: *Sid Sergeant came to see me. Charlie has asked him to look in now and then. He insisted on giving me some money. Said he owed it to Charlie. I'm not sure if I believe that, but it's very kind of him and we can certainly use it.*

A while later she was writing: *We had a visit from Sid, who brought some meat and tinned food. Irene said it was black market stuff, but she took it and we've had a couple of lovely meals, which is just as well because I'm hungry all the time! It's strange, but although Sid is so kind and Charlie is really fond of him, Irene doesn't seem to like him. Says he's in with a bad crowd and that's where he gets the black market food.*

The *bad crowd* Irene was talking about was probably Ernie Georgious's gang, if what Tommy Green said was right. There was nothing after that except the mention of Charlie rejoining the act when he was demobbed. Something else in one of the letters from 1946 caught her eye however: *It's wonderful to have Charlie back home and now Joycie has got used to him she's becoming a real daddy's girl. The war has changed him, but I'm sure we'll get back to the way we were soon.*

Joycie remembered what Cora had said about her dad realizing he was attracted to men when he was in the army. That would surely have changed the way he was with his wife. There were no more references to Sid until 1949: *Charlie and Sid are playing the Chiswick Empire again this year and we've found new lodgings in Acton. We used to stay at the same place as Sid and Cora, but I wanted to be on our own. To be honest with you, I've never liked Cora and I'm not keen on Sid either.*

It was clear her mum's feeling towards the comic had changed over the years, which might explain why she hadn't mentioned him for so long even though she must have come into contact with him and Cora all the time.

Then, in early '52, just over a year before she disappeared, she wrote: *Charlie's not happy because he hasn't had a raise for ages and Sid always pleads poverty when he asks for one. Yet he and Cora* seem to do very well for themselves. Charlie has started to think seriously about leaving the act. I'll be honest – that would suit me. Of course Charlie is so loyal to Sid he won't hear a word against him.

So her dad had considered breaking with Sid even before he met Dennis. Joycie knew how difficult that must have been for him. He had told her many times how Sid virtually adopted him as a teenager. He had never known his parents and had grown up in a Dr Barnardo's home in the East End of London. Sid had given him a job and they had shared lodgings until Charlie went into the army and Sid married Cora.

In the final year, 1953, there were only two letters: both very short. One she sent in January to wish her family a happy new year. She said they'd had a quiet Christmas and that Joycie was becoming really tall. *We'll be in a new place for the summer season this year. Hastings, which will make a nice change.*

The final letter was sent just a day or two before she disappeared. *I'm coming back home. Please tell Dad I only need to stay for a day or so until I find somewhere permanent. Charlie won't be with me, just Joycie …* then there was that scribbled out phrase. Joycie held the paper under the lamp. She thought she could make out a couple of words: *persuade … later.* Had her mum started to say she'd been trying to persuade Charlie to come with them or to follow on when he'd finished the summer season? Or was that just Joycie's wishful thinking?

And what about that mysterious sentence: *Please, Mam, something has happened and I have to get away from here and to get Joycie away too.*

'Something has happened, something has happened, something has happened.' She said the phrase aloud over and over, but was no closer to knowing what it meant.

And niggling at the edge of her consciousness was the sense of having missed a significant clue.

***

When Marcus called up to her, Fatty leapt from the sheepskin rug and raced down, dancing around him, her tail wagging furiously. From the top of the stairs Joycie said, 'She definitely loves you best.'

She must have looked as tired as she felt because when she ran down to kiss him he moved back and looked at her. 'I'll take her for her walk tonight. You look done in.'

While he was gone she rooted in the kitchen cupboards for something they could eat, coming out with a couple of packets of Vesta chicken curry. They would only take a few minutes to heat up so while she waited for Marcus she brought down the keepsake box. Still feeling that she'd missed something crucial.

She reread the cuttings, but could find nothing significant. Fresh eyes might help so perhaps she'd ask Marcus to look at them. The *Hastings Observer* from the week before her mum's disappearance was dusty and yellowing and the entertainments page featured a review of the Disney cartoon *Peter Pan* and of a local amateur dramatic production of *An Inspector Calls.* No mention of the variety show at all.

She looked through the photo album. She had always been disappointed that her parents had no pictures of their wedding, and she remembered her mum saying they couldn't afford a photographer. 'In any case, I didn't have a white dress or anything like that because, even if we'd had the money, it was wartime and that kind of thing was all rationed. People managed as best they could.'

She wondered now if they'd ever actually been married because her aunt had said their father refused his permission.

The only picture of her parents together was a tiny snap. They were walking along a seaside promenade somewhere. The smudge of white in her mum's arms must have been Joycie as a tiny child, but the dazzle of sunshine made their faces so hazy it was impossible to tell if they were smiling.

After that the photos were mostly of Joycie with her mum,

and she remembered her dad taking some of them. There was one professional picture of him, very handsome in his dinner jacket and bow tie. The back was stamped with the name and studio of the photographer and dated January 1952. Perhaps he'd had it done to try for other jobs. That would certainly match with her mum's letter saying he was thinking of leaving the act.

Although she remembered the incident with Mr Grant and knew her mum had occasionally had male visitors when Joycie was in bed and her dad at the theatre she had thought her parents were happy with each other. They were always laughing and joking and …

She wakes to hear a Frank Sinatra song playing softly in the other room. It's called 'Blue Skies' *and when she peeps through her door she sees her mum and dad dancing slowly together, her mum's head on his shoulder, eyes closed …*

Joycie closed her own eyes at the memory. She must have been about eight or nine at the time.

Marcus and Fatty crashed through the door and she closed the album, almost angry with them for coming back so soon. But Marcus was laughing and it looked as if Fatty was too. Tongue lolling from her mouth as she panted and bounced, her lead tangling around Marcus's legs. It was impossible not to laugh with them.

Marcus pulled two bottles of light ale and a couple of packets of crisps from the pockets of his mac. 'I'm thirsty and I didn't know if we had any food in so I popped into the pub and got these.'

Chelsea – July 1965

The weather had been cool and cloudy all month, but today the sun was shining when Joycie got home. It was only just after lunchtime. She'd been booked for an all-day shoot, but some of

140

the clothes hadn't arrived at the magazine so they'd done as much as they could and rescheduled the rest.

Joycie was glad because she wasn't sleeping well and the photographer had kept moving her about and shaking his head. When he sent her to put more concealer under her eyes and a bit of colour on her cheeks she guessed she must look as tired as she felt. She wanted nothing more than to crawl into bed, but Fatty met her at the door clearly longing for a walk, so she clipped on the lead and headed out again.

A taxi drove slowly past her, obviously searching for somewhere, and she wasn't surprised to see it stop just before the Italian restaurant on the corner, but when the cab door opened a chill went through her. The woman getting out was Cora, and she was looking back at Joycie with a beaming smile. Joycie pulled on Fatty's lead, but it was too late to stop her colliding with Cora's legs. Cora gave a smoke-infused laugh and crouched down.

'Oooh what a lovely boy. What a beautiful lad, you are, yes you are.'

The chill sensation turned to a burst of irritation and Joycie dragged Fatty away. 'She's a bitch, Cora.'

As she tried to stand Cora staggered and Joycie had to put out a hand to help her.

'Oops, shouldn't have had that last glass,' she said. 'Just been at a lovely long lunch with a big TV producer. Don't spread it about, but they're doing a show with that Irish singer, whatshisname, and they want a regular comedy spot to liven it up. Very interested in Sid.'

Joycie began to walk away. 'I'm sorry, I can't stop. Fatima has to have her walk.'

'That's all right, darling, I could do with a stroll to clear my head, and I was on my way to see you when I spotted you leaving the house.'

Joycie wanted to hurry on, but she felt obliged to slow her pace to allow Cora to teeter along next to her. The taxi stayed creeping behind them, and when she glanced back she felt the driver's eyes on her. His face was just a fuzzy profile, but she wanted very much for him to go away. 'There's no need to waste your money keeping the taxi with you, Cora,' she said. 'It's easy to hail one on the King's Road.'

Cora took Joycie's arm, a waft of her perfume cloying the space between them. 'It's OK, love, he's a friend. Doesn't charge me.'

Chilly fingers crawled up and down Joycie's spine, but she forced herself not to look round again.

When they got to the park next to St Luke's Church she stopped to fiddle with the clasp on Fatty's lead, saying, 'What was it you wanted?'

Fatty began to whine and strain towards the park gate. Cora turned back to the cab making a circling movement with her index finger. The taxi pulled slowly away, and she headed through the gate.

Released from her lead, Fatty shot inside. Joycie followed, and when Cora sat on a bench near the gate she seemed to have no choice but to sit there too, trying to keep as far away as she could.

'This is nice,' Cora said, slipping off her red stilettos, raising her legs, and wiggling her toes in their black stockings. 'Ooh, that's better.' Her teeth were rather too even and too white and Joycie guessed they must be false, but expensive. 'I do hope you've brightened up a bit now, darling. You seemed very low the last time I saw you. Irene's death must have hit you hard. Brought back too many memories I expect. But it doesn't do any good to mope over things that can't be changed, does it?' A sidelong glance. 'And you've got so much to be grateful for.'

A surge of anger. If Cora wanted to talk to her she'd have to listen to what Joycie had to say too. She walked over to where Fatty stood panting and staring longingly at a stick on the ground, and without looking at Cora she said, 'I've been hoping to see you as a matter of fact. I wanted to ask why you felt the need to lie about the day my mum disappeared.' She threw the stick, moving to stand in front of Cora as Fatty dashed away.

Cora was scrabbling in her handbag; the shiny teeth hidden behind pursed lips; the lines standing out sharply in the sunlight. Joycie saw that beneath the powder she had the shadow of a moustache. But she also saw something else. Cora was rattled.

'What do you mean?' A wavering laugh.

'You said you found a bloodstained mat and disposed of it.'

'And so I did, the morning after.' It was too quick, and her hands were unsteady as she rooted in her bag, pulling out cigarettes and a lighter.

'But you also said you didn't tell Sid what you found and I happen to know you did.'

Cora lit up and breathed out a gust of smoke, which carried a small chuckle with it. 'Did I? It's such a long time ago and my memory's not as good as it was, but you could well be right because Sid and I don't have secrets from each other.' She leaned back taking another drag from the cigarette. If she had been worried she wasn't any longer.

Joycie wanted to tell her exactly what her husband was like. What he'd tried to do to Joycie herself, what she was sure he'd done to other young girls. But for some reason she couldn't do it.

Fatty came back without the stick and stood looking from one to the other. Cora chuckled and patted the bench to bring Fatty to her side. She ruffled the soft hair on the dog's back as she spoke. 'I'm glad you told me what's been worrying you because I had the feeling you weren't satisfied when we had our last chat. That's why I wanted to see you today. Hated to think of you fretting over a silly misunderstanding.'

Joycie found another stick, waving it in front of Fatty until she began to yelp impatiently. That sense of watching eyes was creeping over her again, but when she'd thrown the stick and turned back there was no sign of the taxi, and Cora was staring at the curls of smoke rising from her cigarette. Joycie stood over her: anger spiking again.

'There's something else I need to ask you.'

But Cora slipped her feet into her shoes, and when Fatty bounded back empty mouthed she said, 'Another time, eh? We're keeping this lovely girl from her walk.' She stood and patted Fatty's head, and the traitorous animal batted her eyelashes and wagged her tail until Joycie raised her hand and pretended to throw something and she charged away again.

'I've been followed and threatened by a man from one of the big London gangs and I know you and Sid have friends among them. Did he send someone after me because I was asking questions?'

Cora threw her cigarette on the ground and pressed it under the toe of her shoe. 'Don't be silly, darling. Sid is just a comic and I'm a businesswoman. Anyone working in the clubs has to deal with the gangs, but that doesn't mean we get chummy with them.'

Fatty seemed to have disappeared and Joycie scanned the park for her. Cora pushed her handbag into the crook of her arm, the heavy charm bracelet rattling. 'But you're a sensible girl and you've got so much going for you. So as I said, it's best to leave the past alone and be grateful for what you have.' She glanced towards the road and back at Joycie. 'Now I'd better go and let you look for your dog. Don't want to lose her, do you?'

The taxi had drawn up by the gate again. That urge to shout the truth about Sid surged back. But what was the point? Cora was just a pathetic old woman who probably knew what he'd been up to all these years, but couldn't face it. So why, as she watched her wobble away through the gate and clamber into the taxi, did she feel another shudder of fear?

She shook herself to shrug it off and walked through to the other part of the park calling for Fatty. A couple of girls were sitting on the swings hardly moving as they sucked on ice lollies. One of them took the lolly from her bright red mouth to say, 'Nah, Mrs,' when Joycie asked if they'd seen a dog on its own.

The man walking a collie hadn't seen anything either. By the time she had searched every inch of the park her voice had begun to crack. 'Where are you, you stupid animal?' she whispered.

The road circling the park was busy, but Fatty would surely have been too scared to venture out there on her own and there had been no sounds of screeching brakes. Still, she walked up and down, crossed over and walked the other way, looking along side streets and into the entrances to basement flats. After that she searched the park again, but it was no good. She headed home, biting her lip to hold back the tears.

Chapter Fifteen

Joycie had hoped Fatty might be waiting outside the house, but there was no sign of her. Although it was impossible for her to have got inside Joycie couldn't stop herself running from room to room clutching the useless lead to her chest and calling; making her voice gentle in case Fatty thought she was angry. In the bedroom she pushed up the window and scanned the gardens and the back lane, calling loudly now.

Still nothing.

For a while she leaned on the window ledge staring out, but then her legs seemed to give way and she sat at the dressing table and let the tears come. She was crying for Fatty, but also because she was scared again in a way she hadn't been for weeks. The meeting with Cora had unnerved her and that sense of something important in the back of her mind that she couldn't quite grasp was disturbing.

When the front door opened she wiped her face with the back of her hand and waited, hardly daring to breath. *Please, Marcus, tell me you've found her.* But when he called up it was just to ask if she was in.

She ran down, her voice cracking again. 'It's Fatty. I've lost her.' She was tempted to add that she thought the dog had been taken, but for some reason she felt as if saying it out loud would make it more likely.

After he'd asked if she'd looked everywhere in the park and in the roads around; if she'd checked the back garden and the lane behind it, Marcus said, 'You wait here in case she turns up and I'll have another look all over.'

She stood outside on the top step scanning the street when he'd gone, calling out Fatty's name every few minutes and hearing Marcus doing the same from different places.

It was getting close to midsummer and wouldn't be properly dark for ages, but the cloudy evening had the kind of dreary look about it that always made Joycie feel sad. No sun, but no stars either just a dull light making even the elegant Georgian street seem grim.

Marcus came back alone; his lips pressed tightly together as if he too was afraid he might cry. He shook his head as soon as he saw her. 'I'll pop down to the police station. Her collar has our phone number on it, but if anyone's found her they might have called the cops instead or even taken her there.'

As she watched him walk away Joycie grabbed a jacket from just inside the door and sat on the house steps with the jacket clutched around her, rubbing her bare legs to get rid of the goosebumps. Was she being paranoid in imagining that Fatty's disappearance had something to do with the meeting with Cora? Or that it might be another warning from Bill and his gang?

She stared down the street in the direction Marcus had gone imagining that he'd turn the corner by the Italian restaurant any minute with Fatty by his side.

He appeared, walking slowly, head down: alone. The lump that had been stuck in Joycie's chest rose into her throat. She wanted to shout at him to go back, to look again and keep looking until he found Fatty. But when he reached her and she saw how beaten he looked she stood and they held each other for a long while.

'Let's go in,' Marcus said finally. 'I need a drink.'

Joycie headed straight for the kitchen. 'I'll make us some sandwiches. We've got to meet Helen and her sister tonight.'

'Oh God, do we have to?'

She couldn't see him, but it sounded as if he was stretching out on the sofa.

'I can't let them down and anyway they might have remembered something about Pauline.' The bread was a bit stale so she put it under the grill and sliced some cheese to go on top. 'I'd love to have something hopeful to tell Mrs Shaw.'

'I don't know how you managed to lose Fatty in that little park,' Marcus said, his voice tight.

The cheese was sizzling as she put the toast on plates. She didn't speak, just carried in the food and waited until he swung his feet down and she could sit next to him.

He twisted to look at her. 'What is it?'

And she told him about Cora, the taxi, and her feeling that Fatty's disappearance might even have been managed by Bill's gang. She was expecting him to laugh it off and half hoping he would.

Instead he looked hard at her. 'We should cancel tonight with those girls. Being seen with you might put them in danger.'

'I can't do that.'

'Joycie, you're being followed. We can't get any protection, and now you're telling me you think our dog might have been stolen to warn you off.'

'We won't pick them up then. If we arrive separately no one's likely to connect us.'

Marcus dumped his plate onto the coffee table. 'How the hell can you be sure of that?'

All she could say was, 'I have to see them. It might be my only chance to find out about Pauline. I owe that to Mrs Shaw.'

Marcus jumped up, his toast untouched, and headed for the stairs, stopping at the bottom to turn and shake his head at her.

'They won't get into the Ad Lib without you if they're not members.' Then he pounded up to his room, his face set hard.

Joycie could hear him moving about, but she forced herself not to follow him and to eat some of her toast. She looked at the phone. She'd need to call Helen soon if she wanted to cancel. Instead she walked slowly upstairs and, without thinking, began to get changed.

Marcus came to stand at her bedroom door. He had changed too. 'If you're determined to go I'd better come with you.' His face was still grim.

Joycie had a thought. 'What about that mate of yours, Richie? He's a member. You could ask him to pick them up.'

'I thought you couldn't stand him.'

'I can't. Helen might fancy him though.'

He shook his head at her, but as he turned away he said, 'Better ring Richie now then.'

Richie was actually the Honourable Richard Prescott, and he was tall, blond, and handsome. He was well known in all the London clubs so he would have no trouble getting Helen and Sally through the doors of the Ad Lib. When Marcus told him one of the girls worked in a boutique Joycie could imagine him licking his lips at the thought of impressing a little dolly bird. Marcus had made the mistake once of telling Joycie that Richie had referred to her as *your dolly bird*, but it only confirmed what she thought of him anyway.

When they got out of the tiny lift that took them up to the club Richie waved at them from a table near the big window. There was a wonderful view over the city lights of central London from here: the best thing about the place, in Joycie's opinion. Richie's mouth was moving as they pushed their way through the dancers, but the music was so loud it was impossible to hear what he was saying. The lights glittering from outside and in were reflected by big mirrors hung around the walls, but as they got close to the table Joycie thought Helen's huge eyes outshone them all. Richie's arm was round her shoulder, his other hand on her dimpled knee.

Sitting opposite them, smiling, but with folded arms, was a young woman who must be Helen's sister, Sally. Joycie sat next to her, and Marcus pulled up a stool to sit at the end of the table. Helen, laughing, flapped a hand at her sister and shouted something that might have been, 'Sally.'

Joycie turned to smile at Sally, and Marcus mouthed, *hello*, to both girls and grabbed Richie's shoulder. Richie took his hand briefly from Helen's knee to slap Marcus on the back with a, 'Hi mate. Great to see you.'

There were several bottles of champagne on the little table and Richie filled two empty glasses and pushed them towards Joycie and Marcus. Joycie raised her glass to him, but Richie was whispering something to Helen. Probably telling her he'd been a Guards officer, but had to give it up through injury – his usual chat-up line so Marcus told her. In fact he'd only lasted a couple of months' training before buying himself out.

She turned to Sally, knowing she couldn't be heard by Richie and Helen on the other side of the table. 'Richie's a real poser, I'm afraid. You should tell Helen to be careful.'

Sally pulled a face. 'Fat chance of her listening to me,' she shouted with a gruff little laugh.

Joycie guessed she must be in her late twenties. Her red hair was cut in a neat old-fashioned style and unlike her sister she was wearing hardly any make-up: just a dusting of powder and a touch of pink lipstick. In her plain black dress, a string of pearls at the neckline she was obviously out of place in the Ad Lib. But Joycie thought the look suited her and when she smiled her face was very pretty.

Joycie waved her hand at the dinner jacketed DJ and the girls waving feather boas as they wiggled on the tiny dance floor, then leaned close to Sally and shouted, 'What do you think?'

150

Sally's eyes twinkled. 'Not what I'm used to, but perfect for Helen,' she said.

Joycie laughed. 'It's not really my scene, but it can be fun.'

Sally shook her head. 'Your friend Richie called it, "The place where everyone is either famous, or beautiful or both." Don't think he's impressed with me, though.' Her imitation of Richie's upper class drawl was perfect and Marcus must have heard because he turned and gave a silent handclap. Richie and Helen looked over, clearly wondering what the country mouse could have said that might amuse anyone.

Sally touched her throat, pulling another funny face, and Joycie nodded and raised her glass. Even after a few minutes her own throat was feeling rough from shouting through the music and the smoke that filled the air. Richie and Helen stood up and headed for the dance floor, and Sally and Joycie sipped their champagne in silence for a while, still smiling at each other. Then Sally leaned over again and shouted, 'Helen said you were asking about your mate, Pauline Shaw?'

'You remember her?'

'Yeah, poor love. I …' She shook her head and waved her hand to her ear, her throat, and then to the noisy room with such a comical expression on her face that Joycie couldn't help laughing again.

She stood and whispered to Marcus, 'Sally might have something to tell me,' and pointed back towards the lift.

As they all headed over, Marcus pulled at Joycie's arm. 'We don't know who might be outside.' But Sally was already in the lift so Joycie followed her. Marcus joined them, leaning back against the mirrored wall and shaking his head. 'We need to tell Sally about Bill first.'

Joycie put her hand on Sally's arm. 'The thing is you probably shouldn't be seen talking to me. Someone has been following me. Seems to think I'm poking my nose in where it doesn't belong.'

Sally's forehead creased. 'About Pauline, you mean?'

'I don't know, but I don't want to cause you any trouble. Perhaps we should talk on the phone instead.'

Sally giggled. 'Ooh I say,' and reached around Marcus to press the button to go down. 'I could do with a bit of excitement.'

Marcus said, 'This is serious,' and as the lift doors opened he stepped out, holding the door with one arm as he looked along the wide alleyway. 'No one around,' he said, 'but I'll keep a lookout while you talk, and don't be too long.'

As they left the lift he walked to the corner and the start of Chinatown to stare up and down Lisle Street. Then headed back past them towards Leicester Square.

Joycie looked at Sally. 'Are you OK?'

Sally nodded and lit a cigarette, offering the packet to Joycie. Joycie shook her head. 'Ian, my hubby, doesn't like me smoking. Says it's burning money, but I'm on holiday so what the hell,' Sally said. When she laughed it was still the gruff chuckle that was impossible not to echo.

They walked along the side street away from the noise coming down from the club. It had been very hot inside and Joycie was glad of the cool breeze.

'When Sally told me you were wondering about Pauline I asked Mandy, the girl who told me about her being in trouble in the first place, what she remembered. Pauline wouldn't tell her much apparently, just said the father wasn't in the picture and couldn't help. Mandy could hardly believe it – a kid like Pauline – but then, as she says, it can happen to anyone.'

They had paused under a street light for a moment as Sally dropped her half-finished cigarette and ground it underfoot, and Joycie heard herself saying, 'I don't think Pauline … I mean I think someone …' She stopped. Sally was too easy to talk to.

Sally's eyes, as big and blue as her sister's, glittered up at her. Her pink mouth making a little *O* of shock. 'You think someone forced himself on her? Oh my God, poor little thing.'

'Look, please don't mention it to anyone. I hadn't seen Pauline for a while so I've no real reason to think that. And you're right, it can happen to anyone.'

Another of those hoarse chuckles as Sally jabbed at her own chest with her thumb. 'Yeah, I should know. But Ian stuck by me and we wanted to get married anyway, just not so soon.'

They reached the corner of Leicester Square where Marcus was still waiting then headed back towards the club. It was very late; the last restaurants in the square and at the other end in Chinatown must be closing up, the only sounds coming from the odd car or taxi passing by and the music echoing down from the Ad Lib.

Sally said, 'But, you know, Mandy says she had an idea something wasn't right. Not just because no one had ever seen Pauline with a boy but because, when Mandy told her how much it would cost to get rid of the baby, Pauline said she'd find the money okay. And I don't imagine she was going to ask her mum and dad.'

They paused at the entrance to the club, the music blasting out above them. 'So what happened?' Joycie said.

'Mandy only saw Pauline once more. It was really early one Sunday morning. There was a fair on at Walton and Mandy had been over there to see one of the blokes working the dodgem cars. He brought her back on his motorbike. She knew all the nosy parkers would be looking out if they heard the bike so she made him stop at the end of the road. Pauline walked past them with a little case, but she crossed over pretending she hadn't clocked Mandy.'

'She must have been heading for the station, for London,' Joycie said.

'Yeah. Although it was hours before the first train.'

'And Mandy hadn't given her an address to go to?'

'No and that seems to have been the last anyone saw of her.'

They looked at each other and Joycie saw herself reflected in Sally's clear blue eyes for just a moment before her own eyes blurred with tears. Sally reached out and held her in a warm hug. 'You never know,' she said, 'she might have been going to meet the father after all. Perhaps they'd decided to run off together.'

Joycie bit back the question: 'Well why has she never come back?' Sally was trying to comfort her. To make them both feel better because it was far too late to help Pauline.

That night Joycie got up twice imagining she heard Fatty whining or scratching at the front door, but the street was still and silent. The second time, she opened the back door and scanned the overgrown garden, but there was no sign of movement out there either. She made a cup of tea and stood in the kitchen drinking it and going over and over what Sally had said.

It was hours before the first train. So had Pauline really been heading for the station when Mandy saw her that morning? It would make sense because she would have wanted to be sure her parents were still asleep. But maybe she'd been sneaking away to meet someone. Even though it was difficult to believe of the Pauline she remembered, Joycie knew there had to be a chance that there was a boyfriend on the scene somewhere. As Sally said, falling for a baby was something that happened to plenty of respectable girls.

But if she was going to see a backstreet abortionist then she hadn't got the name and address from Mandy. So where – *who* – had she got it from? She reminded herself that it was possible Pauline had gone to meet a boyfriend and left with him for a new, happily ever after, life. Whatever the truth there was nothing she could tell Mrs Shaw and was never likely to be.

Marcus woke her with a cup of tea. 'Are you able to have a lie-in this morning? Looks as if you could do with it.' They had hardly spoken when they got back last night, but he was smiling at her now, although it was a bit forced.

'They're going to ring me if and when the rest of the clothes for the shoot arrive at the studio, but I doubt that'll be until mid-morning. So, yes, I might sleep on a bit.'

As soon as he was gone however she was out of bed, washed and dressed. She grabbed a biscuit from the kitchen and, holding it in her mouth, struggled into a jacket. It was likely to be at least a couple of hours before they rang about the clothes. Time to have another look for Fatty.

But as she opened the front door the phone rang. She grabbed it from the hall table, kicking the door closed again and reminding herself to sound bright and ready to work. 'Hi.'

'You lost your dog.'

Her stomach clenched and she almost dropped the phone. She recognized the voice – Bill – and he wasn't even trying to disguise it. She couldn't speak.

'Lovely animal, very friendly. You should take better care of her.'

The words, when she forced them out, were a breathy squeak, her heart thumping so hard she had to press her hand to her chest to try to calm it. 'Where is she? What have you done with her?'

'And you shouldn't stand in the kitchen in your nightie with the light on, you know. Anyone might be watching.'

The phone slipped in her hand and when she caught it she held it to her chest for a moment, slowing her breathing; trying to find the right words.

But when she listened again she heard only the dialling tone.

Chapter Sixteen

Joycie stood holding the phone. He must have been in the garden last night, watching, as she drank her tea. And how often had he been there before?

And Fatty, poor scared Fatty, what had they done to her?

Suddenly her mind cleared – *the garden* – and she found herself in the kitchen scrabbling to unlock the back door. Before she opened it she looked round, her breath choking in her throat, heart pounding, and grabbed a steak knife from the cutlery drawer.

Stepping out she looked down the garden. *Damn it, why hadn't they cleared it, got rid of all the bushes, trimmed the trees?* Nothing moved. Breath held, heart no longer pounding but seeming almost to have stopped, she walked slowly towards the fence at the end, the wet grass tickling her bare ankles.

Still nothing. The morning was dank and silent. No bird song; no breeze.

Then something. Not a movement, but a dark shape under one of the trees.

A cry echoed through the silence, and she stopped; shocked by the sound, until she realized that the cry must have burst from her own throat.

The dark shape was Fatty. Lying utterly still.

Joycie managed to get her legs moving and to run, calling, 'Fatty, Fatty girl, come here.'

Nothing.

'Oh no, no. Please God, no.' She fell on her knees in the cold grass, her hands in Fatty's long soft hair.

Warm. She was warm. And, *thank God, thank God,* she was breathing. Joycie shook her and she gave a little moan and one leg twitched, but her eyes stayed closed. She was hurt.

But when Joycie touched her, pressing all over as hard as she dared, there was no reaction, no blood. Maybe she was drugged rather than injured.

It was no good trying to move her. So she ran to the phone in the hall, fumbling with the phone book. *Where the hell was the vet's number?*

At last she found it and, her voice trembling and breaking, managed to tell the receptionist they needed the vet to call. 'It's an emergency. I think my dog has been drugged. I think she's dying.'

The receptionist obviously thought she was making a fuss about nothing, but when Joycie told her Fatty had been stolen and was now unconscious she promised the vet would call. 'But it's surgery now so he won't be able to get there for a couple of hours.'

She wanted so much to speak to Marcus, to tell him what had happened, but he was doing an outdoor shoot so there was no way to reach him. Afraid to leave Fatty for long she grabbed Marcus's duffel coat and her own mac from the hatstand and ran back outside.

Fatty was lying in the same place, but seemed to have shifted and Joycie thought her breathing sounded easier. It was chilly under the trees so she put the duffel coat over Fatty and sat on the mac, rubbing the dog's head and speaking softly to her, only dimly aware of what she was saying.

After a while she stopped speaking and leaned back against the tree to look up at the clouds stacked overhead: grey and heavy. A noise from the alley jolted her alert, and the knife was in her hand. But it was just someone riding past on a bike.

And when she looked back, Fatty moved and gave a whine that turned into a yawn. Then slowly opened her eyes.

**

When the vet turned up Joycie half expected him to walk right out again because after Fatty had staggered into the house, lapped up a bowl of water, and slept for another half an hour, she was bouncing around like a puppy. But the vet was all concern. He said it wasn't unusual for pedigree dogs like Fatty to be stolen. 'And Afghans are very fashionable at the moment.' It seemed that the thieves frequently drugged dogs who barked or whined too much. 'But it's not in their interest to harm them. I've never known them to return a dog, though. So you're very lucky.'

Joycie nodded and smiled, although she felt like telling him how wrong he was. If only it was as simple as that.

The vet told her to keep Fatty in the house or garden until tomorrow because she might still be shaky and best not to leave her alone for a few hours. So when he had gone she rang the magazine and told them she was ill and couldn't make the shoot today. They weren't pleased, but since the delay over the clothes was their fault they couldn't object.

After she had fed Fatty she went into the garden with her. Fatty stayed close to the house, nosing among the overgrown rhododendron bushes, but Joycie made herself walk down to the end. This was where they must have got in last night: through the back gate from the lane. The gate was padlocked, but she'd never looked at it before. Had no idea if it was the same as always. The chain could easily have been cut and then replaced.

She looked back at the house. From here you could see the

whole kitchen. This was where they had stood watching her as she drank her tea worrying about Fatty and staring out into the darkness.

And in a moment that left her breathless the sick feeling that had been lodged in her stomach turned into something else. A burst of rage, hot and raw as a flame. She had tried to keep her head down and it had got her nowhere. Maybe she needed to confront this thing head on. And Sid was at the centre of it; she was sure of that. She needed to go and see him.

As soon as they were back inside she grabbed the phone book and looked up the number of Cora's theatrical agency. Without allowing herself to think about what she was doing she dialled the number, breathing easier when the call was answered by a young woman who must be Cora's assistant. She remembered Sally's imitation last night of Richie's posh tones and twisted her own voice into a female version. 'I'm following up on Mrs Sergeant's lunch meeting yesterday.'

'Oh yes, about the Val Doonican Show?'

This might be easier than she'd expected. 'That's right. I'm Mr Doonican's assistant, and I need to meet with Mr Sergeant himself today.'

'Oh.' The girl was flustered. Had she made a mistake and given herself away? She didn't speak. 'He's on stage tonight, and Mrs Sergeant isn't in the office at the moment.'

She made her voice impatient. 'Where's he appearing?'

'The Camberwell Empire but—'

'That's fine. I can see him before the show. Please call the theatre and get a message to Mr Sergeant to expect me and tell the stage doorman to make a note of my name. It's Miss Jones, Charlotte Jones.'

'OK, Miss Jones, but you should talk to Mrs Sergeant first.'

'I'm sorry, we're in the recording studio for the rest of the day. Can't be disturbed. I'm sure it'll be fine. I only need half an hour or so.'

She threw the phone down on the hall table as if it had burnt her fingers and collapsed on the sofa breathing hard. Fatty ambled over to lay her head on Joycie's knee, giving a tiny whine.

'Oh Fatty, baby, what have I done?'

When the phone rang she jumped up expecting it to be Cora, furious at the deception, or even Bill with more threats. She didn't dare speak.

'Joycie, are you there?' Just Marcus. 'I phoned the mag and they said you'd called in sick.'

She let out a long breath. 'It's all right, she's back, Fatty's back.' When she'd explained it all he said he'd try to get home early. 'But I thought your dad was in town and you were meeting him this evening.'

'It's only a drink at his club. I can put him off.'

Joycie spoke quickly; she didn't want him to know where she was going until it was too late. 'No, don't do that. I'm fine, we're both fine. Just having a lazy day in together.'

'All right, but I'll keep it short and get back as soon as I can.'

When he'd rung off she forced herself to eat a sandwich, feed Fatty, and write a note:

I'm sorry, Marcus, but I lied to you. I've gone to see Sid at the Camberwell Empire. Can't go on like this looking over my shoulder all the time. If they can kidnap our dog and get into our back garden I need to do something to finish it. Don't worry I'll be quite safe.

I love you, Joycie XXX

The letter was for Marcus, of course, but in the back of her mind there was also the thought that it could be useful evidence if anything did happen to her. Because, whatever she had said to him, she wasn't at all sure she would be safe.

***

Joycie had never performed at the Camberwell Empire and she couldn't remember her dad and Sid being on the bill there either, but it was so like all the other old theatres they had worked that it seemed familiar.

Stone steps leading to heavy oak doors studded with small bevelled windows that showed glimpses of the dark foyer; the tiny cage-like box office to one side and posters for old shows in glass-fronted frames on the other. When the bulbs in the dusty chandelier were switched on the place would be all sparkle, but in the half-light of a grey summer evening it looked shabby.

She paid for the taxi and walked round to the stage door. Here there had been no effort to make the place glamorous. A plain wooden door and, inside, brick walls painted dull yellow over a grubby floor. But still Joycie felt that old pang of excitement as she stepped inside. If there was any magic left, this was where you could feel it.

She had dressed in her only suit, navy blue and straight-skirted, a plain silk blouse under the jacket. Her hair was twisted and lacquered into a French pleat. The doorman wasn't the old codger she'd been hoping for but a young lad with a Beatle fringe and as he looked up she saw something spark in his eyes. She still looked too much like Orchid. She lowered her head, pretending to search her bag for something, and making her voice into a commanding snap. 'Miss Jones, Charlotte Jones, for Mr Sergeant please. He's expecting me.'

Thank goodness: he must have decided he'd made a mistake and flipped open a book on the desk in front of him. 'Oh right, yeah. Dressing room three just through there, Miss.'

The dressing rooms were close enough that the doorman would hear her if she needed to shout for help, although she told herself Sid wouldn't dare to touch her. She was someone these days, not a little girl dependent on him for her wages and those of her dad. He might have set Bill on her, but he wouldn't dare to do anything openly.

161

A pause and a deep breath, willing her hands and knees not to quiver and her voice to stay firm. She knocked on the door and called, 'Mr Sergeant, it's Charlotte Jones, Mr Doonican's assistant. You're expecting me.'

His stage voice, loud and hearty, the northern accent exaggerated. 'Come in, love.'

He was sitting, as she'd expected, at the dressing table, in a paisley patterned dressing gown, like a cut-price Noel Coward. He turned and flashed his professional comic's grin. The grin died. His eyes widened and for a blink she saw fear flit across his face, before he replaced it with a false smile.

'Joyce my darling, how lovely to see you but I can't talk right now I'm …' A crack of laughter. 'Oh, I see, you're Miss Jones, are you? Clever girl.' He slapped his palms on his knees. The laugh turning into a long chuckle.

Joycie stayed where she was, one hand behind her on the doorknob ready to pull it open if she needed to. 'I've come to ask if it was you who set that bloke Bill on me, and why.'

Sid moved his chair round to face her. In the harsh light he looked old and worn, much more so than when she'd seen him at Irene's funeral.

'Cora told me about that,' he said. 'You being pestered by someone, but we can't understand it. Why would anyone want to scare you? And why on earth do you think it might be us, darling?' By the end of the speech he was breathless and his final few words came out on a wheeze. His face was mottled with red and purple, his lips almost blue.

'I've been looking into the past and I think you were frightened about what I might find.'

He coughed and shook his head, trying to get the breath to speak. Joycie waited, realizing that she had only planned those first two sentences and had no idea where to go from here.

Finally Sid took in a rattling breath and said, 'Look, Joyce love, I admit I've been a bad boy. Always was one for the girls. Couldn't help myself when I was younger. I'm older and wiser now and I'll never forgive myself for the way I treated my poor Cora over the years. She didn't deserve it.' He looked down and brushed a fleck of cotton from his dressing gown before saying almost to himself. 'But it was harmless, you know, just a bit of fun.' When he looked at her again his faded brown eyes were glassy.

'So you call what you did to me when I was fourteen harmless fun, do you?' He started to say something, but she spoke over him. 'You attacked me. If Dad hadn't come in and stopped it I dread to think how far you would have gone.'

He stretched his hands out towards her, palms open in surrender. 'I'm so sorry about that, my love. Trying it on with you was unforgivable. But I just couldn't help it; you were so lovely. I can't tell you how grateful I am that your dad stopped me making an even worse fool of myself. But you must know I would never have done anything to hurt you.'

A hot, hot gush of rage that made her want to slam her fist into his fat, smiling face. Instead she tightened her fingers on the door handle until they tingled and thrust her other hand into her pocket. 'But you did hurt me and it still hurts.'

He was looking down again, shaking his head, his voice almost a whisper. 'If that's true then I apologize. I honestly didn't realize.'

'And what about the other girls? The ones who didn't have a dad to save them?'

When he spoke again his voice was firm. 'Look, I can understand why you're angry with me and I can only say again how sorry I am. I'll never understand why Cora put up with me for all those years. Thank the Lord I'm too old for that kind of stuff now, but I did betray her more than once. You must believe me though, Joyce my darling, it was only with girls who were willing.'

'What about Pauline Shaw? I bet she wasn't willing.' She hated her voice for trembling. He didn't speak; just shook his head as if he'd never heard the name. So she said, 'Pauline Shaw, from Clacton. Mrs Shaw's daughter.'

His hand went to his mouth, rubbing his lips, and although he continued to shake his head, she was sure he knew who she was talking about. A shaky laugh. 'Blimey, Clacton, we haven't been back there for years. Wasn't Mrs Shaw's girl your mate?'

'Yes, and she got pregnant the summer after my dad died. When you were appearing there.'

Sid flopped back in his chair with a heavy sigh. 'I see. So she got herself knocked up, and she's told you it was me, has she? Well why wait all this time to come out with it?'

'She hasn't told me or anyone because the chances are she's dead.'

The blue tinge was beginning to ebb away from his lips, the purple in his cheeks to fade back to red. He either knew already or just didn't care. 'I'm sorry about that, but it's got nothing to do with me.'

This was hopeless. She took a long breath, trying to organize her thoughts. 'I don't believe you, but we both know I can't prove you *tried it on* with Pauline. Nobody can now. And you must know there would be no point in me going to the police about what you did to me. So I can't understand why you feel the need to scare me.'

He sighed and began to stand, holding onto the dressing table to lever himself upright. 'OK, I've had enough now.' A coughing fit seized him and he sank into the chair again, leaning over and gasping for breath.

When he finally tried to speak she didn't give him time. 'Is it something to do with my mum? Is that what you're so worried about?'

'This is madness, Joyce. You're not going to try and blame me for that now, are you?'

'I only know you seem to have something serious to hide. Otherwise why would you need to get someone to follow me, watch me, steal my dog?' It was all going wrong. She felt out of control. 'Just tell me the truth, Sid. The truth about it all. That's the only thing I want.' She hated the pleading note she could hear in her own voice.

The door behind her banged against her back.

'Hello, hello. Who's in there? Sid, what's going on?'

Cora's voice, and the door handle rattling against her fingers. Joycie stepped back to let her in.

Cora's face was glossy under the make-up, her eyes hard, and Joycie couldn't stop herself from flinching back from her furious stare. 'I thought it had to be something to do with you,' she said. 'That idiot girl in my office, letting you sneak your way in here.' She looked at Sid, her face softening. 'Are you all right, love?'

His breath was loud. 'It's fine, Cora. No harm done. Poor Joyce is a bit upset that's all.' Joycie could almost believe he was concerned about her when he smiled over at her and wheezed, 'I can understand why you can't forget what happened with your mum, darling, but you should let it be.'

Cora went to him and smoothed his wispy hair. 'You relax now and take it easy, love. Let me deal with this.'

She grabbed Joycie's arm, her fingers biting into the soft flesh above her elbow. 'Now, look, this is not on. I don't care how famous you are you've no right to behave like this. Lying about being someone else, accusing people of all sorts.'

Joycie went to speak, but there was too much swirling around in her head and she couldn't find the words. She felt sick and everything looked distorted, as if in a dream; a nightmare.

Cora moved back into the corridor and Joycie found herself there too; whether pushed by Cora or of her own volition she wasn't sure. Cora spoke in a hoarse whisper. 'Sid's not well. Surely you can see that. I can't let you upset him like this.'

'All I want is to know what really happened to my mum. Just tell me everything and that'll be it. You don't need to see or hear from me again.'

Cora stood back and folded her arms. Her eyes were slivers of blue ice almost hidden in thick folds of flesh. 'I've told you. I've told you all I know. Your dad got drunk as a skunk that night and was crying and raving for hours. Sid wouldn't tell me everything he said, but we guessed something had happened between them: something nasty. And that's why Sid sent me round to your lodgings. And – well – you know what I found.'

Joycie's chest seemed to have squeezed closed. She leaned her forehead against the brick wall, but it was warm and clammy and she was sure she was about to be sick.

When Cora touched her she flinched away.

'See what you've done, you silly girl. You've upset Sid and now you've upset yourself. We all know what really happened to your mum, don't we? But at the time me and Sid thought it best to say nothing and we were right. At least that way you still had Charlie. And we knew he didn't mean to hurt your mum, so blabbing about it would have done more harm than good.'

She had to get away from this clammy corridor, from Cora's cloying scent, but when she tried to walk she staggered and clutched the wall.

Cora shouted, 'Darren,' and the doorman appeared. 'The young lady's feeling faint, needs some fresh air.'

Joycie let him take her arm. She felt as if she was walking on cotton wool, but when he opened the door and made to come out with her she managed to shake her head and say, 'It's all right, I'm fine.'

Thank goodness, he dropped her arm and closed the door. She leaned back on it for a moment, breathing in the cool air. It was gloomy and must have been raining while she was inside because the street lights were reflected in dozens of little puddles. She told herself not to think about it yet. She would be all right when she got home. But as she moved away from the door a surge of dizziness caught her and she had to lean over, clutching her stomach, and throw up in the puddled gutter.

Chapter Seventeen

She should have asked the taxi driver to come back for her, but when she arrived she'd been so focused on what she was about to do it hadn't entered her head. The rain started up again, heavy and steady this time, as she headed to the front of the theatre and along the road to where she thought the railway station might be. She'd find a taxi rank there.

A car splashed through the puddles and slowed to a stop. She flinched into her jacket. *Please God, not Bill, not now.*

It was the Morgan. And Marcus, flinging the passenger door open as he stopped. She stumbled round and climbed in. Her skirt clung to her and a hank of wet hair, escaping from the French pleat, trailed across her cheek.

Marcus pulled the car away so hard she jerked back in her seat. The windscreen wipers were going fast and he had to rub steam from inside the glass with the sleeve of his jacket. When they were moving steadily again he said, his voice tight with anger, 'What the hell are you playing at?'

She bit her lip, the aftertaste of vomit still in her mouth. *Don't, don't be like that, I can't bear it.* He looked over and his voice softened just a touch. 'Why didn't you at least wait for me? Anything could have happened to you.'

She managed to say, 'I got so angry about it all. Just had to do something to stop it.'

They pulled up at traffic lights and she saw that his jaw was set hard. 'And have you?' he said. 'Stopped it, I mean?'

When she shook her head wet strands of hair plastered themselves across her lips, making her feel sick again. She pushed the hair away and groped at the clips to undo the rest, but only succeeded in bringing down another wet hank. 'No. I was so sure Sid must have had something to do with whatever happened to my mum, but I don't know any more.'

'So did you find out anything at all that was useful?' His voice was still tight.

It was too much. When she tried to speak the hot tears began to pour down her cold cheeks. She didn't try to wipe them away, just sat staring ahead and feeling something close to relief as she let the misery flood out. Marcus shot a quick look over at her and didn't speak for the rest of the journey.

When they got home she went to the kitchen for a glass of water then started up the stairs. 'I'm going to have a bath.'

She had peeled off her wet clothes and was sitting wrapped in a big towel on the edge of the bath, waiting for it to fill, when he knocked on the door. For a moment she regretted not locking it but, no, she had to talk to him. 'It's open.'

Marcus perched on the toilet. 'I'm sorry, Joycie, it's just that you scared the fuck out of me. What were you thinking going there on your own?'

'I needed to talk to Sid alone. To see his reaction.'

'And did it help?'

She turned off the taps and trailed her fingers in the water. It was too hot. 'Not really.' She tried to smile at him, but her chin wobbled and she looked away again, adding more cold water to the bath. 'Cora arrived and threw me out, but I did have a few minutes with Sid and …' She couldn't go on.

Marcus reached over to test the bath water. 'It's perfect now. I'll leave you to it.'

She stepped in, lying back in the warmth as he closed the door. 'Marcus?'

He looked in again.

'Stay and talk to me please,' she said.

He knelt on the mat beside the bath and she closed her eyes trying to get her muddle of thoughts to make some kind of sense.

'They both seem pretty sure my dad killed Mum, or at least hurt her so much that he scared her away.'

'And do you believe that?'

A sharp spasm in her throat. 'I suppose it's what I've thought for all these years. That Dad must have killed her. That was what I couldn't bear to believe. And this whole thing started because I wanted so much to find her alive and prove myself wrong.'

Marcus kissed her forehead. 'I'm sorry,' he said softly.

They were silent for so long that Joycie felt herself beginning to doze in the warm water until Marcus said, 'You hardly slept last night. Why don't you go straight to bed?'

He handed her the towel and turned away, while she clambered out, feeling so tired that when she'd wrapped it around her she leaned against him and closed her eyes.

'The thing is I still can't make sense of why they've got Bill trying to scare me. Sid must know I can't do anything about what he might have done to Pauline or what he did to me. So why set the gang on us?'

'Don't forget you're a famous name now. Even if you can't go to the police he may be afraid you might talk to the papers, expose him for what he is. That would certainly damage his career if nothing else.'

It made sense. 'Well I told him tonight I wasn't going to do anything at all so that should be enough to make him call the dogs off.'

'And then we can get on with our lives.'

He kissed her and she stayed warm in his arms for a long time. When she broke away he raised his eyebrows and gave her the smile she loved.

After that it was so easy and natural she couldn't believe it. He carried her into her bedroom and lay on the bed with her. She helped him undress.

And they made love.

Afterwards he whispered. 'Are you all right?'

And she laughed. 'Oh yes.'

He didn't laugh and his voice was serious. 'The oddest thing happened. I almost felt as if it was the first time I'd ever made love.' Then he kissed her and their kiss was so sweet she knew that in spite of everything she had never been this happy, and probably never would be again. But it didn't matter. This was enough.

Eventually Marcus fell asleep and she lay listening to him breathing, wondering why it had finally been all right. It must be to do with seeing Sid as he really was – a pathetic old man – and facing up to him. Facing up to what he had done to her. Tonight, with Marcus, was something so different she couldn't even think of it in connection with Sid.

She knew she wouldn't sleep, and she got up, pulled on a long sweater and went downstairs. Thinking of the dark garden with its shadowed trees she didn't dare go into the kitchen, but huddled on the sofa. Fatty came over and lay at her feet, and Joycie kicked off one of her slippers and rubbed the soft hair on the dog's back with her toes.

Tonight had been wonderful, but could she trust herself not to go back to the way she had been? And if she finally found out the whole truth about her parents, would that help or make things worse? The one thing she was sure of was that she loved Marcus and would do anything to avoid hurting him.

The upstairs light went on and he came down, dragging his

arms through Joycie's old candlewick dressing gown and pulling it tight across his chest. 'Joycie? Are you all right?'

She smiled at him. 'Of course I am, just didn't want to wake you.'

He sat beside her and she felt herself blush, suddenly shy, but when he pulled her to him and she nestled into his warmth it was all right again. His voice was very soft. 'And you're sure you're OK?'

She pulled back to look into his eyes. 'It may not always be as easy as it was tonight, but I do love you. I want to be with you. I want this to work. So will you be patient with me?'

He gave her a tiny kiss on the nose. 'I'll try. Now I don't know about you but I'm starving. I'm going to make some sandwiches.'

When he stood she flicked the hem of the dressing gown with her toe. 'You look so daft in that. Remind me to buy you a nice one when I go shopping next.'

He pulled up the collar as he headed for the kitchen putting on a silly, girlish voice. 'No I want one just like this.' Then he pressed his nose into the fabric taking a deep breath, his voice dropping low again. 'And it has to smell the same too. Of gorgeous eau de Joycie.'

She threw her slipper at him and when they laughed Fatty ran round in circles tongue hanging out. But when Marcus turned on the kitchen light Joycie couldn't help shivering. The image of someone watching from the dark garden was still all too clear.

She woke to find Marcus leaning on his elbow, looking down at her as light filtered through the bedroom curtains. They had brought the cheese sandwiches up with them and when they finished eating she lay cuddled against him feeling so safe and happy she was able to forget about the darkness outside and drift into a deep, dreamless sleep.

Now she reached up to touch his cheek. 'Last night …'

His hand came up to cover hers. 'I know and don't worry. This is still your room and I won't expect to spend every night here.'

She smiled and closed her fingers over his. 'I was going to say that last night was just perfect and that I love you.'

He said her name quietly and smiled into her eyes. As if hearing her thoughts, he said, 'Do you think perfect can ever be repeated or does it happen just once?'

She gave him the answer she knew he wanted. 'There's only one way to find out.'

And it was perfect again.

She had to do the delayed magazine shoot that morning and as she'd already cancelled once she didn't want to let them down by being late. So she left without breakfast with Marcus still in bed. He was going to work in the darkroom first thing then had a meeting about a job they were booked for in New York.

At first her delight over last night with him kept her going, but as the day wore on she grew more and more tired. It wasn't late when she got home and Marcus was still out, but she couldn't face taking Fatty for a walk before she had a rest. She fed her and let her out into the garden then sat on the sofa and closed her eyes.

She wanted to keep hold of the feeling she'd had last night and this morning, but it had gone and all the old worries were back.

Marcus had tried to understand, but even he couldn't really do that. No matter how many times she told herself he was right she couldn't stop feeling the pain and the guilt. And it wasn't just about Sid. She had made herself believe her dad was a good man. She had loved him when she should have hated him for what he had done.

If only she could work out what it was that had been niggling at her for the last few days. Somehow she knew she'd missed something important. She went upstairs and brought down the keepsake box, taking out her mum's last letter.

After she left, Joycie and her dad hadn't talked much about her but when they did it had all been about the good times. And those were the memories Joycie had treasured. And yet, if she was honest with herself, she did remember arguments, angry rows, and even weeks at a time when her parents hardly spoke to each other. Had her dad been trying to make her forget the bad parts? To make himself forget how it had really been?

She looked at the letter with the phrase that kept playing over and over in her head: *something has happened and I have to get away from here.* If only she could find out what that *something* might have been. And then there were the words that were crossed out. Last time she had guessed at them as: *persuade* and *later,* imagining they meant her mum hoped Charlie would follow them after the season was over. But, even if she had read the words correctly, they could mean anything.

When she heard Fatty come back into the kitchen she locked the door, put the key in the drawer, and lay full length on the sofa, staring at the ceiling and trying to remember anything significant about the days before her mum disappeared. *Something has happened, something has happened.*

Hastings – August 1953

Joycie is sitting at the table, a pile of spuds she's supposed to be peeling in front of her. Mum is downstairs talking to the landlady, Mrs Palmer, but Joycie isn't doing much because when she spread out a newspaper to collect the peelings she spotted photos of the carnival they had at the weekend.

Her dad took Joycie to see it and she thought it was wonderful, but it's a shame the newspaper pictures aren't in colour because the floats and the costumes don't look so good. The carnival queen had been beautiful, with a bouffant of shining blonde hair like Marilyn Monroe's and a floaty white dress. But she's just a pale blur in the photo.

When Mum comes up again Joycie grabs a potato and starts to peel it. Dad will be in soon and he'll need to eat and be off to the theatre. Mum pours herself some tea even though it's been made for ages and must be cold. She sits in the armchair with her back to Joycie, but Joycie can hear the spoon stirring and stirring. The stirring stops; Mum puts down her cup and gives an enormous sigh as she leans back in her chair.

'What's wrong, Mum?' She doesn't answer so Joycie goes round to her. Her eyes are closed and her mouth looks funny. 'Mum?'

A headshake and Mum's eyes open and focus on Joycie. 'I'm all right, love. Just tired.'

'Shall I make you some hot tea?'

Mum shakes her head and takes her cup back to the table, but just stands there staring as if she's hypnotized by Joycie's half-peeled potato. Her cup tips in her hand and some tea spills onto the paper.

'Bugger it!'

Mum grabs a tea towel from the sideboard and dabs the newspaper and the cloth beneath it, muttering, 'Damn, damn it.' Her voice is wobbling as if she's going to cry. Then she grabs the potato. 'Is this all you've done?' Her voice is harsh, not like Mum's voice at all. 'Bring me the big knife and the breadboard. I'll do it myself. Can't wait all day.'

Joycie wants to shout at her. *It's not fair. You spilled the stupid tea.* Instead she puts the knife and board on the table with a bang. Mum doesn't even seem to notice, just starts peeling away as if she's in a race, so Joycie goes into her bedroom and slams the door. She lies on her bed, too cross even to read, wanting only to think about how mean Mum is being.

At last she hears Dad whistling as he comes in, but she stays where she is. She won't answer when they call her. One of them will have to come and get her.

Dad must have thrown his jacket onto the sofa as usual because Mum says in a nasty voice, 'Hang that up, can't you?'

'Ooer, what's got your goat?'

Dad's laugh makes Joycie smile even though she's determined to keep being cross. Mum's answer is so quiet she can't make out the words. She creeps to her door. Then she hears Dad say, 'Come on, Mary, darling. You're getting yourself worked up about nothing.'

Joycie turns the door handle, oh so slowly, and opens it just a crack, peering through the tiny gap. Mum has pushed the board and the potatoes aside and sits folding the newspaper into smaller and smaller squares. Dad is standing looking down at her, but she just keeps folding, her eyes fixed on her fingers.

'It's not nothing, Charlie. Mrs Palmer downstairs said she saw the three of you together the other week.' Mum sounds as if she's got something in her throat, something that's making it hard to speak.

And when Dad answers it's in a cold quiet way that scares Joycie: 'So what are you getting at? What do you want me to do?'

Mum pushes her chair back so hard the screech makes Joycie jump. She shakes her head at Dad. 'You'd better sort it out. 'Cos if you don't, I will.' Then she walks away, leaving the potatoes half peeled, goes into her room and closes the door very quietly behind her.

After a few minutes Joycie peeps out and sees Dad still sitting at the table staring into space. He must have heard her door creak because he turns with a big smile and says, 'Hey, Joycie. Mum's not feeling too good so how's about you and me go out for fish and chips.'

Joycie sat up on the sofa. Fatty, who had been lying on the floor nearby, stood to look from her to the front door and back again. 'All right, let's go.' With Fatty dancing around her legs she clipped on the lead and they went out. She headed for St Luke's Gardens: the park where she'd talked to Cora. It was the first time they'd been back since Fatty was kidnapped, but she'd just have to be careful. Keep the dog close. Couldn't let them win.

That strange argument happened not long before her mum disappeared. She'd forgotten all about it, but she remembered now that Dad had taken her out for fish and chips in a café. They brought some back for Mum and Joycie wanted to call her to eat them before they got cold, but Dad said best to leave her.

They were still wrapped up on the table next morning and Mum just picked them up and tossed the whole packet in the bin. She made Joycie a boiled egg for breakfast like always, but hardly spoke to her and didn't have anything to eat herself. Just sat holding a cup of tea until the 9 o'clock pips came on the wireless. Then she tipped the whole cupful down the sink, grabbed a shopping bag and told Joycie they needed to go to the greengrocer's.

Joycie couldn't remember her parents arguing again. But then she couldn't remember them actually talking to each other after that. And then Mum was gone.

Keeping close to Fatty was not easy and after chasing her up and down the park for twenty minutes Joycie was exhausted and hungry too. Luckily Marcus was in when they got home and he was making some toast.

Fatty jumped up at him, tongue hanging out, before Joycie could take off her lead. Marcus managed to do it while she lay on the floor and he rubbed and patted her. He smiled over at Joycie. 'You should have waited for me. I've been missing you.'

Finally Fatty moved away to nose at her empty food bowl, rattling it across the quarry-tiled floor, and Joycie put her arms around Marcus. After a while he looked down at her, head to one side.

'What's wrong?'

'Oh, you know. The same as always.'

'You've been looking through your mum's things again,' he said, pointing to the sofa where the keepsake box still sat.

'There's something there, I know there is. Something I've seen, but haven't understood.'

'Go on then. Look through it again and I'll bring the toast.'

The argument she'd remembered must surely have been connected to the *something* that her mum's letter said had happened. And, if Joycie's memory was right, she'd been angry about the landlady seeing *the three of you together*. But who could the other two be? Sid and Cora? Or more likely Sid and some girl they met at the stage door. But Joycie knew they'd taken girls out before. So why would her mum react so badly this time?

She pulled out a few playbills. There wasn't one for the show just before Mum went, but another caught her eye. It was for Eastbourne, in June, just a couple of months earlier.

Marcus plonked down beside her, holding out a plate of toast. She took a slice and handed him the playbill. 'I've remembered an argument Mum and Dad had just before she disappeared. She was angry because someone had seen him with two other people. I thought it might be Sid and a girl.'

'That would make sense.'

Joycie pointed to the playbill. 'But look who was in the show with them a couple of months before that.'

'The Bluebirds – that's Dennis is it?'

'Yes, Dennis and Kay. And Dennis told me it was love at first sight for him. He also said Dad insisted he loved Mum and would never leave her, but …'

Marcus nodded and tapped the paper against his chin. 'So the two people he was with might have been Dennis and Kay? Are you thinking your mum guessed there was something going on with Dennis?'

She sat back. 'Dennis said nothing happened between them before my mum left, but I think it must have been pretty soon afterwards. So maybe my mum suspected Dad was attracted to Dennis even if he hadn't acted on it. I think I need to talk to Dennis and maybe to Kay as well to see how close they were to Dad before Mum left us.'

***

They were working together next day doing a studio shoot for wedding dresses and all morning Joycie had to fight to keep focused on the job. But when Marcus said, 'I like the dreamy look through the veil, but don't overdo it,' she knew she wasn't managing very well.

Two other models would be posing as her bridesmaids, but they were only booked for the afternoon so they didn't arrive until lunchtime. Marcus sent them to the make-up girl and dashed down the stairs, shouting, 'Got to pick up those lenses from the repairers and I'll bring back some sandwiches. Don't change, Joycie, we'll start with that dress.'

There was a phone in the office just off the studio, but she didn't want to be overheard. Luckily the dress was a short and simple little thing so she slipped on a mac and her own shoes, grabbed her purse and ran down to the phone box on the corner of the street.

She slotted in her pennies and rang the theatre at Clacton; relieved when a male voice answered because she had been dreading having to tell Mrs Shaw that she had no more news about Pauline. She pressed button A, letting the coins clank down into the box. 'I wonder if you could give a message to one of The Bluebirds for me. Just ask Dennis or Kay if they could ring Joyce. They've got my number.'

'I'd better get Kay for you now. They won't be here after today.' While Joycie waited the pips went and she had to feed in more pennies, glad she'd thought to fill her purse with change that morning.

Kay sounded breathless. 'I've just been clearing our stuff from the dressing room.'

'I thought you were there for a few more weeks.'

'Dennis is gone, Joyce. Upped and left the other day. So it looks like The Bluebirds have done their last flight.' Her laugh ended on what sounded like a sob.

'I'm sorry, Kay. He seemed so much better when I spoke to him. I thought you'd be all right.'

'Me too, but I could tell something was worrying him. And it just got worse and worse. Then yesterday he left me a note saying I'd be better off without him, which he knows is ridiculous.'

'What will you do?'

'Back to Mum and Dad in Cornwall for a bit, I suppose. Then find some kind of job.' Those wretched pips again and the last of Joycie's pennies rattling in. 'But that's not why you're ringing me, is it?' Kay continued.

'No, I need to ask you something more about Dad and Dennis.' She thought she heard Kay sigh, but there was no time to waste. 'Dennis said it was love at first sight for him. When did you first suspect there was something between them?'

A definite sigh. 'I really don't know, it's all so long ago.'

'Well, did the three of you ever go out together in those early days? After the show maybe?'

'I honestly can't remember.' Joycie could almost hear the *but* so she bit her lip and stayed silent. After a few seconds Kay said, 'I'm sure we would have jumped at the chance, though. We both fancied Charlie at first.'

'So there could have been gossip backstage?'

'Not about Charlie and me. That was never a goer, but Dennis was besotted, and it was obvious to me that your dad had a thing for him too, so I'm pretty sure other people in the show must have noticed. But Charlie told Dennis he was married and planned to stay that way.'

'And Dennis accepted it?'

'He had to. Wasn't happy about it, of course, and ...'

'What?'

'Well at one stage I seem to remember he talked about going to see your mum; to ask her to give Charlie up.'

Joycie's heart gave a thump. 'And did he?'

'When I told him not to be stupid he laughed it off, said he was joking, but who knows.'

Joycie was aware that her money must be running out. 'Thank

you, Kay. When you do see Dennis will you ask him to call me?'

The pips were going again and Joycie had no more coins, but she heard Kay say, 'I don't think that's going to be any time soon. If he's run away from me and from the act something must really have spooked him.'

Chapter Eighteen

It had been hot in the studio, but it was a lovely evening, and as they drove home with the top of the Morgan down Joycie leaned back on her seat and closed her eyes, letting the breeze ripple over her face and through her hair. But it didn't help to calm her. Her brain was buzzing, and she sat up and told Marcus about the phone call to Kay.

'Kay says Dennis didn't try to hide the fact that he had fallen for Dad and that even though Dad insisted he was married and loved Mum it was obvious he was attracted to Dennis as well.'

'Which means your mum could have seen it too.'

'I suppose so.'

After a few moments Marcus said, 'So Kay thinks Dennis has run away because something scared him?'

'Yes, and I'm wondering if Bill put the frighteners on him. I mean, he followed me to Clacton so he probably saw me with Dennis.'

'But why would he threaten Dennis?'

'To stop him talking to me again. Telling me whatever it is they're so keen to keep quiet.'

'You think Dennis might know something important?'

Joycie swallowed and raked at her hair. If so then it was her fault that he was terrified and Kay's life and career were in ruins. 'I can't think of any other explanation, can you?'

'Yes, I can think of plenty.'

Marcus stopped at a zebra crossing for a woman with a pram. She glanced at them and Joycie saw recognition spark in her eyes. The woman slowed to a stop. A car on the opposite side hooted and she jumped and moved away, still looking back at them. Marcus gave a little chuckle. 'Well she's got something to tell the old man when she gets home.'

Joycie didn't feel like laughing. 'What were you going to say about Dennis?'

'Only that there could be any number of reasons why he might have wanted to disappear. After all, you don't really know anything about him.'

Hastings – September 1953

Joycie is holding a pillow to her face to muffle the sound of her crying. She had been dreaming about Mum, thinking she was still with them and they were all happy, but when she woke she remembered.

It's almost exactly a month since her mum went missing, and Joycie knows she won't be coming back. Dad doesn't talk about her much, nor does anyone else when Joycie is around, but she can guess what they're saying. They all think Mum has gone off with her fancy man. Joycie isn't a baby and she understands what that means, but she doesn't believe it. Mum would never have left without her.

There's a noise coming through the wall from the other bedroom, what she still thinks of as Mum and Dad's room, and as she puts down the pillow and listens she hears Dad moving about and mumbling. She knows he hasn't been sleeping well and he stayed up late last night. Those two singers from the show, The Bluebirds, came to see him and they sat drinking together for ages. Were still there when Dad sent her to bed.

Joycie likes them. Kay is so pretty and Dennis is handsome and they are a lot younger than the other acts in the show. They brought Joycie some sweets and a bottle of lemonade so she could have a drink with them. Dennis even offered her a sip of his whisky, but Dad said, 'No,' and Kay smacked Dennis on the arm and told him not to be wicked. When Kay laughed it was almost like singing, and Joycie felt happy for the first time in ages. Then Dad told Joycie it was time for her to go to bed, and Kay said they should be off too. But Joycie heard them talking until she fell asleep.

Maybe it's because of Kay and Dennis that Joycie had that happy dream. But now she feels bad that she forgot about Mum going away even in her dreams.

It sounds like Dad is crying and she wants to go to him. If she does he might talk to her: tell her everything about what really happened to Mum. But the thought of that makes her scared and she huddles down into the warm bed trying not to hear Dad.

After a while his crying gets softer and she decides to make them both some tea. That will cheer them up and they won't need to talk about anything. Her feet are warm, but the lino beside her bed is cool and a little shiver goes through her.

At her own door she freezes because she can hear two voices and for a tiny moment her heart seems to jump up into her throat. But it isn't Mum; it's a man's voice. Surely Kay and Dennis can't still be here – and if they are then why are they in Dad's bedroom?

His door is closed and Joycie presses her ear against it. She knows it's wrong to be listening at the door like this, but she stays where she is until she's so cold her knees are shaking.

Dad is letting out little sobs and someone else is muttering to him. It's Dennis. They keep talking and Dad's sobs slowly die away. She doesn't hear a lady's voice, so Kay must have gone home and Dennis has stayed because he could see Dad was upset.

Then the voices stop and there are only rustling sounds that go on and on. And after a while Joycie creeps back to her own room and lies awake listening to the creak of the bed next door.

Joycie was no cook, but she could make a good omelette so she told Marcus she would do the dinner if he'd take Fatty for her walk. Although it was still light outside she pulled the kitchen curtains. They were ugly things covered in alternating rows of huge orange onions and scarlet tomatoes. Marcus's mother had chosen them, presumably to give the kitchen a Continental atmosphere. Joycie and Marcus never used to close them, but since Fatty's disappearance Joycie was far too aware of the long garden looming outside the windows.

While she mixed the eggs and grated some cheese she tried not to think about Dennis, but it was impossible. What reason did he have to be scared? Marcus was right that she didn't know him at all well. So it was quite possible that his running away had nothing to do with her visit. But surely it was too much of a coincidence.

Fatty burst through the front door, with Marcus in tow, and charged into the kitchen; her big red tongue dangling out of the side of her mouth; eyes bright at the thought of food. Joycie threw down the grater – what was the point of all this? Every question just led to more confusion and she seemed to be getting further and further away from finding out what had happened to her mum. And to her dad for that matter.

She jerked open the cupboard, grabbed a can of dog food, and cursed as the hopeless can opener did its usual stop/start act. Pushing the tin towards Marcus, she said, 'Can you open this?'

He hummed to himself as he tipped the pungent meat into Fatty's dish and refreshed her water bowl. 'There you are, girl.' His cheeriness and Fatty's delight as she wagged her tail and slobbered down her dinner made Joycie smile despite herself.

When she carried the plates in and put them on the coffee table she pushed all the letters and playbills still scattered on the sofa back into the keepsake box. She'd shove it on top of the wardrobe when they'd eaten. Try to forget it all, at least for now. She and Marcus were going to New York next week and she would let herself enjoy that.

Marcus handed her a glass of red wine and plonked down beside her on the sofa. 'This smells good,' he said leaning back. He sat up again at once and pulled out a folded newspaper from behind one of the cushions, handing it to Joycie. It was the one from the keepsake box.

'My mum must have put this in by mistake. There's nothing about the show or any of the acts.'

A flash of memory and she saw her mum staring down at the table where Joycie had spread out the newspaper to catch the potato peelings. Another flash: peering from her bedroom door to hear her parents' argument and seeing Mum folding and refolding the same paper. Then something she had hardly noticed at the time, but remembered now. As her mother walked away to shut herself in her bedroom she was putting something into the pocket on the front of her apron.

'It must have been the paper.'

'What?'

She had said it aloud and Marcus stopped eating, his fork halfway to his mouth.

'Mum saw something in the newspaper that upset her and that's why she kept it.' She went to put her plate on the floor but Fatty, who had been lying on the rug by the fireplace, looked up and ambled over, her tail wagging. Marcus chuckled and held out his hand and Joycie passed the plate to him then spread the newspaper on the coffee table, pushing Fatty gently away. 'And it must have been on the same page as the carnival pictures because that was where I'd opened it.'

One whole page was covered with snaps of the parade. The

spectators lining the narrow streets as they watched the carnival floats and people in fancy dress. But the opposite page had ordinary news. And one item drew Joycie's eye: a blurry photo of a smiling young girl. 'This is it,' she said. 'It's got to be.' She read it aloud:

'"*The body of missing teenager, Sharon Madison, 16, was discovered on Thursday morning by fishermen at Rye. It is thought that she drowned. Sharon was last seen leaving her home in Hastings Old Town on Monday. Our reporter talked to her mother, Margaret Madison, 45. Mrs Madison said Sharon was a happy girl, but had been upset after a recent split from her boyfriend. 'I couldn't understand it, they were childhood sweethearts,' she said.*

When we talked to Nigel Godwin, 17, however, he claimed that the couple had parted over a week before. 'Sharon found someone else and I hadn't seen her since we broke up,' he said."'

I heard Mum tell my dad that the landlady had seen *the three of you together,*' Joycie said. 'I thought that might have been Dad and the two Bluebirds, but my first idea was that it was him with Sid and some girl.' She tapped the paper. 'So what if it was this Sharon?'

Marcus read through the story again. 'She was sixteen, which would make her Sid's type, but ...'

'And the girls used to hang about at the stage door to see Dad. If Sid saw someone he fancied they used to go out together after the show, but Dad would make himself scarce before the end of the evening.'

'So if this Sharon killed herself, you're thinking it could have been because she was upset when it turned out your dad wasn't interested?'

'Or more likely because of what Sid did to her when Dad left them alone.'

'He attacked her you mean?'

'Something like that. After all it was only Dad turning up that saved me. And who knows what might have happened if a girl resisted him and there was no one to help her.'

Marcus put his hand on her forearm. 'You do realize this is all complete guesswork?'

'No, Marcus, it isn't. Mum saw something on this page.' She stabbed her finger at the print. 'And there's nothing else it could be. She said the landlady saw *the three of you together*. That had to be Dad, Sid, and this girl. Then she saw that the girl had drowned.'

'Come on, Joycie, that's a bit of a leap. Are you saying Sid was responsible? That he might even have murdered her, and your mum guessed?'

'I don't know what happened and I doubt Mum did either. She just thought Dad should admit they'd seen her around the time she died. I remember her saying if Dad didn't do something about it she would. And if Sid knew what she intended …'

'Now hang on there. You don't even know if this Sharon met your Dad or Sid.'

'But if I could find out that she'd been to the show …'

His grip tightened. 'It would prove nothing. And even then it would get you no further.'

She pulled away to cross her arms tight over her chest. 'If my mum was going to expose the connection with this girl it might explain her disappearance.'

Marcus took her shoulders and turned her to face him, his clear blue eyes gleaming. 'You don't really think that, do you?'

Joycie could feel herself flushing and she shook him off. 'I don't know, but I've got to try and find out. Go to Hastings and track down this Sharon's family and the boyfriend.'

He took a slug of wine and slumped back on the sofa. 'OK, if you think it'll help let's go down as soon as we get back from New York.'

'No, I can't wait that long. I want to go tomorrow.'

'You know I've got to redo some of those pictures of the bridesmaids this weekend. I've no idea how long that might take.' His voice was tight.

'I'm fine to go on my own. It'll stop me being bored while you're busy.' She tried to sound casual, suddenly knowing she didn't want him to come with her. He was staring at her and she jumped up and took their plates into the kitchen. Her own food was untouched, a yellow congealing mess on the plate, and she slid it into the bin and began splashing water into the sink.

Marcus followed and stood, arms crossed, leaning against the wall. Fatty sat beside him giving a little whimper. 'You realize it might be a waste of time,' Marcus said. 'Or, worse, you might find out things you'd rather not know.'

She plunged her hands into the water. It was too hot and she had to add some cold to make it bearable, holding her fingers under the tap to cool them. She could feel Marcus's eyes on her, but refused to turn and look at him. 'I might find out that my dad killed Mum, you mean? Deep down, I've always realized that was possible and at least I'd finally know for sure. In some ways it would be a relief.' Even as she said it she wondered if that was true.

'And what will you do if it turns out there are no answers?'

'I don't know.' She'd hardly eaten any of the omelette, but there was a sour eggy taste in her mouth. She swallowed down hard.

He came behind her, his arms around her waist, his breath fluttering a strand of hair against her cheek. 'You shouldn't go on your own. We can have a bit of a holiday when we get back from the States. Drive down there and afterwards take a tour along the coast.'

She was hot, pressed against the sink, trapped by his weight and the warmth of him, but when she twisted round holding her wet hands out to each side he moved even closer. 'I'll book us into a nice hotel. Get a room with a huge bed and a bath big enough for two.' He nuzzled her neck.

Dirty little tart, I know what you want.

She pushed him away, grabbing a tea towel and drying her hands. 'I'd rather go tomorrow – get it over with.'

He stood, hands by his side, just looking at her. She knew she should put her arms around him, tell him she was sorry, that it wasn't him she had pushed away, but she couldn't speak. And she couldn't bear to see his expression; to see how she had hurt him. She turned back to the washing up, hearing him move into the living room, Fatty's claws rattling on the parquet floor as she followed him.

'I'll take the dog out. Might pop into the pub as well,' he said. 'No need to wait up.'

She finished the washing up. *Don't think about it, don't think.* Then dried the dishes and put them away and scrubbed the sink with Vim. After that she mopped the kitchen floor and tidied the living room, putting everything but the newspaper into the keep-sake box. She would take the paper with her tomorrow.

She had hoped the work would help her to sleep, but once in bed it was still not dark outside and she lay staring at the ceiling trying not to think about anything. It seemed hours later when she heard Marcus come in, talking softly to Fatty then coming upstairs. She closed her eyes pretending to be asleep, but he carried on past her door and into his own bedroom.

Hastings – July 1965

Joycie threw her bag onto the hotel bed and walked over to look out along the busy promenade and towards the Old Town of Hastings where the local fishing boats were drawn up on the shingle. It was a warm and cloudy afternoon and the grey-blue sea looked like pleated silk frilled with white at the shoreline. She picked up the phone to call Marcus.

In the end she had slept later than she meant to and he had woken her with some tea. He sat on the bed, not looking at her as he spoke. 'Are you still planning on the Hastings trip today?'

'Yes, I have to.'

'Well I don't want you going on your own, so I've called one of my mates. Andy Pugh, known him since school,' he said. 'Not much up top brain-wise, but he's a big bloke. Scrum half in the rugby first fifteen. You'll be safe with him.'

She pulled her fingers through her hair, not sure whether she was touched or annoyed. 'What did you tell him?'

He walked towards the door. 'I said you were being bothered by a fan. Told Andy to make himself visible, but to let you get on with some delicate family business you had to sort out down there. Don't worry, he won't ask questions; he never was the curious type.' As he opened the door a car horn sounded. 'That'll be him. Shall I tell him you're OK with it?'

'Of course, I'll get ready. Thank you, Marcus, I ...' But he was gone.

She dressed and packed quickly, listening to the two voices rumbling away downstairs. She'd call Marcus up here before they left and clear the air with him.

When she went down carrying her overnight bag Andy was sitting on the couch, long legs stretched out in front of him, the coffee cup looking tiny in his beefy hands.

He stood when he saw her. 'Hi there, Orchid, or should I call you Joyce like old Marky does?' Unlike Marcus, who overlaid his posh accent with a fake cockney twang, Andy was trying to disguise his with a kind of Elvis drawl.

'Joyce is fine. It's my real name and anyway ...'

'You want to keep a low profile.' He tapped the side of his nose. 'Understood.' He grabbed her bag as she looked around for Marcus. 'Marky's gone. Needed to get to the studio, says to phone him from the hotel.'

If Joycie had assumed Andy would be the strong and silent type she was wrong. He talked constantly in a surprisingly high-pitched voice as he drove his E-type Jag with delicate skill through the London traffic and along the winding country roads.

'I'm going to ring Marcus and then I want to look up an old

friend,' she said when they'd checked in. 'So shall we meet down here in an hour? And let's eat in the hotel tonight?'

Andy looked disappointed. He had been asking her about the nightlife in the town as they drove down.

'I was just a kid last time I was here so I wouldn't know.'

'Well the Mods and Rockers seem to love coming on bank holidays so it must be lively enough.'

Marcus had told Andy he needed to stick with her, but only when they went out. Joycie smiled and said. 'After dinner I want an early night so you can hit the town then.'

Chapter Nineteen

'Marcus all right?' Andy asked as they walked out of the hotel.

'There was no answer so he must still be at work.'

After ringing their home phone Joycie had tried the studio, but it was Saturday so there was probably no one in the office and Marcus and the models wouldn't hear it from where they were working. Joycie had given him the hotel's number, which was one reason she wanted to eat in the restaurant tonight. She mustn't miss a call from him.

She had remembered how to get to the lodgings they'd stayed in all those years ago, but the young woman who answered the door was clearly not Mrs Palmer. 'We bought the place from Mr Palmer after his wife passed away, I'm afraid.' The woman hadn't heard of either the Madison family or the boyfriend, Nigel Godwin, so it was a dead end.

Andy took Joycie's arm as they turned away, obviously interpreting her disappointment as shock. 'Are you OK, Joyce? Need a drink or something?'

'No, I'm fine. I didn't know Mrs Palmer well, she was just a friend of my mum.'

As they passed the pier Joycie looked away. Didn't want to remember the time she spent there. The days when her mum's absence felt so raw. On the other side of the road a sign for the public library caught her eye. She looked at her watch. It was five o'clock so it might still be open and she could check the electoral roll. The newspaper said Sharon Madison's mother lived in the Old Town and it was quite likely she was still there, which should narrow the search for an address. And the boyfriend, Nigel, was Sharon's childhood sweetheart, which meant there was a good chance he had lived nearby. With any luck he'd have stayed in the same area. Surely she could locate at least one of the two.

The library was airless and very warm. They were directed upstairs to the reference section and when Joycie asked for the voters' register the librarian handed her a book that was much thicker than she'd expected. A few large tables were dotted among the shelves. She headed for an empty one next to a rack of newspapers.

Andy was shifting from foot to foot beside her, looking totally out of place. She whispered, 'Why don't you have a wander for half an hour. Meet me outside. It looks safe enough in here,' and with a little salute and a look of profound relief he headed for the door.

She had borrowed a ruler from the girl behind the counter and when she found the Old Town section she worked through it street by street, moving the ruler down the addresses. It was slow going and by the time she'd been at it for five or six minutes her eyes were blurring and she had to look around for a few seconds to get them to focus again. An old man came to the newspaper rack beside her. He looked and smelled like a tramp and, sod's law, he settled at her table, sniffing loudly and rattling his paper. Every few minutes he gave a rasping cough accompanied by the occasional burp as gusts of old sweat and grime wafted over from him on the warm air.

At last she found an entry for Madison and, yes, the names were Stanley and Margaret. They could be Sharon's parents. And in the very next street there was a family called Godwin with two voters named Nigel: probably a father and son. She noted down the addresses and arrived at the library entrance as Andy was loping up to meet her.

'Hey, guess what?' he said, his voice soaring with excitement. 'They had PJ Proby on at the pier the other week. Shame we didn't come down then.'

She nodded, keeping her head down to hide her smile, and taking deep breaths of the fresh sea air.

At the hotel she went straight to her room. With any luck there would be time to phone Marcus and have a bath before meeting Andy for dinner. Her clothes seemed to carry the smell of the tramp on them so she stripped off, wrapped herself in a towel, and hung them near the open window. There was still no answer when she rang home and when she put down the receiver her stomach was churning. Was Marcus ignoring her? Had she upset him even more than she'd realized? But looking at her watch she told herself he was probably taking Fatty for her walk. She was being silly. They would be fine once they'd talked.

The cool bath was perfect after the sticky weather and, dressed only in her underwear, she lay on the bed to try Marcus again, but there was still no reply. She told herself he'd decided to eat out, that was all.

In the restaurant they were given a table by the window. The promenade was deserted, everyone having tea at home or in their guest houses. The sky had cleared to a translucent baby blue. The sea was motionless: a misted mirror of the sky above it. It was too lovely and Joycie wanted to cry, wishing Marcus was here.

Andy was busy studying the menu and she swallowed, blinked away the tears, and put on a smile. 'What are you having?'

'Roast beef for me and they've got my favourite for pud.' He rubbed his hands together and grinned showing huge white teeth. 'Rhubarb crumble and custard.'

The restaurant was busy with several groups apparently celebrating special occasions. They were all middle-aged or older and none of them seemed to recognize her. When she looked back outside she saw that coloured lights had come on along the promenade and the sea was a dark shadow. The prom was getting busy with holidaymakers again, in bright clothes and silly hats, and the melancholy air she'd imagined earlier had disappeared.

Andy swallowed down his roast beef with all the trimmings in a few minutes and while Joycie, who always thought of herself as a quick eater, chewed her overdone Barnsley chop, he gazed around, his foot tapping under the table, obviously desperate to get on to the rhubarb crumble. She asked for cheese and biscuits, but when it arrived – Jacob's cream crackers, a lump of cheddar, and a bit of dry Stilton – she pushed the plate towards him. He'd already wolfed down his crumble – 'Good grub this!' – and he demolished the cheese and biscuits with a large brandy as she drank her watery coffee.

'Tomorrow I need to visit a couple of people then we can leave whenever you're ready.'

'Shall we have lunch here?' he said and she nodded, although she wanted to get away as early as possible. The food would all go on her bill and he deserved that at least for coming with her.

Up in her room she reread the newspaper article then called home again. Still no answer. If he was in the darkroom he often didn't hear the phone, but why didn't he ring her?

She sat in bed trying to read an Agatha Christie paperback, but it was a creepy story about girls whose hair was falling out and a strange house where women practised witchcraft, and it made her feel unsettled.

Ten o'clock. Marcus should be back by now even if he'd been out for dinner. She let the phone ring and ring, but eventually had to hang up. He was on a tight deadline and it wasn't unknown for him to stay at the studio until late then work in the darkroom through the night.

***

If she slept at all Joycie wasn't aware of it, but the night passed eventually and when the sky began to lighten she got up and dressed. It was too early to ring Marcus and in a way she was relieved about that, wondering how she would feel, what she would say, if a girl picked up the phone or it was obvious he had someone there.

It was a brilliantly sunny morning and she was almost tempted to take a walk along the seafront on her own. She was pretty sure no one had followed the car down and there had been no sign of Bill or anyone like him in town yesterday. Bill's approach seemed to involve trying to intimidate her by making his presence obvious. So it looked as if they had managed to get away with it. Joycie had to hope so because she didn't want to put Sharon's family in danger and she told herself that if she spotted any suspicious characters today she wouldn't go to see them after all.

She had been flipping through the Sunday paper and now her hands were black with newsprint so she went back to her room, washed, grabbed the floppy hat she had brought as a gesture at disguise and stood looking at the phone for long minutes, her heart thumping hard and fast. Finally she grabbed it and dialled.

It rang and rang and she could almost hear it echoing through the empty house. It was nearly 8 a.m. and she told herself it was just possible that Marcus hadn't finished the shoot yesterday and was already back at the studio. More likely he was taking Fatty for a walk. But her knees were quivering as she walked down to the foyer again and the lump that had been lodged in her stomach all night was threatening to rise into her mouth. *Please, please, Marcus, call me.* Perhaps she had missed something from him yesterday.

The man at the desk shook his head. 'No messages for you, *Miss Todd.*' He laid emphasis on the name, just about resisting a wink.

Andy waved to her from the restaurant and she joined him. At least no one there seemed to take an interest in her. Andy was wearing a short-sleeved shirt with a floppy collar and thick stripes in purple and pink, reminding Joycie of a large and comfortable deck chair. He was eating a huge fried breakfast, liberally slathered with brown HP sauce, and the smell clashed with the whiff of stale booze from last night that hovered in the air.

Joycie pressed her napkin to her lips and asked for some toast and black coffee, but could only nibble on half a slice. She longed to tell Andy to drive her home right now, but that would make the whole visit pointless and she would have upset Marcus for nothing.

Andy, who had cleared his plate at lightning speed last night, seemed to take an age to eat his breakfast. Joycie pushed her plate and cup away, looked at her watch pointedly and told him she'd wait for him in the foyer.

'Oh right.' He folded a slice of toast and crammed the whole thing into his mouth, standing at the same time. 'Mustn't dawdle, eh? Lead on McDuff.'

His high-pitched American twang sounded even more ridiculous through a mouthful of toast and made Joycie grin despite her anxiety.

As they walked along the seafront the sun shone down hard and she was grateful for her big white hat. Andy mopped his face.

'Bloody hot.'

Joycie nodded, forcing herself to match his slow, slow pace even as her mind said, *hurry, hurry.* There was no point in rushing. The people she needed to see were likely to be having a Sunday morning lie-in and she'd promised Andy they'd have lunch at the hotel before leaving, but she longed to be back on the road and heading home to Marcus. At least Andy hadn't asked about him this morning.

The promenade was quiet in the heat haze. The only sound the low *shush, shush* from the sea: a sheet of blue glass rippled here and there with a few imperfections. There was certainly no one following them. They were passing the Italian café where she

used to eat with her dad in those weeks after her mum disappeared. It looked exactly the same and she had to turn away and
take a deep breath, but Andy was too busy looking at a couple
of girls in bikinis covering themselves with sun oil to notice.

When they reached the Old Town Joycie touched his arm. 'The
people I'm going to see are a bit shy of strangers so will you wait
at the end of the street? I won't be long.'

They were passing a pub and Andy glanced at it longingly but,
of course, it was closed until midday.

The house where Sharon Madison's parents lived was down a
narrow lane off the old High Street. It was a tiny terraced cottage,
and the door was opened very quickly by a woman who looked
to be in her fifties. She was wearing an apron and wiping her
hands on a towel. The smell of roasting meat came from inside
and the woman's face was shiny with the heat.

'Mrs Madison?' When she nodded, Joycie said, 'I lived here for
a while in the '50s and my older sister was a friend of your daughter,
Sharon. I've been looking up some other friends and they told me
Sharon had died and I just wanted to say how sorry I am.'

The woman's face was red, but white blotches stood out on
each side of her nose and she swayed and grabbed at the door
frame. *This was awful.* Joycie wanted to turn and run but it was
too late: the damage was done. Sharon's mother raised her eyes
and they were filled with tears, but her face was twisted in what
looked more like anger than grief.

'Did they say she killed herself or she was so drunk she fell
off the pier?'

What an idiot she was blundering in like this. 'I'm very sorry.
I didn't mean to upset you.'

She turned to go, but Mrs Madison touched her arm. 'I'm
sorry too, love. You didn't mean any harm. It's just that I have
to set people straight. That inquest was a joke. *Accidental
drowning*, they said.'

Joycie could hear her own heart thumping so hard she was

surprised the other woman didn't notice. *Careful, careful.* 'But you don't believe the verdict was right?' Mrs Madison looked at her, twisting the tea towel around her fingers. Joycie could see she wanted to talk. 'So what do you think really happened?'

The towel was tortured into a misshapen knot, the knuckles on Mrs Madison's hands standing out. She jerked her head towards the main street, speaking in that harsh half whisper again. 'He did it, that Nigel. Couldn't bear it 'cos she'd found someone else. Always was jealous of her.'

'So why didn't the police charge him?'

She raised her voice, glancing around as if wanting to be heard. 'Got his mates to lie for him. And it was what the police wanted to believe. Made it easier for them if no one was to blame.'

Joycie had been aware of Andy moving down the little lane towards them and now she turned and shook her head at him. He stood with his arms folded like a nightclub bouncer. Mrs Madison looked at him and began to shut her door. 'I've got dinner to make, can't stand here talking.'

Joycie said, 'I'm so sorry,' but the door was already closed and she didn't think the poor woman heard her.

'I thought you might be in trouble for a minute there,' Andy said when she joined him.

'She was a bit upset, but it's all right.' After Mrs Madison's reaction Joycie knew she needed to be more honest with Andy because if Sharon's mum was right Nigel Godwin might be dangerous.

As they walked towards his address she told Andy that she was really down here trying to find out what had happened to a young girl who had been a family friend and had died in suspicious circumstances. 'That was her mother and I'm going to talk to her boyfriend now. It all happened years ago, but I'm guessing he might have strong feelings about it too. So perhaps you'd better come to the door with me.'

Andy gave one of his mock salutes, clearly enjoying this. 'You're the boss, Joyce. Whatever you say.'

'I'm sure he'll be fine, but I'll feel happier with you beside me.'

That made him flush and look down to scuff at a pebble on the pavement.

Nigel Godwin's family lived only a few hundred yards from the Madisons. Their place was a flat above a hardware store. When Joycie knocked at the narrow door to the side of the shop window she heard heavy footsteps running downstairs. It was a man who answered, but too old to be the boyfriend. She smiled. 'I was hoping to see Nigel Godwin junior. Is he at home?'

The man, who was wearing an old-fashioned collarless shirt and an equally outdated pinstriped jacket, was almost as tall and broad as Andy. When he answered he was looking at Andy, not her. 'Who wants to know?'

She told the same story, but adding that her sister had known both Sharon and Nigel.

The man buttoned his jacket. 'Well she's dead and my son's working in London so you're wasting your time, darling.'

'I know about Sharon. I spoke to her mum.'

'Don't talk to me about that cow. My Nigel couldn't stay here because of the lies she spread. Telling everyone he had something to do with it.'

'What did Nigel think happened?'

'Like the inquest said, it was an accident. She fell off the pier. Probably drunk. Her mum tries to make out the girl was some kind of angel, but she led our Nigel a merry dance. Dumped him, really upset him.'

'You don't think she killed herself then?'

'Nah. Last time I saw her, couple of days before, she was dressed up to the nines and happy as Larry.'

She took a chance. 'I heard she went to the show on the pier. Did she go with Nigel?'

A harsh laugh. 'She did and he paid for the tickets, as well. Then she made him go round to the stage door. He said he felt like a right idiot.'

Joycie's heart gave a huge thump. 'Who did she want to see?'

'Some kind of singer, I think. Nigel said he looked like a proper poofter, but she was drooling over him. Now, do you mind, I've got to be somewhere.'

He pulled the door closed and pushed between Joycie and Andy. She shook her head at Andy, anxious he shouldn't make a fuss, and followed the man.

'Please Mr Godwin, just one more thing. Was the singer Sharon was interested in from the duo – The Bluebirds?'

'Don't know what they were called, but there was two of them 'cos Nigel said he sang with a nice-looking girl. So if he wasn't a poofter he was probably with her and Sharon was wasting her time anyway. But she wouldn't listen, said she'd read the programme and the girl was his sister.'

The journey home seemed to take forever. Andy kept up a non-stop commentary, for which Joycie was grateful. She was able to say the occasional yes and no while she thought about what she'd found out in Hastings, all the time trying to shut her mind to her worries about Marcus.

The main thing was that Sharon Madison had seen the show and gone round to the stage door afterwards. Even if it was Dennis she was interested in, not Joycie's dad, she could still have caught Sid's eye. Maybe Sid persuaded Dennis to invite her out with a group from the show or just waylaid the girl and offered to introduce her. And, of course, Dennis could know about it and that could be why they'd scared him off.

She told herself this was what she needed to focus on, but every time she let her guard down her thoughts came back to one thing: *Marcus, Marcus, Marcus*. What was wrong? And what would happen when she got home?

By the time they pulled into the street she was feeling sick. It was filled with bright sunshine. The white houses gleaming in the quiet emptiness of a lazy Sunday evening. But it was too quiet, too empty, and there was no sign of the Morgan outside the house. Marcus wasn't home.

She could hear Andy talking: 'Marky's out, I see. Must be still hard at it.' She sensed rather than saw him getting out of the car, grabbing her bag, opening her door. Was somehow able to take the bag, to smile and thank him. He had told her he had a date later that evening so she said, 'You get going. No point in waiting for Marcus. He could be hours yet.'

He looked at his watch. 'Sure you'll be all right?'

'Of course and thank you again. You've been wonderful.' She stood on tiptoe and kissed his warm cheek.

He blushed red, hovered awkwardly for a moment, did one of his little salutes and jumped back into the Jag. 'Ciao then, Joyce, say hi to Marky.'

He tooted his horn as he drove off, and she climbed the steps to the house, pulling her key slowly from her bag. The sound of the Jag's engine died away and the street fell silent again. Although it was less than two days, she felt as if she'd been away for weeks and almost expected Marcus to have changed the locks.

Inside she called out to him, although she knew there would be no answer. The kitchen door was closed – Fatty must be in there – at least someone would be glad to see her. She ran upstairs.

'Hello, anyone home?'

Her bedroom was just as she'd left it, the bed roughly made and her dressing gown thrown on top of the satin eiderdown. The door of Marcus's room was open, but the rumpled bed didn't tell her anything, because he'd used it the night before she went to Hastings.

She walked slowly down. No sign of a note in the sitting room, but maybe in the kitchen.

The kitchen was empty. Marcus must have taken Fatty with him, wherever he'd gone. Joycie picked up the kettle – she wasn't thirsty, but it was something to do. As she stood by the sink she saw a movement in the garden. It was Fatty: running up to the kitchen door and scratching at the wood.

When Joycie opened it the dog rushed in leaping and licking, tail wagging furiously. Finally she calmed down, panting and leaning her back against Joycie's calf. Her food and water bowls were just outside the back door. Marcus had obviously planned on being away for some time. Both bowls were empty, and when Joycie refilled them, putting them in their usual place on the kitchen floor, Fatty went first to the water.

Joycie made her tea and sat at the kitchen table, watching, as Fatty slurped up the water then turned to swallow down the meat. All the while keeping one eye on Joycie. 'You poor girl. Did that naughty Marcus leave you all alone?' She felt a sob rise in her throat as she said it, wondering if he'd left them both.

That was when she heard a car; the familiar sound of a Morgan drawing up outside. *What to do?* It might be best to stay where she was and let him make the first move. But, no, she would act normally. Go to the door, put her arms around him and wait for him to explain.

The top of the Morgan was up despite the warm sunshine, but she could make out two people inside. He wasn't alone. And when the passenger door opened a pair of slender legs in high heels slid out.

Joycie stepped back from the window, not breathing yet somehow aware of Fatty beside her pressed hard against her leg. The driver's door opened and for a moment she thought she'd made a mistake. The car wasn't Marcus's at all. But then she recognized the driver, although she'd met him only once. It was Marcus's father. And the woman: an elegant and well-preserved fifty-year-old, was his mother.

Joycie felt herself flush, as if she was an intruder, although Marcus's parents knew she was his *lodger*. They stood together for a moment beside the car, looking up at the house.

And the world seemed to jolt, turning fuzzy and out of focus, as Marcus's mother threw herself into her husband's arms and began to sob as if her heart was broken.

Chapter Twenty

The windows were dusty and, despite the bright sun, Marcus's parents seemed to be huddled in a blur of mist. Joycie was reminded of Irene's funeral service with its haze of incense, but there was no Latin chanting this time. No sound at all. The glass blocked everything. The world outside was utterly silent and Joycie felt as if she had become a pair of staring eyes, watching something terrifying.

When she was able to force her feet and hands to work and to open the front door she flinched and put up her hand to shade her eyes. No longer muted by the dusty window, the light was too bright.

Joycie had met Mrs Blake only once, but this was not the elegant and youthful woman she remembered. Her hair, big strands falling from the knot at the back of her head, looked more grey than blonde and as she came up the steps she clutched the railing, the bones and veins in her hands standing out sharply in the cruel light.

Mr Blake's silver hair was neatly slicked back, but he needed a shave and he too seemed shrunken. He looked up at Joycie as he followed his wife up the steps and made a shushing sound; whether to stop her from speaking or to comfort his wife, Joycie wasn't sure. Perhaps it was both.

She couldn't have spoken anyway. Couldn't bear to hear them speak. *Don't say it, don't say it, please don't.* All she could do was step aside and stand leaning against the front door, knowing her legs wouldn't support her if she tried to move.

Marcus's mother sat bolt upright on the sofa, staring into the distance through faded-denim eyes. His father stood behind her and gave Joycie a gentle smile. It was no good. This was happening and she had to let herself hear it. She looked back at him with a tiny nod. He rubbed his wife's shoulder and coughed, but before he could speak Mrs Blake shook her head and pressed her hand over his.

'My son, Marcus ...' Her voice quavered. '... this house was broken into last night and my son beaten so badly he's in a coma.'

A coma, a coma. He's not dead, thank God. She had opened the door before she knew what she was doing. She had to get to him.

But his mother was speaking again. 'If he does come round he may never be the same.'

Her hand went to her mouth. She had short neat nails and Joycie could hear Marcus's voice telling her that his mother rode her horse every day. 'Loves that thing more than me and certainly more than Dad.' *I'm coming, Marcus, I'm coming.* She turned back to the door.

'Only next of kin allowed to visit for now, my dear.' His father's words came from far, far away. 'We're just here to get a few bits and pieces he might need.' He went over to the drinks cabinet and held up a bottle of Scotch. 'May I?' Joycie managed to nod at him and he filled a glass, the bottle clinking on the side.

Mrs Blake's voice was needle-sharp this time. 'They say it was something to do with drugs. There were drugs in the house.' She shook her head with a sound that was half sigh, half angry gasp.

'It's not the girl's fault, Blanche. She wasn't even here.' He gulped from his drink.

Blanche – the name suited her – swayed when she stood,

steadying herself with a hand on the arm of the sofa. 'I'll go and collect those things for him. We want to be back for visiting hour.'

'I'd like to come to the hospital.' Joycie's voice sounded too loud.

Mrs Blake turned at the foot of the stairs. 'They won't let you see him.'

Was she angry? Joycie registered what she'd said about drugs in the house. Marcus never bought drugs. They'd smoked a joint or two at parties and that was all, but this wasn't the time for arguments. She picked up her handbag.

'Where is he?'

Mr Blake gave a smile that was so like Marcus's it sent a spike of agony through Joycie's heart. 'It's St Thomas's Hospital, my dear, but as Blanche said we're the only ones allowed to see him and then only for a short while.'

'I'll take a taxi,' Joycie said.

It was true. They wouldn't let her see Marcus; wouldn't even tell her which ward he was in. So all she could do was hang around in the cavernous hospital entrance hall. It was gloomy with dark walls and a chilly tiled floor. Empty except for an occasional nurse in her white starched apron and cap hurrying past. Finally Marcus's parents arrived. His dad, carrying a small leather holdall, smiled a weary smile at her, but his mother pretended to be searching for something in her bag.

Joycie sat on a bench and waited. It was her fault, although not at all in the way Mrs Blake seemed to think. She had no doubt this was Bill or those he worked for. They had planted the drugs so that only she would know why they had attacked Marcus. Why, why, had she carried on after his threats? Why had she imagined she was the only one in danger? They'd taken Fatty, hadn't they?

She wondered about Fatty for a moment. Couldn't remember if she'd left her in the house or the garden. And who had shut her out there with food and drink? If Marcus had been attacked in the house that meant he was home, so why would he do that?

After what seemed an age, but was probably less than an hour, Marcus's parents came back. They were with a man in a crumpled grey suit: tall, solid, early thirties. He didn't look like a doctor. Joycie stood up and this time Marcus's mother looked straight at her.

'This is my son's colleague and lodger,' she said.

The man smiled at her, his face flushing in a way that told Joycie he knew who she was. 'I'm Inspector Flynn from the Metropolitan Police. I wonder if I could have a word with you, Miss …?'

'Todd, Joyce Todd.'

Marcus's mother moved away, but his father touched Joycie's arm and spoke softly. 'There's no change. They say they'll call us at the hotel if anything happens.'

'You're not going to sleep at the house?'

'No, no, we'll leave you in peace.'

Marcus's mother was already standing by the row of swing doors at the entrance. She turned back when Joycie spoke.

'Please, will you phone me when you hear?'

The smallest nod and a glance at her husband, who squeezed Joycie's arm. 'Of course we will, right away.'

After they'd gone Joycie sat on the bench again, too weak to stand. The policeman sat very close to her. She could feel the warmth from him and smell a hint of Old Spice. He rubbed his hands over his knees, the rough material of his trousers making a noise that set Joycie's teeth on edge.

'So.' His voice echoed in the big tiled foyer and a doctor in a white coat, stethoscope hanging from his pocket, turned to look. Inspector Flynn twisted towards Joycie and spoke more quietly. 'You don't call yourself Orchid in normal life, then?'

'No, that's just for modelling.'

'You've known Mr Blake for several years, I gather.'

'Yes, he gave me my first break and we've worked together a lot since.' She had to tell him everything – about Bill and the rest of it. Should have talked to the police before. But now she must make sure they didn't get away with it. A deep breath, then: 'I think I know who did this and why.'

Inspector Flynn smiled. It was a sweet smile. She thought she might be able to trust him.

'That's great news, Miss Todd. I've called a car to pick me up so what say we stop off at the station and you can tell me everything? Make a statement then I'll get someone to take you home.'

The police car pulled up just as they came out of the doors. Inspector Flynn shepherded Joycie into the back and joined the PC in front. Joycie leaned back and closed her eyes, too tired even to think about Marcus. She must have dozed because the next thing she was aware of was the car doors opening and the PC getting out.

Inspector Flynn opened her door and leaned in. 'I'll be a minute or two, but I'll organize a cup of tea while you wait.'

She followed him, still dazed with sleep, and he led her to a small room with a table and a few wooden chairs. When he left she rested her head on the table, but almost immediately a young WPC came in with a cup rattling in its saucer. The tea was weak and not all that hot and the thick white cup had a chip in it, but Joycie was so thirsty she drank it down quickly. Longing to get this over with and go home.

Inspector Flynn came in and she spoke as he pulled out a chair opposite her.

'It was a man named Bill who did this to Marcus.'

'And his other name?'

'I don't know, but I could describe him. He's a gangster and I think he's with Ernie Georgiou's mob.' Inspector Flynn nodded, seemed to be taking it seriously, although she knew how flimsy it must seem. 'He's been threatening me, you see, and he kidnapped our dog.' Her voice sounded high and silly in the cold bare room and even when the inspector smiled, encouraging her to go on, she began to doubt she could make him understand.

'You see my mother disappeared and I started to think someone had killed her, but when I talked to people about it this Bill threatened me.'

'Your mother disappeared? When was this?'

'Oh, a long time ago, 1953.'

He leaned forward, forearms on the table. 'So what's this got to do with the drugs? Was Bill Marcus's supplier?'

'No, of course not. Marcus doesn't take drugs.'

Inspector Flynn was looking hard into her eyes now. His were so dark as to seem black with no visible pupil. He spoke slowly, as if to a child. 'Miss Todd, Joyce, we found a large amount of cannabis in your house as well as quantities of illegal pills. So the likelihood is that Marcus was beaten for not paying up or maybe for selling to his mates. Stepping on the toes of the big boys.'

It was difficult to breathe. She stared down at the scratched tabletop and the pale rings left by endless cups of tea. She could feel his eyes boring into her. What a fool she was. Their minds were already made up. There was no point in going on, but she had to try.

'Where were these drugs?'

'In the darkroom, which was where the attack took place. So it's likely they'd just been delivered.'

'Marcus doesn't buy drugs or sell them.'

Flynn leaned back and folded his arms. 'His parents say the same.'

'They're right.'

'But then parents are always a bit naive, aren't they? Old-fashioned and out of touch.' He chuckled. 'I mean, they think you and Marcus are just flatmates.' Joycie folded her arms too, trying to calm her breathing. She was still staring down at the table, but she could hear the smile in his voice. 'And Marcus's mother claims the drugs must have belonged to you.'

Her heart began to drum. She wanted to jump up and run out, but would she be allowed to? A vision of handcuffs and police cells. *Keep calm, talk firmly.* 'Neither of us has ever bought or sold drugs of any kind, Inspector.'

'It's possible, though isn't it, that Marcus kept them in the darkroom to make sure you didn't find them.'

His smile said he was offering her a way out, but she shook her head. 'We have no secrets from each other and as I told you, I've been threatened because I was delving into my mother's disappearance and those of two young girls.'

'Okaaay.' That smile was still in his voice. 'And you'd like to make a statement about all this, would you?'

'Yes.'

He went out and returned a moment later with a uniformed policewoman, who carried a large writing pad.

'WPC Williams here will take down your statement.'

While she talked he leaned back in his chair, arms folded, watching her. No expression on his face even when she described how Sid Sergeant had attacked her and that she thought he might have killed her mother and the girl in Hastings. It took a long time to go through the whole thing and the WPC stopped to rub her wrist a couple of times. By the end Joycie felt sick.

When she'd finished Inspector Flynn said, 'Please sign if this is a true record of your statement.' As she was reading through the pages he said, 'The problem is that all this happened a long time ago and from what you've told us no one seemed to think there was anything suspicious at the time. There are no investigations to reopen and I'm afraid I'd need to have some pretty solid evidence to start one.'

She scribbled her signature and looked up at him. 'And the threats to me and the attack on Marcus aren't good enough?'

'If we can find this Bill you've accused and are able to link him to the assault on Mr Blake we'll put those charges to him, of course.'

'What about Sid Sergeant?'

'The advances he made to you were obviously unpleasant, but we have only your word to go on and you weren't actually hurt were you? And you say there are no witnesses. So I doubt we'd get anywhere with that.'

It was hopeless; just as she'd told Marcus it would be. She stood. 'Can I go? I need to be home in case Mrs Blake calls with news from the hospital.'

'Of course. Thank you for your help. It's been very interesting. I'll have a closer look at your statement and see if there is anything we can move on but, as I say, it's all a long time ago. We may have to talk to you again, but if you wait there a minute I'll get someone to drive you.' And he smiled that sweet useless smile again.

When Joycie arrived home in the police car, the elderly next door neighbours came out to talk to her. They had overheard the sound of Marcus's attack and became alarmed in the silence that followed. Marcus's parents had left a spare key with them so the old man let himself in when his knocks brought no response.
Joycie didn't really know them, but found herself sitting on their lumpy sofa with a cup of sweetened tea as they explained that they discovered Marcus unconscious in his darkroom and called the emergency services and his parents. 'I'm sorry we didn't know how to contact you, my dear,' the old lady said. She gave a little shiver. 'And to be honest we were so shocked we weren't thinking straight. You don't imagine something like that happening around here.'

The old man took his wife's plump hand. 'We were so upset. We've known Marcus since he was a boy.' He looked at her from under bushy white eyebrows. 'You haven't been into that room have you?'

When Joycie shook her head he said, 'Well don't go now. Just keep the door closed and leave it.'

His wife smiled at her. 'And don't even think of trying to clear up. I'll send my cleaning lady over to sort it out for you.'

Of course as soon as she could get away she went straight to the darkroom. She stood in the doorway, her hand pressed against her mouth, relying on the light from the hall to show Marcus's chair tipped on its side, the floor littered with photographs and negatives and the overturned bottles on the worktop. It was when she saw the dark stain on the floor that she flinched back and slammed the door shut.

She spent the rest of the evening downstairs staring at the silent phone until she decided she should try to sleep. She let Fatty come with her; couldn't bear to be alone in the bedroom. And when Fatty jumped up next to her she didn't push her down. After one thump of her tail Fatty fell asleep. Joycie could only lie dead tired but wide awake.

Would Marcus's parents actually call if they heard anything? Wasn't it likely that good news or – *please God, no* – bad news would drive everything else from their minds? And she wasn't even sure that Mrs Blake would want her to know.

She swung her feet to the floor. Couldn't lie still any longer. Fatty let out a little growl of protest, but stayed where she was. Dragging on her candlewick dressing gown, Joycie headed downstairs. She'd ring the hospital herself and *make* them tell her how he was. But she stood, her arms clutched round her, looking at the phone. What if it was bad? Could she bear to know?

She grabbed the directory and looked up St Thomas's Hospital, her trembling hands tearing the thin paper of one of the pages. She copied the number onto the telephone pad, heart beating so hard it was difficult to breathe, and dialled. But when she heard ringing on the other end she dropped the phone back onto its cradle. Hot tears flooded her eyes.

How long she stood there she couldn't tell, but eventually she found herself in the kitchen. As she waited for the milk to boil for coffee her eyes were fixed on the lurid curtains with their ugly patterns of onions and tomatoes. They made the kitchen seem so much smaller and airless, but she didn't dare to open them.

When she saw she'd got out two cups, as always, a sob rose from somewhere deep inside. It hurt with a pain as real as any she'd ever felt, and she pressed her hand to her chest where something seemed to be rupturing. The misery she'd been feeling all these hours felt more like terror now.

A sound from the garden, and the flare of a different kind of fear. She went towards the stairs to call Fatty down, but all was quiet. She had imagined it. She opened a cupboard and stopped. A definite noise now – something rattling – very close by. She spun around, staring at the back door handle.

The rattle was coming from there as someone tried to open it.

Chapter Twenty-One

The back door was locked; she'd checked it enough times yesterday to be certain of that. But the rattling continued and there was no bolt at the bottom. Whoever was there must know she was here because of the light. She reached behind her. All the knives were in a drawer, way out of reach, but she was able to grab the handle of the milk pan. The milk was boiling hot. Her heart beat a heavy thump, thump, thump in her ears.

The door opened – Bill – as dapper as always. His face the same shiny mask. She pressed back against the sink gripping the pan handle tight.

He closed the door carefully, all the time holding her stare. One hand was behind him and Joycie heard that rattling again. He was relocking the door. Trapping her.

'We need to talk.'

His voice was as soft as ever. It was a voice that always made Joycie want to scream and run away, but today she had to be strong. She set her jaw, fighting the urge to speak because if she did she was likely to cry.

'How's Marcus doing?' It was almost a whisper.

'Have you killed him, you mean?' Her voice didn't quaver, thank God, although her knees felt like water.

'I hope not, Orchid love, I really do hope not.'

A surge of anger. 'So you hurt him more than you intended, did you?'

He moved towards the sitting room and she lifted the pan behind her back. *Now Joycie, now.*

But then: 'I shouldn't do anything silly,' he said, turning back with a shake of his head and gesturing for her to go into the sitting room ahead of him.

Don't cry. She shook her hair over her face so he wouldn't see the tears of rage and frustration. She wanted to hurt him, to beat some kind of reaction onto that perfectly shaven face. Instead she followed him and when he sat on the sofa, feet in their shiny shoes stretched out in front, she crouched on the armchair opposite.

He gave a deep sigh, rubbing his chin and shaking his head at the same time. 'Marcus shouldn't have been here. The plan was to plant the stuff, let the police know where to find it and Bob's your uncle.'

'But Marcus was in the darkroom.'

'I could have handled him without too much bother, without doing him any real damage, but I had a young lad with me and, well, your boy put up a fight. Got my lad riled.'

'So none of it was your fault?' She hated her voice for quivering.

He wasn't even looking at her now, but smiling up at the stairs and a tousled Fatty plodding her way down. 'How's my girl,' he said, holding out one hand. Fatty ran up to lick him and let herself be stroked. Her expression was half ecstatic, half embarrassed.

Still stroking her, Bill said, 'Don't blame the dog. She got to know me when we had her for those few hours. Couldn't defend her master because we'd already shut her in the kitchen.'

'So it was you who put her in the garden with food and water?' His nod brought a surge of hatred. 'You took care of the dog, but left Marcus to die.'

Another of those headshakes. 'That was different. And we alerted the coppers.'

'So they would find the drugs. Am I meant to thank you?'

A tight smile, looking at Fatty as he stroked her head and she leaned against his knee. Then silence. Joycie let it go on as long as she could bear, but the words forced themselves out.

'So what now?'

Bill carried on stroking. Finally he leaned away and rubbed his palms together very slowly. After one longing look at him Fatty lay by his feet and closed her eyes. Joycie bit the inside of her cheek to stop herself from speaking. Watching Bill's hands as he slid them back and forth, back and forth. He was looking at them too until one finger shot out to point at Joycie and she found herself forced to meet his pale eyes.

'Whatever happens to Marcus is out of our hands now,' he said, 'but there's still the drugs. And you two are going to get it in the neck for them unless I help you out.'

'And you can do that?'

'Of course. All you've got to do is stop all this rubbish about Sid Sergeant. Concentrate on looking after your boyfriend and leave me to sort the cops.'

Nothing mattered any more but Marcus. 'All right.' She sank back into the armchair.

When he stood Fatty raised her head and he rubbed her back with the tip of his gleaming shoe. 'I knew you'd see sense in the end. Just a shame it took so long.' He held out his hand.

She stood to face him. Wanting to shout at him to get out and leave her alone. Instead she took the cold, smooth hand.

'Believe it or not,' he said, 'I've got fond of you and I'd hate to see you hurt.'

She pulled her hand away. Something about that touch had filled her with so much rage she was no longer scared. 'I've been hurt already, Bill.' She used his name deliberately and for the first time felt in control. 'Hurt so much that I'll never get over it. Hurt by the man you're helping. And I'm not the only one.' He rubbed his jaw as if checking for stubble on his shiny cheek. She went on. 'Sid Sergeant tried to rape me when I was fourteen. Did you know that? And I think he raped my friend so she had to have the backstreet abortion that killed her. He may have murdered another girl in Hastings, and I'm sure he was behind my mother's death and probably my dad's too.' She couldn't stop the tears now. *Damn, damn it.*

His face was grim. 'There's bad people in the world, love. And they're the ones with the power.'

'Only because people like you help them.'

He nodded and shrugged, glancing back at Fatty, who ambled over to lean against him again.

Joycie gave a little laugh that was half sob. 'But you don't need to worry. There was never any way I could stop him. He'll go on hurting girls and using you or someone like you to help him get away with it. Now, would you please go and leave me alone so I can call the hospital.'

He headed for the kitchen and she followed him. When he opened the back door he handed her the key. 'You'd better have this. We got it copied.'

She didn't want to ask him, but couldn't stop herself: 'How did you do that?'

'You thought you were being so careful, with the dog and all that, but you should lock the door even when you're in.'

'I do.'

'Not every time and just once is enough. It only takes a second to get an impression of a key.'

That day she had been upstairs with Fatty and came down to find the back door open. The cigarette smell. She folded her arms tight over her chest, squeezing the key so tightly it hurt her fingers.

He turned away. 'There's just that one duplicate, as far as I know, but you should get some bolts too and maybe change the locks.' When he'd opened the door he paused and seemed about to say something more, but shook his head instead, and she watched until he disappeared into the dark at the end of the garden.

No phone call came from Marcus's parents and, despite her pleas, the hospital wouldn't tell her anything, but by 8 a.m. Joycie couldn't wait around any longer. She got ready and walked Fatty, filling the time before visiting hours started. When 10 a.m. finally arrived Joycie took a taxi to the hospital, determined to get in to see him. She had dressed inconspicuously in black slacks and flat pumps with a plain blue blouse, no make-up, and her hair tied back. It looked like news of the attack had got out – there was a little group of men with cameras on the road outside – but no one seemed to notice her.

She didn't try to ask where Marcus was this time, just waited on a bench in a corner of the foyer until Mr and Mrs Blake walked through the doors. She held a magazine in front of her face until they passed, then followed them.

He was in a private room, and when his parents went in she headed back to the foyer to wait until they left. They were in there for the full hour and a half while she paced up and down, flipping through the magazine and watching the visitors, doctors, and nurses passing through the various doors or up and down the stairs. Eventually Mr and Mrs Blake walked out and she went back to Marcus's room.

At the door she almost turned away. This wasn't Marcus. The person in the bed was dark-skinned, his face very plump. But, with a jolt that had her clutching at the end of the bed frame to keep standing, she realized his face was so bruised and swollen it was unrecognizable. His head was bandaged and so were his hands, lying absolutely still on the covers, but the name on the chart was Marcus Blake all right.

'Oh, baby, I'm so sorry.'

She sat on the hard wooden chair by the bed and began to

talk to him, hardly knowing what she said. Telling him she was here and he would be better soon. She said Fatty was missing him, wanting him home again. All that mattered was that he should get better. 'Come back to me please, my darling, I love you so much,' she said as the tears that had been hurting her chest and throat forced their way out.

After that all she could do was to sit and stroke a small area of his forearm: the only part of him that was not bruised, bandaged, or hidden under the bedcovers.

The door opened and a young nurse in her neat striped dress and starched apron and cap stopped and stared, her face and neck mottling bright pink. She was carrying an enamel kidney bowl, which must have held something metal or glass because it rattled as her hand shook.

'Oh, I'm sorry, Miss, Miss Orchid, is it? I think it's only family allowed to visit.'

'Yes, of course. I just had to see him for a minute. Please don't tell.'

The girl giggled. 'I won't if you won't, but sister will be here soon so you should …'

Joycie stood. 'I'll go.' The last thing she wanted was get the nurse into trouble, but she had to ask. 'Do you know how he is?'

'No change. I'm really sorry, but that's all the doctors are saying.'

The shock began to set in when she was in the taxi. Surely that hadn't been Marcus so still and swollen back there. She thought of him running through the park with Fatty. Laughing when a shoot was going well. Stomping about, changing lenses and shouting at her to wake up and make an effort, when things weren't working. And holding her, kissing her. His lips, oh his poor torn lips. It looked like they'd knocked out some of his teeth and his familiar smile flashed into her mind, white and whole again, bringing the tears choking up from deep inside.

220

She was aware of the taxi driver looking at her in his mirror, but she couldn't stop crying. At the house she shoved some money at him. 'Sorry, sorry, keep the change.' Ran up the steps; scrabbling to open the front door and cursing as she dropped her keys and had to try again.

She went straight upstairs to lie on the bed, clutching the pillow and sobbing until she was exhausted, while Fatty paced beside her, letting out little yelps of distress.

When she'd cried herself dry she lay staring at the ceiling with swollen eyes until Fatty's yelps turned into whines and she had to force herself downstairs to open the back door and drag a can of dog food from the cupboard. There was nothing she could do now but wait for the phone call from Marcus's parents. The call she longed for – and dreaded.

Fatty wolfed down her food and was soon up on the sofa, her head on Joycie's lap. As Joycie stroked her she saw the newspaper on the mat by the door. She must have stumbled over it as she came in. There was a photo of Marcus in one corner of the front page. *Photographer in coma after attack.* The story was brief, talking about a break-in at *his luxury Chelsea home* and that he was *famous for his partnership with top model, Orchid.* No mention of drugs, at least.

The phoned shrilled through the silence. *Please God, please God.* 'Hello.' *Don't say it, please don't say it.*

A man's voice, but not Mr Blake, and for more than a moment she couldn't make out what he was saying. '… wondered if you have any news of Marcus, Orchid, darling. Or anything to say about what's happened. You live there with him, don't you?'

She couldn't speak, couldn't think – finally hearing her own voice. 'Who is this? What do you want?'

'*Daily Express,* love. It's a difficult time for you I know, but our readers would love to hear how the poor chap is getting on.'

She replaced the phone very slowly in its cradle, hardly able to keep standing.

The next two days passed in a daze. The phone rang several times. More newspapers wanting her story, but she had to answer in case it was the Blakes. When Marcus's dad did call he just said there was no change and still only family visitors allowed.

She managed to sneak in again and see him the next morning, sitting holding his hand for ten minutes, hardly able to speak to him through her tears because she was certain he looked even worse than he had done on the first day. But the next time Mr Blake called he told her, 'They've had to move Marcus's room because reporters have been trying to get to him.'

She waited in the foyer for what seemed hours after that, but didn't catch sight of the Blakes again so had no idea where the new room might be.

On the afternoon of the third day she took Fatty for a walk, keeping her on her lead and sticking to the streets although she knew the poor dog was desperate for a run in the park. When she got home she found an envelope on the mat. There was no stamp or address, just the name: *Joyce Todd*. Delivered by hand so it was probably another approach from a newspaper and she was tempted to put it straight in the bin, but she tore it open.

My dear, dear Joyce,

I read about what happened to poor Marcus and I'm so very sorry. You may have heard from Kay that I've been threatened myself and that's why I've been lying low. However I can't keep being a coward and I feel I owe it to you and to dear Charlie's memory to set the record straight about Mary, your mum.

I realize this isn't the best of times for you to leave town, but I daren't come there. In fact I've decided to go abroad and I'm leaving very soon. For my safety and yours I can't tell you where I'm staying, but if you take the 7.15 train for Uckfield from Victoria tonight and get off at a village called Eridge I'll see you there. Just cross over and wait on the London-bound platform.

Please come on your own and make sure you're not followed!

Joyce, sweetheart, do try to get there. I won't be able to rest until you know everything.

Yours ever,

Dennis.

Chapter Twenty-Two

No change expected, no change expected, no change expected – the train wheels seemed to be chanting Mr Blake's words. He'd rung just after she found Dennis's note to say the doctors were sure nothing would happen overnight. She'd been telling herself that she couldn't leave town for even a few hours, but it seemed almost as if Marcus was giving her permission to go. Though she needed to be extra careful, like Dennis said.

Before she left the house she closed all the curtains and left the light on in the living room, the radio playing in the kitchen. Then she put on a dark dress and tied a silk scarf over her hair.

She had time to walk to Victoria Station, but instead she headed towards Sloane Square Tube, doubling back on herself a couple of times. The station was busy, but she took the tube in the wrong direction: getting off at Earls Court where it was even busier before crossing the platform to go to Victoria. At the ticket office in the mainline station she bought a return all the way to Uckfield hoping to confuse anyone who might be lurking behind her in the queue.

By the time she was on the 7.15 she was almost sure she had avoided being followed. But as she watched the countryside slide by her heart began to beat faster and her mouth grew dry. The sky was splashed with orange and red. She was alone in the carriage and the world outside looked empty too. Everyone staying in because they could feel a storm in the air.

It was ridiculous to imagine that Marcus would want her to do this. He'd tell her she was putting herself in danger. And how could the doctors really know that nothing would happen to him before morning? They'd probably only said that to reassure the Blakes. As the train pulled into a station she put her hand on the door. She'd get off here and go straight back.

But something stopped her. This might be her last chance to find out the truth about her mum. And if she could do that at least it would mean that all the hurt she'd brought onto other people hadn't been for nothing. She owed it to Marcus, and to poor Dennis.

She sat back, feeling sick and tearing at a piece of loose skin near her thumbnail. When she looked down there was blood on her hand. She sucked it off, but was back to worrying at it right away. She slipped her hand under her thigh, feeling the rough pile of the seat press into the sore place, but keeping it there despite the pain.

The carriage was gloomy and there were banks of dark cloud ahead. This was all wrong. She had promised Bill she was done with probing into the past and she couldn't bear to think what might happen if he found out she was meeting Dennis. Marcus might not even be safe in his hospital bed.

The train whistled and they slowed to a crawl. Would Dennis wait if they were delayed? And what could he tell her anyway? If it was just backstage gossip that would be no use. If he'd seen something himself it would only help if he was prepared to talk to the police. She hoped he might have some actual evidence to give her, but after Bill's visit she wasn't sure she would dare take it to Inspector Flynn.

The train moved on fast for a few minutes, rattling over the points, then with a long moan from the wheels and a shriek of brakes they pulled into Eridge. She was the only passenger to get out and when she slammed the door the crash echoed all around. But as she made her way over the footbridge she heard a blackbird singing somewhere close by.

'Evening, Miss. Looks like rain, don't it?'

She jumped at the voice, but as she came down the steps she saw the stationmaster pottering about in a little garden next to the main entrance and ticket office.

'You won't find a taxi at this time of day,' he said, straightening up and rubbing his hands together.

'It's all right, I'm going straight back. Just meeting a friend here.'

'You'll have a wait. The next London train's not for nearly an hour and it's the last one tonight.' He threw his trowel and rake into the wheelbarrow beside him and she was relieved when he said, 'Cheerio then,' and trundled it along the platform to the little house at one end. She suspected Dennis would want to avoid being seen.

She sat on a bench and waited as the sky turned from red and orange to purple, the dark clouds building more and more. It was so quiet. Even the blackbird had stopped singing. She couldn't sit still so she paced up and down the platform for a few minutes. Then walked out through the ticket office.

Outside was as deserted as the platform. Just an empty space covered in gravel, edged by bushes and trees. The village, if there was a village, must be some distance away. There was a lovely smell of cut grass in the air, but she thought she could also detect the scent of rain on its way. Back on the platform she sat on the bench again. Day was shading into twilight, but it was still warm. Joycie closed her eyes. She was so tired.

A car door slamming and footsteps walking through the ticket office jolted her awake. She stood, trying to force a smile for Dennis.

The door opened and she felt her face grow rigid.

Because it wasn't Dennis.

Even as Joycie realized who it was, she struggled to believe her eyes. Cora was dressed, as always, in a too-tight skirt with black stilettos, but she seemed to have aged ten years since Joycie last saw her. Her red lipstick was smudged and there was a streak of mascara under one eye that reminded Joycie of a clown's painted tear.

She tottered over and sat on the bench, leaning back with a huge sigh. Joycie thumped down at the other end, unable to do more than stare.

'So you came.' The words were slurred and Cora's eyes were fixed on something in the distance.

'Did *you* send me the note? Not Dennis?'

A laugh or cough, it was impossible to tell. 'Knew you wouldn't come if I asked you.'

'Where is Dennis?'

'Search me. Hiding out somewhere like the snivelling little worm he always was, I expect.'

Joycie's stomach twisted. 'What do you want?' she said.

Cora's eyes were glazed. 'He's dead.' It was almost a whisper and for a fraction of a second Joycie's heart shuddered. But it couldn't be Marcus.

'Do you mean Sid? Sid is dead?' she asked. The hint of a nod. 'What happened to him?'

The eyes focused, boring into Joycie. The voice rasping. 'You should know.'

'What do you mean?'

'What do you mean? What do you mean?' It was a high-pitched trill; a bad imitation of Joycie's voice. 'Butter wouldn't melt, would it? I should have known you'd get round him with your sob stories. I can just hear it now. "Poor little me. That nasty Sid was cruel to me. It wasn't my fault. I was just a little girl. I couldn't have led him on."'

'Cora, what are you talking about?'

A lamp had come on just over the bench and Cora's eyes glittered with dark tears. 'You got him killed. Run down in the street like a dog. And the bastard will get away with it.'

A cold hand around her heart and she could only say. 'Who do you mean?' No answer, but she had guessed anyway. 'Was it Bill?'

'You told him a pack of lies and the stupid sod was taken in. I warned Sid not to get Bill or any of them involved this time. Told him to let me deal with it.' Her voice was bitter. 'But, no, "It's Charlie's girl," he said. "Bill can give her a fright. That's all we need."'

Her sob was a groan of pain. She pulled a hankie already blotched with lipstick from her bag and blew her nose.

Joycie reached out again. 'Cora, I'm sorry, I ...'

'Don't you touch me.' She pulled back and the handkerchief fell to the platform: a white bird, shot through with red. She turned to stare away down the line. 'He was everything to me. There's nothing left now.' The rasping voice was softened by tears. 'Oh, I knew there were others, but he only ever loved me.'

The pity Joycie had been feeling dissolved in a fierce surge of anger. 'I was just a kid when he forced himself on me, Cora. I wasn't one of *the others* as you call them. I wasn't much more than a child.'

'You weren't too young to lead a man on. Don't think I didn't see it – from you and the rest of them.'

Joycie's anger forced her to keep going. Cora had to know everything; to understand what Sid really was. 'But he did other things, dreadful things, Cora, and you need to face that. I think he killed people. Murdered my mum and a girl in Hastings.'

Those eyes were on her again, the tears gone. Only the darkness remaining. The tiniest smile playing on the smeared lips.

And Joycie's insides clenched as she saw the truth. 'You?' It came out as a gasp.

'Sid was too soft. Never understood what evil cows women can be.'

Oh God, oh God. Joycie was on her feet wanting to run away, but needing to stay. She stared down at Cora. Seeing the same blowsy drunk she always had, but so, so, different.

When she had forced her brain to work again she managed to say, 'But why bring me here? Why are you telling me now?'

'Because he's gone. Sid's gone so none of it matters any more.'

A gust of booze and stale perfume as she stood turning to look up at the clock hanging just in front of the departures board. Joycie followed her gaze. Fifteen minutes until the London train.

She had to calm her racing heart. Had to hear it all.

'The girl in Hastings. That was you?'

Cora's eyes were fixed far into the distance along the track; her voice a monotone that Joycie struggled to hear. 'It was an accident. Poor Sid came running home. He'd met her on the pier after the show. They had a few drinks and things got out of hand. She knocked herself out somehow. He was frantic so I went to see what I could do. The little tart was staggering about in the dark. I tried to help her, but she was saying terrible things about my Sid, threatening all sorts. I couldn't let her carry on like that. I was just trying to shut her up.'

'And?'

A shrug. 'She fell.'

'And you just left her there?' It was difficult to breathe.

'What could I do? It was dark and the sea was rough. No one could have helped her – the state she was in.'

As she spoke Cora had been pacing slowly forward, still staring down the track. Now she looked up at the clock again, and Joycie went cold. Saw what she was planning.

Ten minutes until the train. No sign of the stationmaster.

A lump of something hard as rock was lodged in Joycie's chest. She wanted to scream, but she had to keep control. 'Please come and sit down so we can talk properly.' But Cora didn't move, and

Joycie had to find out. 'My mum?' Her voice broke on the words, but she carried on. 'Did my mum guess?'

'Silly bitch came to see me. She'd read about the girl in the paper and said she thought Sid had something to do with it.'

'And you killed her too?' Even as she said it a tiny hope flickered.

'I didn't want to. Came to your place that night to talk some sense into her.' Cora turned back, speaking more clearly. 'It was quick, if that's what's bothering you. Used a sharp knitting needle. I did a bit of nursing in the war and if you know the right spot there's not much blood. Just a bit on the mat.'

That painful lump was in Joycie's throat now. She felt she might choke, but had to hear it all.

'I knew the landlady went to her daughter's on Wednesday nights and I arranged to go then. The rest of the lodgers were all in our show so the house was empty except for you and your mum. She told me to come after you were in bed, which was perfect. She had to open the main door to me herself. Was surprised to see I'd come by car. But I'd brought an old blackout curtain with me. Told her Charlie had been complaining he had trouble sleeping and I thought it might help.' She sounded almost proud.

The noises Joycie had heard that night: the rustling and dragging. 'And you rolled her in the blackout curtain and just carried her down to your car.' Her own voice sounded like a stranger's.

A chuckle. 'Lucky she was as thin as you and short with it. And I was strong in those days. Had to get Sid to help me with her afterwards though. He was so upset. Felt sorry for Charlie and you.' The chuckle turned into a little sob and she rubbed her fist under her eyes, dragging the mascara stain further down her cheek.

'Where did you …? Where did you take her?' The words hurt.

'Drove out to the country next day. Sid said a few words. It was a nice spot. Quiet.' Those dark eyes gazed into the past again. She was far away.

230

'Where was it?' *Please, please tell me.*

But when Cora looked at her it was with a little, *wouldn't you like to know,* smile.

Joycie had to wipe that smile off her face. 'You forgot something though, didn't you? The bloodstained mat. And I found it.'

The smile stretched wider. 'Oh no. I was going to take it, but then I thought: what if Charlie didn't believe she'd run off and he called the police? He'd be the first one they'd suspect, and if they found that mat hidden under the bed he'd be done for. So I just packed up her clothes and took them. I went back for the mat once we knew Charlie wasn't going to make a fuss.'

Five minutes until the train. The stationmaster's little house far away in the dusk at the other end of the platform. No lights, no movement.

She fought to keep the hatred out of her voice. 'What about my dad and Dennis?'

'It was fine until Charlie decided to leave. Sid was daft enough to mention that bloody mat and tell him I got rid of it, and we knew he was getting suspicious so …'

'You had them jailed?'

'Filthy bastards deserved it.'

Joycie bit hard on her lip and clenched her fists, holding back the vicious words she wanted to use. *Don't let her see how you feel.* Finally she managed to speak almost normally. 'Did Sid know you arranged for my dad to be killed in prison?'

'I told you. He was always too soft. Needed me to sort everything out for him. I told Ernie Georgiou I knew your dad had killed your mum and got away with it. Ernie doesn't like men who hurt women for no reason. So he had a word with some friends doing time in Wandsworth Prison where your dad was.'

A sudden urge to run at her. To hurt her. Push her onto the rails. If she wanted to die why not help her? But that would be the easy way out. And there was more she needed to know. 'Did you sort Pauline out too?'

'Who?'

'You don't even remember her, do you? My friend from Clacton, Mrs Shaw's daughter. The girl Sid raped and made pregnant.'

'Oh her.' A little laugh. 'I guessed she'd got herself into trouble and I helped her, if that's what you mean.'

This time she couldn't stop a single sob filled with pain and rage from escaping. 'She never came home again. Your help killed her.'

'I just gave her the money and the address. It must have gone wrong.'

Not the whole truth. Joycie was sure none of it was. But she needed to let Cora talk. It was three minutes until the London train. Big spots of rain beginning to fall from dark clouds – and the two of them alone on the platform.

Cora's smile was almost kindly now. She spoke softly. 'Would you like to know where we put your mum? That's what I really wanted to tell you.' Joycie held her breath, moving close. 'It was a little wood in the country, an hour or so outside Hastings.'

'Where? Cora, what was it called?'

Cora looked along the track again; poised on the edge of the platform.

Less than a minute. The rumble of the train. And still so much more Joycie needed to know. She grabbed Cora's arm. Fingers digging into the plump flesh. Smelling stale perfume, booze, and sweat. Shouting against the roar. 'Cora, don't. Don't do it.'

Cora looked back. Her eyes were dark pits.

And she smiled.

Her hands latched onto the collar of Joycie's dress and she jerked her forward. Joycie's feet slipped. They swayed together. She pulled hard back and they tilted upright; the soft heavy body almost crushing her. Another sickening pitch forward. The black rails surging into view. The dark glitter of Cora's eyes as Joycie tried to push her away.

Running feet. A shout. A piercing whistle, and a roar from the train. So close, so close.

Flashes of light. Screaming metal. And something – someone – dragging her back.

Her dress ripping. Pain screaming through her head as Cora clutched at her hair.

But those other hands wrenched her back, tearing out hair. And she crashed onto her knees on the platform.

A huge black shape, brakes squealing.

And no Cora.

Just something warm and wet spattering Joycie's face.

Chapter Twenty-Three

They took her to the local cottage hospital along with the station-master who had dragged her away from Cora. He kept talking and talking. Patting her hand and telling her how he had guessed what *that poor lady* was about to do as he came out of his house to meet the train.

'And you grabbed her. Such a brave little girl. But she was so much bigger. You never stood a chance. At the last minute she must have panicked, changed her mind. I thought you'd had it too. I knew there was nothing I could do for her, but I got hold of you.'

Joycie let him talk. Then let a doctor examine her and a nurse clean her up. But she wasn't really there. Her mind was still on the platform, replaying it over and over. Seeing Cora's eyes. Hearing the train shriek and roar. Feeling the warm blood spattering her face.

A uniformed policeman asked her some questions, and she heard her own voice saying her name and address and Cora's name. Nodding when he asked if Mrs Sergeant seemed upset. Her own voice again: 'Her husband has just died.'

The doctor came and rescued her. Said she was in shock and needed to stay in overnight. When he put a blanket round her she realized she was shaking, although she didn't feel cold. Didn't feel anything.

Lying in the dimly lit ward she began to think again. Cora had done it all for love of Sid. A strange, twisted love. And when he was dead she wanted to die, but planned to take Joycie with her. Blamed Joycie for his death and wanted to torment her by almost telling her where her mother was buried.

Somehow she must have slept because the ward lights were on. A trolley rattling from bed to bed. Smells of sausages and baked beans and loud voices shouting, 'Good morning.'

Marcus. She had to get back to him. The nurse tried to stop her getting out of bed, but she demanded her clothes, knowing she needed to sound calm, but unable to stop the tears.

Then the doctor was there. Sitting beside her and patting her hand. Why did they keep patting her hand? But he spoke gently. 'I know you're worried about your friend in hospital, but you won't help him by making yourself ill.' A vague memory of gabbling about Marcus last night. 'I'm just off-duty so please let me check you over then drive you somewhere you can get a train. The local station will be closed.'

On the way to London the businessmen, their bowlers on the racks, glanced very casually around their papers at her. Her dress was navy blue so the blood didn't show, but the torn collar, plasters on her knees, and the missing clump of hair must have made her a startling sight on the morning commute.

Finally London and another taxi. *Hurry, hurry.* Longing to get to the hospital and yet dreading it. She leapt out before they'd properly stopped. Then had to go back when the driver's shout of 'Oi!' tore through the air. She paid him. Forcing herself to walk more steadily this time. To comb her fingers through her hair. She had to look respectable.

In the entrance hall she stopped. And the world stopped too.

Marcus's parents sitting on a bench. Holding each other.

She couldn't move. Her legs were marble. And yet she was moving. Closer and closer. Somehow she was standing in front of them. Wanting and not wanting to ask.

His father's eyes focused on her and he seemed to speak, but she could only hear the word, *Marcus.*

Then his mother turned to her and she was smiling and Mr Blake was smiling too. Mrs Blake said, 'He's awake. And he's been asking for you.'

That first day she was only allowed to sit with Marcus for a few minutes. He was still bandaged and bruised and she didn't dare to kiss his poor sore lips. He mumbled, 'I love you,' before closing his eyes and lying as still as before. She called a nurse who smiled and said, 'He'll be groggy for a while, but much better tomorrow.'

When she arrived next morning Inspector Flynn was standing in the foyer. His face was grim and her heart did a sickening little flip. 'I'm glad to say Mr Blake was well enough to give us a statement,' he said. 'Unfortunately he says he didn't see his assailants so it looks like they may get away with it.' He looked hard at her. 'You'll be happy to know that we won't be bringing any charges about the drugs. Insufficient evidence there too, apparently.' Bill had made good on his promise.

Inspector Flynn held up a newspaper. 'I see you've been in the wars as well.'

There was a picture of Eridge station with the stationmaster standing, chest thrust out, at the edge of the platform. The story was a shortened version of the one he'd told over and over that night. He was quoted as saying: 'I just thought she was a very brave girl. Had no idea she was famous.'

Inspector Flynn gestured to one of the benches. Joycie looked up at the clock, desperate to get in to see Marcus. Only two visitors were allowed at a time and his parents had said they would stay for just half an hour, generously allowing her the final hour. They were due out soon.

'The woman who went under the train, Mrs Cora Sergeant, was the wife of Sid Sergeant,' the inspector was saying. 'If I'm not mistaken he was the man you mentioned in your statement. And he was killed the day before. Hit and run with no witnesses.'

She watched people coming through the doors to the wards, but forced herself to listen to him. 'Coincidences do happen, of course, and these *accidents* will be dealt with by the local police. Unless there's something you want to add to the statement you gave me.'

All she could think of was Marcus. And Sid and Cora were dead so was there any point in telling him? But ... She swallowed. 'What if I knew for certain that my mum had been murdered and I had some idea where she was buried?'

He let out a sound that was half sigh, half laugh. 'Do you?'

'It's somewhere in East Sussex. A wood about an hour's drive from Hastings.'

'And the person who told you this could pin it down a bit more, could they?'

'She's dead too.'

'Then I'm afraid we'd need more than that to start digging up whole swathes of Sussex. But I want you to know I didn't ignore your statement.' He was looking at her with those very dark eyes and his kind smile was back. 'There's nothing in our files about your mother, so it seems she was never reported missing, but we do have quite a bit on Charles Todd.'

'My father, yes, he died in prison.' It was pointless.

'And you know why he was there?' She nodded unable to speak. His voice became gentle. 'You see, that does explain why she would want to leave him.'

In his room, Marcus was sitting up and when he smiled he looked almost himself again, apart from a missing front tooth. It made Joycie see the schoolboy he must have been and just looking at him brought tears to her eyes. But everything seemed to do that just now.

He reached for her, but she hesitated to take his hand because the knuckles were red and swollen.

'It's all right. My head hurts so much I don't feel anything elsewhere.'

For a long time they just sat smiling at each other. Joycie loving the feel of his warm skin against hers.

Finally, he said, 'So what the hell happened with Cora?'

She slowly explained it all. 'I'm sure she glossed over some of the things she did. I wouldn't be surprised if she killed Pauline Shaw herself. Or made sure the backstreet butcher was someone who could be relied on to make a mess of it.'

'So what now?'

'The police won't help so it was all a waste of time and I got you hurt for nothing.' She scrubbed at her face.

Marcus squeezed her hand. 'Now stop that. It wasn't a waste. You found out what you needed to know. Your mum is dead, but your dad didn't do it.' They sat in silence again until his grip on her hand loosened and his eyes fluttered closed. He was still asleep when the nurse came to tell Joycie she had to leave.

It was a lovely afternoon and she took the bus home – no one ever recognized her on a bus. On the way she thought about Marcus's question, *what now?* There were some things she could do. She'd visit Hastings and talk to the dead girl's family and her boyfriend's too. They needed to know she hadn't killed herself and he had nothing to do with her death. And she must talk to Mrs Shaw.

When she got in she fed and walked Fatty and shoved a jacket potato in the oven to bake. Then poured a drink and, with Fatty's head on her knee, she phoned Mrs Shaw. As soon as she said who it was Mrs Shaw started talking fast.

'Oh Joyce, I read about everything that's been happening to you and I'm so glad you're all right. What about Marcus? How's he?'

'Much better, thank you. They say he's making a remarkable recovery. But Mrs Shaw …'

'I know it's a terrible thing to say, but I never liked Cora or Sid much.' She took a noisy breath and Joycie spoke quickly before she could carry on.

'Cora asked to meet me and she told me things, Mrs Shaw. I'd like to come and see you to talk about what she said.'

A long pause then that rush of words again, punctuated by tiny gasping breaths. 'Did she tell you something about your mum?'

'Yes, but ...'

'Is she dead? I always thought she might be.'

'Well you were right, but I need to talk to you about Pauline. So would it be OK if I visited soon?'

Silence. Only the rapid breaths showing she was still there. 'I'm not sure, Joyce. I'd love to see you, of course, but ...' Those panicky breaths again. Joycie waited, didn't know what to say.

She heard a cough and then Mrs Shaw's voice, slower now. 'Does it help? Knowing your mum's dead, I mean?'

'Yes, I think it does.'

'Well for me it wouldn't.' The voice was firm and clear. 'I'd rather imagine my Pauline alive and happy somewhere.'

After that there was nothing more to say.

Chapter Twenty-Four

It was only a few days before Marcus was so much better that they were talking about when he could come home. She hated leaving the hospital without him and had got into the habit of taking long, meandering walks after visiting. The newspapers had lost interest now he was recovering and the drugs angle had disappeared so there was no one outside to bother her. As she walked the occasional passer-by looked hard at her or nudged a friend, but she'd only been asked for an autograph once and she found she wasn't so worried about being recognized now anyway.

It was a beautiful day; the Thames glittering silver in the sunshine as she crossed Westminster Bridge. After half an hour or so she reached Soho Square and went into the little park to sit on a bench in the sunshine. There was a wedding at the French church in one corner of the square and the bride's white dress fluttered in the breeze as she kissed her new husband amidst a swirl of bright paper confetti.

Joycie touched her own lips, remembering the feel of Marcus's warm mouth on hers, and closed her eyes to let the sun play on her face as she listened to the chime of the church bells.

It wasn't until the bells fell silent that she heard the click of heels approaching.

Her eyes flew open as the bench creaked and Bill lowered himself onto the other end. His face was the same shiny mask as always. She slowed her breathing to still the thump, thump of her heart, but couldn't trust herself to speak.

'Don't worry, love,' he said staring straight ahead. 'I won't be bothering you again. I just wanted to say I'm glad your fella's on the mend and the rest of it has turned out all right for you.'

Although she wanted nothing more than to tell him to go away she had to ask. 'But why did you …?'

He touched her knee before she could say any more and put his finger to his lips. 'Shh.' A waft of his familiar aftershave as he leaned closer; a smell she knew she would never forget. 'Wise monkeys, eh,' he said. 'Let's just say you opened my eyes to a few things. Made me think.'

She couldn't avoid a flinch as he reached into his jacket, but breathed again when he pulled out a large white envelope.

'I've already got your autograph, but would you mind signing this too.'

For a moment she expected some kind of document in which she would have to promise her silence, but it was a glossy photo he took from the envelope.

It was of her – one she'd always liked. She stared at it, wondering what this was all about. But when she looked up at him his face creased into what looked like a real smile and the pale eyes glinted in the sunshine.

'It's for my girl, my daughter. She's fourteen next week, and you're her idol.'

He was holding out a pen and Joycie took it, feeling as if she was in some kind of dream. The thought that he had a daughter, a family, was incredible, and a vision of a young girl's bedroom wall covered with pictures of pop stars and models filled her head. She found herself parroting the words she always used when signing photos. 'What's her name?'

'Christina, but she likes to be called Tina.' His voice was always soft, but this time there was a gentle quality to it she'd never heard before.

But he was a killer and the gentleness had nothing to do with her, and when she gave the picture back to him she kept her voice cold. 'And you'll leave us alone now?'

He put the picture carefully back into the envelope and the envelope into his jacket with a gentle pat. Then he stood looking down on her. 'Yes, love, that's all over now. Thanks for the autograph.' And he turned on his heel and was gone.

She should have been relieved, but her legs were shaking as she left the park, and she hailed a taxi, needing to get home as quickly as she could. In the house Fatty greeted her with delirious waggings and lickings. They had never been more welcome.

The knock on the front door had Fatty rushing past her, alert as always these days to the hope that it would be Marcus arriving home again. Joycie peeped through the window, still shaky from the meeting with Bill.

But it was Dennis on the step. And when she opened the door he gave her a huge smile.

'How lovely to see you,' she said. 'You look good.' It was true. His skin had lost that grey tinge and his eyes were clear.

He raised his brows when she offered him a drink. 'I'll have a cup of Earl Grey if you've got it. I'm off the booze and off the boards too. Kay and I are planning to stay in Cornwall and open a little tea shop.'

They took their mugs into the garden. Fatty followed, wagging her whole body when Dennis patted her, and lying at his feet with one of her gusty sighs.

Joycie told him what Cora had said to her. 'So it was her not Sid who killed my mum, although he was just as much to blame.' When he nodded, but didn't speak she said, 'Why did you disappear, Dennis? Did someone threaten you?'

He put down his cup. 'I'm such a coward. There was a man hanging about who I recognized from one of the big London gangs and I knew it must be to do with the questions you were asking.' He rubbed his hand over his sweet, battered face.

'That was Bill,' she said. 'He followed me to Clacton. I'm so sorry, I was too naïve to know what risks I was taking with other people's lives.'

'You know about Bill?' Dennis stared at her with wide eyes.

She laughed. 'Oh yes, we've had a few chats over the last couple of months.'

He grabbed both her hands and pulled her round to face him, speaking fiercely. 'It's not funny, Joycie, he's dangerous.'

'I know that, but I spoke to him today and he tells me it's all over.' Dennis's fingers tightened on her wrists. 'It's all right,' she said. 'Cora told me he was the one who killed Sid and he more or less admitted it to me today. Said I'd made him think.' He dropped her hands and turned away breathing heavily.

When he didn't speak she said, 'Are you all right?'

His voice was muffled. 'Did he say why he did it? Killed Sid, I mean.'

'Not exactly, but he mentioned his daughter so I think it was to do with what I told him about Sid attacking me and other young girls.'

Dennis stayed turned away, saying nothing, his shoulder blades standing out sharp as he breathed.

'Dennis, what is it?'

'Nothing. I'll be all right in a minute.'

She grabbed his shoulder. 'Look at me, Dennis. And tell me. I have to know.'

His eyes glistened with tears, and he took her hand and kissed it. 'You're wonderful, darling. Charlie would be so proud of you.'

She waited until he dropped her hand and sat looking down the garden rocking gently as he spoke.

'Bill was in Wandsworth Prison at the same time Charlie was on remand there. So when the order came through from Ernie Georgiou I was told it was Bill who actually did it.'

She could only gasp it out. 'Bill killed my dad?'

'That's what I heard.'

'Tommy Green said Bill had come out of retirement because of me. If he killed Dad then maybe he was scared I'd find out and cause him trouble.' She was clenching her fists so tightly that her nails dug into her palms. 'Oh God, Dennis, I wish I could do more than make trouble for him. A whole lot more.'

'No you don't, sweetheart.' He rubbed her knee. 'You need to let it go and concentrate on making a happy life for yourself. I know that's what Charlie would tell you and what your mum would want.'

When she put her hand over his he pulled her into a hug. He was thin and felt fragile compared to Marcus, but it was good to rest her head on his warm shoulder and let the tears come.

After a while he drew back, rubbed his own eyes and handed her a fresh smelling blue handkerchief. 'Don't know how you manage to stay so pretty after you've been crying,' he said as she dabbed at her face. 'I always look like a boiled beetroot.'

She laughed and realized she felt better. The tears had helped to clear her thoughts. 'As Bill followed me around and learned the same things I did he must have begun to see that Dad was innocent all along.'

'And he would have been furious. These people have their own codes. They don't hurt anyone unless they think they have to, or they know the person deserves it.'

He was right. It all made sense and she wasn't sure whether she hated Bill or was grateful to him. One thing was sure, she was probably as close to the truth as she was ever going to get. 'Bill obviously thought it was Sid who wanted my dad killed, but I'm pretty sure it was Cora.'

'Didn't matter anyway did it,' Dennis said. 'Killing Sid was the same as killing her. She couldn't go on without him.'

'Cora sent me a message pretending it was from you, and I hoped you had some evidence to give me.'

His smile made him look like the handsome young man she remembered. 'Well now you mention it I came today to give you something. I don't know if you'd call it evidence, but ...' He pulled a piece of paper from his pocket. 'They found my letters to Charlie and used them as a reason to arrest us, but they never got hold of the ones he sent to me.' He handed the paper to her.

Dearest Dennis,

I've had a big bust up with Sid because he made a pass at my Joycie. Thank the Lord I caught him before he got far but the poor kid's really upset. I told him we were through, but then he said something about Mary. And, Dennis, I think he might have killed her!

All this time I've been telling myself she ran away. Not that I ever really believed it. She might have left me but she would never have left Joycie. And the worse thing is Joycie knows that too and I'm scared she thinks I did something to her mum.

And I keep worrying about all those girls that come round to the stage door. Sid always says nothing ever happens unless they want it. But what if he's lying? What if sometimes he won't take no for an answer? It's me the girls come to see and then I go and leave them alone with him. Mary didn't trust him, but I always defended him because he's been so good to me over the years. So if he's hurt any of those girls it's partly my fault.

We will start again like we planned. Get the nightclub and make a real home for us and for Joycie, but I have to sort this out as well. If Sid killed my Mary he's got to pay for it.

You know I love you, Dennis, but I loved Mary too and I can't rest until Joycie knows the truth.

Joycie stared at the letter for ages before she turned to give it back to Dennis. But he wasn't there, and when she went into the house he had gone. Back in the garden she sat for a long time looking up at the blue and cloudless sky.

Acton – March 1951

Joycie is in bed listening to the gramophone playing very softly in the other room. But it isn't the music that has woken her and she smiles. Before she goes to sleep each night she tells herself to wake up when Dad gets home. It doesn't always work, but it has tonight.

There's his voice. 'Let's have some Frank Sinatra, eh, Mary. I like him.'

The song is called 'Blue Skies', and it's one she likes too. She slips out of bed and opens her door just a crack. Her mum and dad are dancing slowly together, her mum's head on his shoulder, eyes closed.

Joycie watches for a bit until Dad turns towards her. He sees her and winks then reaches out a hand and when she runs to him he swings her up between him and Mum. It's soft and warm and she can smell Mum's flowery perfume mixing with the sharp scent of the aftershave that always makes Dad shout when he slaps it on.

Mum kisses her cheek and whispers, 'You should be asleep, naughty girl.' Then Dad laughs and kisses her too and the three of them sway together to the music. Joycie closes her eyes and sees the blue skies smiling down on them all.

Author's note

For a fascinating account of the Montagu Case by one of the defendants, as well as an insight into the persecution of homosexuals in 1950s Britain, I recommend *Against The Law* by Peter Wildeblood.

Acknowledgements

As always very special thanks, and a bubbly IOU, go to my first readers Sue Curran, Moira McDonnell and Jack Farmer. You help to make my writing, and my life, so much better.

Also to Tricia Gilbey, Jo Reed, Claire Whately, Marlene Brown, Barbara Scott-Emmett, Lorraine Mace, Justine Windsor, Liza Perrat, June Whitaker and Karen Milner – insightful critics and constant allies.

I couldn't be more grateful to the whole team at Killer Reads, especially my wonderful editor, Lucy Dauman, my copyeditor Janette Currie, and the cover designer Cherie Chapman.

To anyone who is passionate about books and takes the time to talk about and review those they have enjoyed I send my heartfelt thanks.

And most of all, for sharing so many perfect days and supporting me through the less than perfect ones, my endless love to my husband, Paul Farmer.

KILLER READS

DISCOVER THE BEST
IN CRIME AND THRILLER

Follow us on social media to get to know the team behind the books, enter exclusive giveaways, learn about the latest competitions, hear from our authors, and lots more:

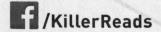 **/KillerReads**   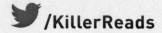 **/KillerReads**